Dancin' In The Moonlight

By

Beverly Rae

Triskelion Publishing
www.triskelionpublishing.net
All about Women, All about Extraordinary

Triskelion Publishing
15327 W. Becker Lane
Surprise, AZ 85379 USA

Printing History
First e Published by Triskelion Publishing
First e publishing March 2006
First printing by Triskelion Publishing
First paperback printing June 2006
ISBN 1-933874-03-1

Ebook and cover design Triskelion Publishing
Wolf graphic by Tyler Johnston

Dedication

To all the "animals" women love.

Beverly Rae

Chapter One

"Five."

"No way. He's not even a four."

"Okay. So how about that guy?"

Two of her friends questioned Carly at the same time. "Which one?"

Carly rolled her eyes at the other women and shook her head. "The lean, mean-looking one by the bar. The one staring at Tala."

Tala darted her eyes toward the bar, found the object of their discussion, and whipped her gaze back to her Cosmopolitan. "Figures."

"Just because he looks mean, doesn't mean he is mean, Tala. Besides," Sara licked sugar off the rim of her glass, "I like 'em a bit rough around the edges."

"Sara, don't razz Tala. She's just being cautious." Carly managed to appear delicate while nibbling on a piece of sushi. "You know what she's been through."

Oh, crap. Pity from her friends was worse than suffering through an abusive relationship with Mark Winston. Well, almost. "You know, ladies, I booted Mark to the curb over four months ago. Can we give the pity party a rest now?"

She glanced around the table at her three closest friends. Carly, the oldest one of their thirty-something group, leaned against the back of her stool and regarded Tala with cool eyes almost the same gray-blue as her own. Sara caught the unspoken communication between the two women and tucked her head, giving her silent agreement to keep the conversation light. Yet Melinda, normally the quietest one of them all, decided to add her two cents.

"I mean, damn, how long can you last, girl? Four months and counting without any sex. How the hell do you keep from going insane?"

"She spends a lot of money on batteries."

Tala started to laugh at Carly's impromptu response. "Hey, I can have a different fantasy every night. One night I can savage Brad and the next night I'm licking up and down Clooney's body." Figures the quiet one in the group was the most sexually active. "Actually, Mel, four months isn't very long. I mean, for most of us."

Mel adopted a perfect coquettish smile and nodded. "I guess. But if you ask me, I'd rather die than go four long, lonely months without male companionship. Much less without the Big O. Still—"

"Still, no man is better than an asshole, right?" Tala flicked back a loose strand of hair. "Okay, here's the deal. I broke up with Mark because he hit me. So maybe I'm not ready to leap into the pond again. It's a sad fact, but all the guys I meet aren't worth the time of day anyway."

Carly opened her mouth to speak, "Honey, we've all been there. Not the violent part, but the lack of quality fish in this pond.

"That's what I'm talking about." Tala jumped in and headed her off. "Besides, I'm good to go, at least until my vibrator dies." She winked at Carly when her friend snorted at her joke.

Tala gulped in a breath of much needed relief, released the air, and relaxed. Now maybe their *Girls' Night Out* tradition would get back to normal. This was the first time she'd gone out with the ladies since she left Mark, and she didn't want anything spoiling the night. "But hey, don't mind me. If you want to search for your perfect man," she added finger quotes to the description, "then, by all means, don't let my self-imposed celibacy stop you."

"Uh-oh, Tala. Don't look now, but Man-At-The-Bar is headed your way." Carly's warning barely made it out of her mouth before the "lean, mean-looking" man appeared at Tala's side.

The stench of alcohol and smoke smothered the atmosphere around Tala and she had to shift her head to the side to gasp in semi-clean air. His hand slid behind her, stopping to rest on the top of her stool. "Hey, beautiful one. Tala, right? Name's Fred. How about you excuse yourself from these other gorgeous ladies and join me for a nice private drink?"

Oh, shit. A fan. He must have recognized her from the zoo's public service and promotional spots, *Tala's Animal Facts.* Just what she needed. Not. She tilted her head up and batted her eyes at him. "Wow, Fred, I haven't had such an enticing invitation in a really, long time. How can I refuse?"

His stained, toothy leer didn't do anything for his bloodshot eyes. "You can't." He snaked his hand around her arm and tugged, "Come on, babe, let's go back to my place and you can show me what you've learned from all those wild animals. In fact, I bet you're the wild animal. You know. In bed. With Fred?"

Tala slipped her thumb under his fingers and ran her fingers over the top of his hand. Putting on her best airhead voice, she tossed her hair away from her shoulders in a perfect imitation of the stereotypical blonde bimbo. "Oh. My. God. You're a poet and don't even know it."

Fred blinked, her barb slipping straight over his head. "Huh?"

"Poet? Know it? Get it?" When he clearly didn't get it, she shook her head, trying not to let her jaw drop to the ground. Was this guy genetically stupid? Or was he drunk stupid? "Never mind. Don't strain your brain."

His face lit up as her joke finally hit home. "Oh, I get it now. Bed and Fred. Strain and brain." His loud horselaugh echoed through the room, stopping conversations and swiveling heads in their direction.

"Let me give you a little tip, Fred. Unless you want a broken hand, back off. Now."

Sara giggled and nodded. "She's been taking karate."

Carly chuckled, "Isn't it *tae kwon do*?"

Fred got a little green around the gills, "Aw, but she wouldn't hurt me." Yet, he carefully withdrew his hand before adding, "Would you, babe?"

Damn, how she hated anyone calling her "babe." But before she could open her mouth, Carly twisted on her stool, knocking over her drink. The cool liquid splashed onto Fred's bright orange shirt and green pants, a dark stain spreading over his crotch.

"Oh, I'm so, so sorry!" Carly feigned a contrite expression while winking at Tala.

Fred's curse only added to the ladies' enjoyment, although they all tried to go along with Carly's ruse. With a groan of disgust, Fred flicked drops of drink off his hands. "You bitches are crazy." Adding a few more choice expletives, he slinked back to his hole at the bar.

Giggles erupted from all four ladies as Tala high-fived Carly. "Thanks, girlfriend. Fred doesn't realize he got off easy."

Carly grabbed the rag from the waitress who'd arrived to clean up the spill. "I'll take care of this." She nodded toward Tala. "You can get the drink my friend here is buying me."

Tala sipped a little of her Cosmopolitan and echoed Carly's nod. "You bet. You deserve it."

Sara pointed an accusing finger at Tala. "You need to let yourself go. Free your inner goddess. Run naked through the woods. Do something and get over it."

Tala tried to control her infamous temper, but some sneaked out anyway. "Well, you know what you can do, don't you, Sara?"

"No. What?"

"Bite me."

"Ooh, Tala. I didn't know you got into women."

Leave it to Sara to turn a jab into a joke. Of course, that was part of the reason she loved these women so much. Sure, they were tough, yet they were loving, too. After all, they'd had to be strong to rise to the top of their professions, but they cared about her. Accepting Sara's lead, she quipped, "I don't usually swing that way, but for you, Beautiful, I might." Sara batted her eyes, ran her tongue over her lips, and wiggled her fingers in a come-and-get-me gesture. Tala faked a lecherous smirk at Sara just as a couple of good-looking men passed by them, shooting them a disgusted look. The two friends reached out for the men, pretending to pull them to the table.

"Hey, don't go. We're only kidding!"

Tala crossed her heart. "Yeah, really. We love men."

Carly slapped her hand down on the table. "Will you two cut it out? Do you want gossip getting around the bar that we're lesbians? Which would be okay if it were true, but when you're trolling for men that's the last message you want to send."

Mel sipped her wine cooler and agreed. "Right. Besides, let's not lose focus. Keep your eyes peeled for the perfect man." She copied Tala's earlier use of finger quotes. "This is the hottest club in town."

Tala's sarcastic laugh turned heads in her direction again. Lowering her voice, she explained. "There's no such thing as the perfect man. It's an oxymoron, not to mention an impossibility. Especially for women our age. And especially for successful women like us."

"Maybe we *should* become lesbians. I wonder if the whole sex thing and finding the perfect partner would be easier if we eliminated men altogether." Tala, Mel, and Carly raised their eyebrows at each other. When Sara caught their reaction, she held up her hands and backpedaled. "Hey, I'm only wondering. I love men, too, you know."

Mollified, Mel picked up where they'd left off. "I agree with Tala. I don't think a perfect man exists. To be perfect, a guy would have to be half man, half god. Like Hercules, or Zeus, or whichever mythical hunk you can think of." Mel sighed. "You know, someone with major brawn."

"Yeah, but he'd have to have brain power, too. I don't want a pretty boy toy. If I wanted a handsome dead-head, I could take home half the men in this bar."

Carly's assessment rang true to Tala. "As long as the head that's dead is on the shoulders instead of in his pants, then at least he'd provide some fun for a little while. But she's right. The perfect man has to possess all the right traits. Looks, intelligence and a—"

"A wild side." Mel ripped tears into the edge of a napkin. "Your definition of the perfect man would include animalistic qualities. Probably need a hairy chest, too."

"Ewww, I like mine smooth."

Tala blushed, hating the heat spreading across her cheeks. Yet she couldn't help telling them more. "Well, if you want to know the truth, I think the perfect man would be like a wolf."

Sara sputtered into her drink. "A wolf?"

"Told you, she wants a man with a hairy chest. Never mind Tala. She's always had a thing for wolves. I think she wants to make it with an animal. Personally, I think she's worked at the zoo a little too long for her own good."

Tala's hair stood up on her neck and she fought the urge to change the subject. "You know what I mean, Mel. I want a man to be *like* a wolf. Beautiful, with muscles and endurance. And loyal to his woman."

"His woman? You make 'woman' sound like female. Or bitch." Sara tilted her head back and gave a teeny howl.

"Yeah. I've heard wolves mate for life." Carly sipped her Chocotini and waved at Tala to go on.

Tala let her mind envision the ideal mate. "Hey, go with it for a sec. I mean who wouldn't want a guy like this? Wolves are tough when times call for tough, but they're also loving and playful, too. And they're rarely cruel."

"You'd have to make monthly appointments for him."

"For his shots?"

"Nah, the groomer."

Tala smacked Carly in the arm. "I'd take him where I get my bikini wax done, thank you very much."

"Forget the grooming. Think about the dough she'd have to shell out for training. I mean he's got to be housebroken. Not to mention taught to sit up and beg. Or should I say, lie down and beg."

Immersed in her thoughts, Sara was the only one not laughing. "Immortal." Sara played with the swizzle stick, tapping it on the table in rhythm to the music blaring through the speakers on the dance floor.

"Immortal?" Tala was aware that sometimes Sara came up with some good ideas. Tala squinted at her in the dim light of the bar and waited.

"Yeah, immortal. Forever young and virile. Forever hunky. Forever mine."

"Yuck. If he were immortal, then you'd grow old while he stayed yummy. I'm not sure even an immortal man would stay with some dried up old prune." Leave it to Carly to pop up with the negative in the situation.

"What if loving him made you immortal, too?" Sara winked, enjoying her dream.

"Okay, I guess we're going deep into this fantasy, aren't we?" Carly raised her glass to Sara. "But I do like the way you think."

The ladies stopped for a moment, letting the thought sink in.

Immortal, huh? The word "immortal" jogged Tala's memory of her cousin's recent visit. Would her friends think she'd gone nuts if she brought up the idea? She checked their faces and decided to risk it. Besides, she could always blame it on the booze later.

"Funny we're on this subject." She hesitated, and then took the plunge. "Because my cousin brought up the same subject not long ago. In fact, she and her friends had a similar discussion."

She searched her memory, dredging up all the details she could remember. "They're like us. Thirty-something, successful, and manless. So they brought up the plan of summoning an immortal man."

Mel leaned forward. "You mean like Hercules? Or Adonis? Or Zeus?"

"Okay, we get it. You want a Greek god." Carly downed the rest of her drink and motioned for the waitress. "Or are those guys Roman?"

"Who cares? I don't care if they built Rome or Athens. I just want *them* built." Mel followed Sara in ordering another drink.

"Maybe mine would be part elf. Like the cute one in the movie we saw last week." Sara grinned and ran her tongue over her lips. "No wait. I've changed my mind. Maybe I'd prefer—"

Carly's sarcastic tone interrupted Sara's musings and brought them back to reality. "And did they have any luck finding their immortal men?"

Sometimes Carly could be a real killjoy. Tala scowled at her, unhappy with her negativity. Which made the truth even better. "Come to think of it, I think they did. Well, at least they found love. I can't say about the immortal part. But here's the really weird part. They did some kind of ceremony to call the men to them."

Carly Killjoy smacked down the others' exuberant reactions. "Now we're getting silly. A ceremony to attract an immortal lover? Get real, Tala."

A stab of embarrassment for letting her whimsy run wild zipped through Tala. Until Sara spoke up, keeping the dream alive. "Let's do it."

Carly sputtered into her drink. Dabbing her chin dry, she threw an exasperated look at the others. "Do what?"

All eyes squared on Sara.

"Let's summon our immortal men."

"Are you kidding?"

"Carly, shut up. Sara, are you serious?" The excitement in Mel's voice mimicked the shiver running through Tala.

"Yeah, I am. I mean, what's the harm in trying? Besides, it'll be fun."

The conversation stalled as the waitress returned with fresh drinks. Once she'd left, Sara took up where she'd left off. "What exactly did they do, Tala?"

Are they seriously considering summoning their perfect men? She tried to recall how they'd ended up on this topic, but the alcohol fogging her brain kept her memory on a leave of absence. Just how desperate could they get? Tala bit her lip and shook her head. "I'm not sure."

Sara clapped her hands. "Hey, I have an idea. Since Tala's perfect man is a wolf," she paused at Tala's warning glare, "uh, wolf-like, then how about we do something under a full moon?"

Mel gasped and slapped her hand over her mouth. Lowering her hand slowly, she whispered, "I think the moon's full tonight." She checked her watch, and met their eyes with wonder in her own. "In fact, the moon should be high in the sky by now."

Without finishing their drinks, the ladies pushed away from the table, grabbed their purses, and headed outside.

*****

"This is so ridiculous. I hope nobody sees us."

Carly stood with her arms crossed, tapping her foot, and glaring at the other women standing in the middle of the bar's parking lot. "Are you all actually going to do this?" Nonetheless, she clasped Tala's hand in her own and reached for Sara's hand.

Ignoring Carly's outstretched hand, Sara giggled, spun around, and let the cool breeze of the summer night ruffle her hair. "Come on, Carly. Let yourself have some fun. And who knows? Maybe we'll get lucky and it'll work."

"Yeah." Mel grabbed Sara's arm to keep her from toppling over. Acting like giggling teenage girls, they hugged, squealed, and hopped up and down.

"Look, Tala." Mel pointed toward the heavens. "I was right. A full moon. Talk about your premium conditions. Perfect for calling up your wolfie, don't you think?"

Tala grinned at them and tapped Carly on the shoulder. "Lighten up and stop worrying. If anyone sees us, we can always claim we were drunk out of our minds. Besides, who's going to care?"

Carly shrugged and linked hands with Mel to begin their circle. After Mel pulled Sara to her side,

Tala grabbed Sara's other hand. Once in place, all eyes fell on Tala.

"Okay, Tala. So how do we do this?" Sara squeezed Tala's hand and scanned the faces around her. "Do we make a silent wish like when you blow out candles on a birthday cake? Or chant something about immortal men?"

Tala paused, trying to recall her cousin's description of the process. But, when she couldn't remember any details, she flung caution to the wind and guessed. "Uh, how about we, one by one, speak our wish out loud? How else are we supposed to know what everyone wants? And I'm dying to hear everyone's wish. Especially Carly's."

Sara shook her head as intense determination creased her forehead. "We need to do something more dramatic along with just wishing." She scanned her friends' faces, searching for suggestions. "Like maybe a dance after we're through describing them."

"Sure. Why not? If we're going to do this nutty thing, then let's go all out." Carly fixed her steely-eyed glower on Tala, making her squirm, but she held her ground. "Any volunteers to go first?"

Mel nodded toward the horizon. "Better hurry. We want to catch the moon at its highest peak. So I'll go first." Staring into the night sky, Mel took a huge breath and described her perfect man. "My Immortal One—"

"Now there's a title to live up to."

"Shush." Tala nudged Carly into silence. "Go on, Mel."

Mel's description went on for several minutes with exact details given to every aspect of her man. From eye color to length of his shaft, Mel left nothing to the imagination. From his spiky white hair to his exact height, she described her perfect man, making it easy for the other ladies to visualize him.

"Wow." Sara's whisper spoke for the group as they all nodded in awe. "Something tells me you've given this some real thought."

"I hope you get him, Mel. He sounds incredible."

Heads turned at Carly's warm declaration and she scowled at them. "What? Just because I think this is stupid doesn't mean I don't want the best for my friends. Sheesh." She tossed back her hair in defiance. "So here's my immortal hunk. He'd be tanned, dark, rippling with muscles, impeccably dressed and..."

Tala stared at the moon above her, allowing her mind to drift away from the sound of Carly's voice. Wouldn't it be great if she really could summon her dream man? If she could beckon her very own half-wolf, half-man stud? A punch in the arm broke her out of her reverie.

Catching Sara watching her quizzically, she wiggled her hand for encouragement. "Okay, Sara. You go next."

Taking a deep breath, Sara spread her lips wider, unable to hide her excitement. "Well, let's see. My Immortal One would be a man like no other."

As Sara continued to describe her version of the faultless male, Tala's mind drifted off again, letting the image form in her mind's eye. Within seconds, the form appeared, drawing her deeper into her trance.

His long, toned body, sleek and glistening in the moonlight, slowly rose from a crouched position. Muscles rippled across his chest, highlighting the broad expanse while large, brown nipples accented his hardened pecs. A sprinkling of silky black hair running from his six-pack abs led to the full, curly patch below and Tala wetted her mouth at the sight of his richly endowed self. Yet more magnificent than his body, his face drew Tala's attention away from his torso. Straight, black hair teased the tips of his shoulders and flowed around his angular face, while his strong, square jaw beckoned for a woman's touch.

And then she saw his eyes.

Amber eyes. Golden, compelling, magnetic eyes drew her to him. He commanded her to be his while he promised to be hers. Eyes she recognized from pleasurable nights of lustful dreams.

Her respiration quickened with the ache, the need clutching at her heart. Could he exist? Even as she wondered, he bent, inching back into a crouch. His image morphed, blurring the lines of his physique while outlining another. She blinked, trying to see him better but, instead, she lost the vision for a moment. She whimpered while a small, tortured sound escaped her lips.

Blinking again, Tala saw the new image. The amber eyes were the same. Golden, compelling, magnetic eyes. She blinked again and stared into the mesmerizing eyes of a black wolf.

"Tala?"

"Hel-lo? Tala? Are you okay?"

She jerked to awareness to find the others gawking at her. All three of her friends had their cell phones pointed at her, snapping pictures. Then she noticed why. She was down on the pavement, on all fours, gravel digging into her knees and palms. She must've fallen over from too much alcohol. "What's going on?"

Sara reached over and helped her to her feet. "Well, for one thing, you're sweating like a pig. Gross!" Releasing Tala's hand, she wiped her palm on her jeans. "Having hot flashes already?"

Tala shook her head to both answer the question and to clear the remnants of the dream lingering inside. "Excuse me?" She lifted her hand, noted the clamminess and copied Sara's gesture. "I, uh, guess I'm a little hot. Probably from too much alcohol."

"Yeah. Sure." Mel's tone left no doubt of her disbelief.

She glanced around her, clarity forming again. She tried to make a joke. "What's the big deal? I zoned out for a minute and fell over. No biggie."

The ladies dropped their hands, but remained focused on Tala. Unnerved by the intense scrutiny, she tried to pick up where she thought they'd left off. "So Sara's finished, right?"

When no one nodded, she swallowed and continued anyway. "Carly, I think it's your turn. It's Carly's turn, right?" Uneasiness crawled down her spine at their lack of response. "Cut the crap, would you? Or are you trying to scare me?"

Carly patted Tala's arm, bringing her into a hug in the process. "I already took my turn, remember? You haven't been ill lately, have you, Tala? I mean, with a fever or anything?"

Tala broke free and stepped away from the group. "Will you stop? You're acting like I've done something crazy. Haven't you ever gotten a little tipsy before? Damn it all to hell and back, knock it off."

The three women glanced at each other and back to Tala. Mel dropped her head while chewing on her bottom lip, but Sara and Carly returned Tala's glare. Carly flipped open her cell phone.

"What is the matter with you guys?" Tala's nerves strung tighter and she tried hard not to fidget. Was this a joke? Or did she have a problem? She gritted her teeth and asked the question she didn't want to ask but had to. "You're acting like I've gone over the edge. What the hell did I do to make you act this odd?"

Several tense moments passed until Carly broke the silence. "We're not the ones acting strangely, Tala. You are."

"Yeah? So what strange thing did I do, huh? And didn't all of you do something just as weird?"

Turning the cell phone to face Tala, she revealed the snapshot. "Just look at the picture." Again her friends exchanged telling looks. Taking a deep breath, Carly gave her an unexpected answer. "You howled."

Tala's mouth dropped. "I did what? You're kidding."

From the expressions on their faces, joking was the last thing on their minds. In fact, Mel still couldn't meet Tala's eyes.

"You lifted your head, stared at the full moon, and howled."

"I did not." No way could she believe such an outlandish accusation. She'd daydreamed, sure. But howled?

Carly lifted an eyebrow at her. "Take a look at the picture, honey. Head laid back, baying at the moon in full color."

Tala shook her head, but held out hope for a better explanation. "No, but—"

Carly dipped her chin and raised both eyebrows. "I swear, girl. I am not lying to you. You stood there and let loose with an actual throw-your-head-back, no-holds-barred, canine-loving howl. Hell, I thought we'd have a wolf pack on us before the sound died out."

Sara nodded. "It's true, Tala. You bayed at the moon."

"I did?" Had she really howled? If she had, she needed to come up with a good explanation and quick. "Hey, I was just kidding around." She forced out a laugh. "And you all fell for it."

"Looked real enough to me."

"Yeah. Too real."

Needing a major diversion, Tala hopped a few feet away, gyrating to an unheard rhythm. "Come on, ladies, let's dance." When the others eventually joined her, she grabbed Carly by the hand, pulling her into a spin. "Dance. Now."

Whooping and shouting, the other ladies stretched out their arms and began twirling in circles. Sara bumped into Mel, sending the two crashing to the ground in a fit of hilarity while Tala and Carly skipped around them.

Exhausted, Tala and Carly pulled the two women to their feet and hugged each other. "Well, if nothing else, dancin' in the moonlight was fun."

Sara's silly smile reinforced Tala's statement. "Yeah, it was."

Mel stumbled to a stop and blew out a long breath. "I don't know about you girls, but I've had enough excitement for one day. But I gotta say I thoroughly enjoyed everyone's performance. Whew! I'm danced out."

Carly caught Tala's eye and rolled her eyes. "Especially Tala's. She proved she deserves her wolf man."

Sara leaned against Tala and nudged her in the arm. "Yeah, who knew you could howl?"

Chapter Two

Dark forms flowed along the trails as more of the pack traveled to the meeting area in the mountains. Wolves of various colors, sizes, and breeds gathered together under the full moon, and waited for their leader to speak. The soft, white glow of the full moon softened their glinting eyes and sharp teeth, giving them the appearance of domesticated dogs. Man's obedient best friends. But the truth lay miles away from their appearance. The members of the Morgan pack were strong. They were the dominate pack among the Werewolf Nation.

Brogan Morgan, leader of the pack, sat on a high rock overlooking the clearing where most of the wolves converged. Tonight was the Time of Choosing. Tonight he would choose his heir.

He studied his sons one last time, noting each of their strengths and weaknesses. They were so much alike, yet so different. Yet he knew, while one of them yearned to be leader and head of the pack's business concerns, the other shunned all responsibilities, preferring to live off the work of others. Too bad Devlin didn't possess Mickale's thirst for power. Yet while Mickale wanted to take charge, he chose only weak females, undesirable partners as co-leaders of the pack. Especially unacceptable was his current female, Chia, who didn't have a dominant bone in her body.

Mickale, the older of his sons, paced the path below his father. He shook his thick, black fur in his impatience and cocked his massive head up to peer at Brogan. A jagged streak of white fur ran along the side of his face, serving to highlight the set of his jaws. As the older son, he considered the decision made long ago at the time of his birth. By birth and by pack law, leadership should be his.

In contrast, Brogan's younger son, Devlin, sat motionless; an obsidian statue amidst a sea of gray. His eyes locked onto Brogan and held for a moment, but Brogan could not read the emotions behind them. Mickale was the larger of the two in size, but Devlin possessed greater intelligence, more agility, and the basic, indefinable character of a leader.   But that character was wasted with his lack of ambition.

Brogan sighed, wishing he could combine the two sons into one. Where had he gone wrong? One son couldn't care less about taking charge, while the other who wanted to rule, spent too much time playing with every bitch in heat.

Devlin didn't have a mate yet, and a wolf could not take leadership until he or she mated.   His frustrated growl rumbled deep in his chest and he made his decision. His best option was to force Devlin to take over. Tonight, he would send Devlin in search of his mate. Once mated, Devlin would have to accept leadership. Whether he wanted it or not.

Brogan's howl ripped through the air, capturing the attention of the wolf pack. An excited murmur traveled through the group, picking up speed as they realized the importance of the meeting. Brogan inhaled and exhaled, building his confidence while buying a moment's reprieve. "I have tried to lead you well."

Cries of agreement lifted into the air along with howls of praise. Brogan nodded his thanks, but knew their approval could fade soon enough.

"But I grow weary and no longer wish to carry the burden of leadership. I have two strong sons. Sons

I am proud to call my own." *Well, for the most part.* Brogan kept his sarcastic thought to himself.

Brogan lifted his head toward the moon and cried out into the sky. "The Time of Choosing is now." All the wolves followed his example and the air filled with the sound of exultation. His people, his pack, was ready to claim a new ruler. Yips, barks, and excited rumblings floated up to Brogan, but he ignored the interruption and continued. "My son will be your new leader."

Mickale stood on all fours and held his head high, poised for the declaration announcing him as their leader. Devlin remained seated and watched his brother with calm, cool eyes.

Gritting his teeth together, Brogan stared into his older son's eyes and spoke the words he knew would slice Mickale to the core. "I have chosen my son, Devlin, as your next leader."

Shock registered in Mickale's eyes and raced back to Brogan. A cacophony of astonishment, agreement, and disbelief struck his sensitive ears, but Brogan held fast. He turned his attention to Devlin who sat as motionless as ever.

"Oh, Sweet Susie, you've got to be kidding. That's as ridiculous as wearing white after Labor Day."

Brogan narrowed his eyes and sought out the one who spoke. Blair, the pack's openly flamboyant gay shifted, his skinny, nude body rising from a crouch to stand, fists on slender hips.

"Are you mad, Big B? Devlin doesn't give a flip about the pack or the business. Mickale on the other hand," Blair winked at Mickale who cringed and pivoted away, grumbling, "is a true leader. And one hunk of a canine, if you ask me. Besides, since you're getting all hoity-toity, may I remind you that a true leader must have a mate? Or are you forgetting our laws?" Blair puckered up and blew a kiss at Mickale. "I'll gladly volunteer as Mickale's mate."

Brogan let the laughter of the others flow over him as he tried to control his anger toward the scraggly challenger. The declaration was offered in jest...or at least, he hoped so...but he couldn't ignore the laws. "I'm forgetting nothing, Blair. I'm well aware of our rules."

"Then how can you choose a successor when neither of your sons has a mate?" Blair shifted again, his frail wolf form sliding closer to Mickale who nipped at him in warning.

"I'm ready to choose a mate now." Mickale jumped away at Blair's quick overture. "A *female* mate." He sprinted over to Chia, who lowered her head in submission. Mickale nudged her with his nose before facing the crowd. "I choose Chia as my mate."

"She is not the one for you."

Brogan stood ready for his son's reaction. Why couldn't Mickale follow tradition and wait for his mate to call him? "Mickale, you can take any willing female for your mate, but you must choose wisely. You must wait for your destined mate."

"Why? If you want a son to lead, then I'm ready to take a mate now. What does it matter who she is?"

Brogan cringed at Mickale's scornful tone, and his heart ached under the glare Mickale sent him, but he held his ground. He had no other choice. He had to select the best leader for the pack. Even if that wolf was a reluctant leader.

Without giving Mickale a chance to continue arguing, Brogan countered with a compromise. He barked, bringing the crowd under his control again. "Since Devlin is not yet mated, I'll retain power for another month. At the end of that time, if Devlin hasn't found his mate, I'll stay on until Mickale's mate calls him."

The group nodded their approval and Brogan relaxed, hoping his plan would work. Even Mickale seemed to accept this concession and remained silent.

Devlin glanced from his father to his brother. Again, Brogan fought to understand the thoughts running through his son's mind, but couldn't. Instead, he asked, "Devlin? What do you say? You're my choice and must do as you're told."

Standing on all fours, Devlin studied his father and the wolves surrounding him. Muscles flexed as he whipped his tail high in the air. His eyes, sparkling against the darkness of his fur, locked with his father's. "I don't want to rule, Father. You know that. But I have heard her call."

Devlin threw his brother a commiserating look before returning his attention to his father. "She called to me tonight. I'll find her, but I don't want to take over the business." A clamor rose around them as father and son glared at each other. At long last, Devlin dropped his gaze, whirled, and loped into the forest.

Mickale snarled at his father and strode from the pack, heading into the woods in the opposite direction. Chia started to follow until Blair hopped in front of her, sticking his nose and tail into the air. "Don't bother, girlfriend. When a male's got to blow off steam, he doesn't need a bitch barking at his heels."

Fluttering his eyes at her, he posed like the diva of dogs, "Not even my sexy self."

*****

Devlin scanned the valley below him, enjoying the twinkling of the city's lights. However, the smell from the city offended him and he rubbed his nose in the dirt to get rid of the stench. Soon he'd change into human form, but traveling progressed faster on four paws than on two feet.

Shit. How could his father force him into this situation? After all the years of ignoring his father's insistence to get involved, how could Brogan still want him to take over? Why not give the power to Mickale who wanted the organization?

He puffed out his frustration. Should he tell his father about the corporation he'd grown on the sly? He'd always wanted to be his own man, mark his own territory, and he had. His import/export company grew larger every year. Wouldn't his accomplishment make his father proud?

Maybe he could tell his father after he'd found his mate? At least Brogan and he agreed on that much. It was time to find her. She was his destiny and she'd called to him. He knew the truth of this in his heart, in his very soul. Like all his ancestors before him, he would find his mate among the humans because she was human. At least, for now.

Sighing, he thought about the pack and its future. The Morgan Pack had lived in the wilderness far too long. Aside from the few who'd helped him grow his company, most of them preferred to live among nature. Oh sure, they went into town, but only when necessary. In fact, he, too, preferred to conduct his business through associates, leaving the interaction with human civilization, its culture, and its technology to others.

But now he'd return to claim his mate, the one destined for him. The one he'd trust with his life. The one he'd trust with his heart.

Taking long strides, he loped toward the train yard spreading out below the hills. The satchel he carried on his back held what few supplies he needed. Stretching out his long legs, he lengthened his gait, anxious to reach the city.

Devlin reached the first track at the same moment the moon reached its zenith in the starlit sky. Ducking behind an empty boxcar, he checked to make sure he'd arrived unnoticed, and let the transformation start. Within seconds, his human form materialized and he stood naked, the night breeze spreading goose bumps over his skin.

Pulling on jeans, a denim shirt, and well-worn boots, Devlin ran a hand through his hair, checking his reflection in the metal of the car. Would his mate consider him handsome? He laughed at the ludicrous thought. They were soul mates. How could she think otherwise?

He rotated in a circle, trying to determine which direction to go. Lifting his head, he sniffed the air and caught her scent, slight and almost nonexistent, but there. Somewhere in this city of brick and steel, his mate waited for him.

Her faint scent drew his attention to the left and he sniffed once more. Pivoting on his boot's heel, he took up long, easy strides and headed in her direction. Although he didn't know her name, age, or exact location, he knew her from her smell. No other female could call to him as she did. Determined to answer her call, he sped up, his feet pounding on the concrete surface.

Office buildings grew fewer and farther between, while neighborhoods and subdivisions sprang up around him. The barking of a dog protecting his turf slammed him to a dead stop until he realized the dog couldn't escape from behind his six-foot fence surrounding a two-story home. Uttering a low growl, he met the canine's gaze, and snarled a dare. The dog whined, tucked his tail between his legs, and scampered into his doghouse.

"Wimp." Devlin cocked his head to the side. Taking care to stay aware, he moved toward his mate's scent.

Her scent, a fragrance filling Devlin's nostrils more with every step he took, drew him forward, bringing him to her as no compass or lighthouse beacon could. The nearer he got to her, the longer his strides became, until he broke into a comfortable run, his panted breaths matching the rhythm of his footfalls.

He was almost there. Along with her smell came a tug at his heart, an excitement, and a thrill at the thought of a future with her. Rounding a corner, he jogged up the sidewalk, past the open gates, and into an apartment complex.

Sounds of humans playing, arguing, and living in the small dwellings stacked one on top of the other drifted to his ears. A young woman standing on a balcony called out to him, waving him over to her. Curious, he crossed the tiny bit of grass behind her building, and crooked his neck toward her.

"Yes?"

Her dark hair draped in front of her when she leaned over the balcony. Full breasts threatened to fall out of her tight top. "Hey, Hunkie, how about joining our party? We're down a few good men in here."

Two other young women exited the apartment to join her at the railing, adding their invitations to hers. The chunkiest of the three wobbled, spilling her drink onto the patio below. "Oops, watch out below."

Devlin jumped out of the way with one graceful movement. Shoving his hair away from his face, he made to leave. None of these women was the prize he sought.

"No wait!" The chunky woman ginned at him and sloshed more of her drink. "It's like Sharla said. We're going down on a few good men in here." She weaved from side to side, gaping at her friends who giggled at her twisted sentence.

Devlin shook his head, tossing them a smile, and picked up his mate's aroma again. Maybe before her call he would have stayed with the party, enjoying the pleasures of the night, but no longer. He couldn't, wouldn't, delay meeting her for anything.

Ignoring the catcalls and jeers from the women as he strode away, Devlin lifted his nose to the air and sniffed. Her spicy scent wiped the stench of the alcohol from him, leading him along the narrow pathway to the rear of the apartment building.

The last row of apartments backed up to a wooded lot, keeping the area more secluded than the rest of the complex. One lamppost lit the area behind the apartments, casting a yellow glow over the ground. Another light shone from a second story window, highlighting a shadow on the blinds. He inhaled, caught her scent in the wind and smiled.

The form playing across the blinds glided back and forth, arms outstretched at times, almost as if in flight. Her enticing shape in silhouette, dipped and weaved, dancing in time with the sensual music coming from inside the apartment. Her movements entreated him, sending a primal urge to dance with her flaring within his soul.

After scanning for any onlookers, he crouched and jumped; hurling his body onto the side of the balcony rails, and pulled up his body for a good look. Secured with both hands, he paused when she stopped moving, holding his breath as he waited. Had she seen him?

"What 'cha doing?"

Devlin dropped in surprise, hanging on with his fingertips, and gaped at the curly-haired girl peeking out of the first story apartment window. He grinned, scrunched up his face, and let one hand release its grip. Scratching under his armpit, he uttered sounds he hoped sounded like a monkey and prayed the little girl found him funny.

The child giggled, and hopped up and down. "Mommy! Mommy!"

Devlin stopped the monkey antics and put a finger to his lips. "No, little girl. Don't tell Mommy or the monkey will go away."

"Tracy? What are you doing out of bed at this time of night?"

Hearing her mother's voice, Devlin prepared to run.

"There's a monkey on the patio, Mommy."

"Don't be silly, honey. You get right back into bed this instant and stop waking up Mommy."

Again, Devlin held his finger to his lips. This time, Tracy copied his gesture, and brought her finger to her lips. Softly, she whispered, "Shush, Mr. Monkey. Don't wake up Mommy." She waved at him, turned, and disappeared.

Devlin let out a relieved sigh and let his body hang loose for a moment. Just as he started to pull himself up to watch again, he heard the glass door...*her* door...slide open. He grabbed the slatted boards of the patio floor and slipped underneath the floorboards. The woman's shadow crossed over him, her feet narrowly missing his fingers, as she moved to the railing.

Taking shallow breaths he waited, knowing he could keep his hold for hours. At last, she went inside and he heard the "click" of the patio door. He waited, seconds turning into minutes, but didn't hear the slide of the blinds.

"Damn it, man. Be careful." Although he chastised himself, his grin grew wider. What harm could a little pre-meeting snooping do? After all, destiny and instinct told him she was the right one for him, so she'd better get used to his playful side, right?

Devlin swung like a kid on a jungle gym to the edge of the patio. Changing his grip to lock his hands around the vertical boards, he did a pull-up and held his head just above the flooring. With his chin braced on the edge and his arms tense under the strain, he peeked into the apartment.

She's magnificent.

Swaying to the sultry music, the woman, his woman, clad in skimpy underwear and bra, flowed in front of him. With her back to him, she stuck out her buttocks toward him, perfect melons below the slope of her hips. His mouth flooded with saliva while his shaft jerked in response. Long, blonde hair rippled like a golden waterfall down her back to kiss the tip of her ass. And then she whirled around.

At the sight of her firm, ripe breasts, perfect in size and shape, he loosened his hold and dropped, scraping his chin in the fall. He dangled, suspended by one hand, and clung on with the other while his head...both heads...rejoiced at what he'd seen. Grunting, he stretched upwards to regain his position and view.

She bent over, facing the sliding door; hands on her knees, letting her breasts fall, and twisted her head to look at her bottom. Wiggling her ass around, she slid one hand under her panties and between her legs, pleasuring her mound. She lifted her head toward the glass, eyes closed, and the rapt expression on her face almost knocked Devlin to the ground.

Was this dance for him? Was this spectacular show for his benefit? After all, she'd called him to her, so maybe she'd planned to entice him with a performance using her female charms? Why else would she have opened the blinds at the perfect time? Devlin considered the chances of her having seen him, and his shaft grew thicker. The idea of her treating him to such an alluring exhibition hardened him further and he groaned at the tight fit of his jeans over his crotch.

She turned with her side to Devlin, but she kept her hand in place. Running her other hand over her breast, she pinched her nipple through the thin, lacy material and continued to dance. Her hair tumbled over her shoulders, slinking over the tops of her breasts and he ached to touch the silky strands. Devlin lowered one hand and tried to reposition the bulge in his pants.

When the music ended, Devlin's heart stopped along with it. *No, don't stop! Keep dancing!* He regained his grip on the railing, forcing down the urge to leap onto the balcony. Would she come out and greet him now?

Instead, she pivoted into the interior of the apartment, placing her back to Devlin. Walking towards a computer sitting on a table, she scooped up the robe on the chair to wrap around her as she slid into the chair. Punching a few buttons, music again filled the room, while an abstract flow of colors bounced across the screen, keeping beat with the rhythm of the music. After awhile, the music grew louder for a moment, reaching a crescendo as the end neared. Devlin held his breath and waited, anxious to see what she'd do next. Swaying in her seat, she sat for several seconds more before rising to cross over to the blinds. Just in time, Devlin ducked his head and dropped, his body stretched to full length below the patio.

"Hey! What're you doing? Yo, Caroline! We got us a pervert peeking inside the apartments."

Devlin glanced to his left. A wiry, unkempt man wearing hunter's camouflage stood a few yards away, with both arms braced to steady the shotgun he carried. Devlin's fight instinct clicked into high gear and he swung forward and backward, gaining the thrust he would need.

"Hoo-ee! You, my man, are b-u-s-t-i-d, bus-ted!"

Twirling around with the skill of an Olympic gymnast, Devlin released his hold on the railing, and flung his body toward the man. Devlin struck the hunter head-on, sending them both reeling to the ground and the gun flying. They tumbled together, rolling over each other until they banged into the trunk of a tree. With a grunt, they stopped, clinging to each other, each fighting to gather his wits and breath.

Landing on top, Devlin fought to control the power surging within him, but couldn't keep the flow of energy from leaking through. The man's eyes went wide as he stared into Devlin's, and a desperate cry escaped his lips when Devlin snarled, exposing long, sharp fangs.

"Shit! What the crap are you?"

He growled and rolled to the side. Crouching, he bared his teeth again at the terrified man as he fought to stay in human form.

He failed.

Clothes ripped from his body as the transformation took over, shifting him from man to wolf in seconds. The hunter, shuddered in fear as he opened his mouth, and yelled a strangled, incomprehensible cry. But it was another's cry that caught Devlin's attention.

"Bobby Lee!"

Devlin, in full wolf glory, wrenched his head around to see a woman in the lower apartment bursting onto her patio. Together, they glanced at the shotgun lying at the edge of the patio. Without further hesitation, she scooped up the gun and pointed the barrel straight at him.

"Get away from him, you beast!"

A loud *pop* fractured the air sending pellets flying toward them, and Devlin hunched his shoulders in reaction. He ducked, twisting his body lower, and prayed for luck.

But luck wasn't on his side. Or Bobby Lee's.

Pain seared through him as the buckshot found its target, wrenching a howl from him and a shout from Bobby Lee.

"Shit, Caroline! You shot me! Shoot the wolf, woman!"

"I did!"

Devlin cringed at the burn coursing through him at the same instant he noticed blood running down Bobby Lee's shirt. He stumbled toward the woods, falling once as the pain raked up his flank.

"Oh, my God. What's going on?"

Devlin skidded to a stop, pivoted in the direction of the voice, and met the woman's stare as she leaned over the railing. *His* woman. Her eyes, sparkling blue against the paleness of her startled face, caught him, making him forget about the man, the gun still in the other woman's hands, and even about the pain. He'd seen those eyes before. In his dreams. In impossible, desire-driven dreams.

Breaking the connection with him, her gaping stare jumped from Devlin to the hunter, taking in the scene. Delicate hands flew to her mouth, yet she didn't scream. She stood stunned, yes, but not frightened.

The hunter's voice, however, grew stronger by the second. His next tortured cry propelled her into action. Yet, instead of coming to Devlin's aide as he'd hoped, she motioned to the man to stay where he was.

"I'll call for help!" Spinning around, she fled back into the building.

Growling his disappointment, Devlin rose and bolted into the woods.

Chapter Three

Damn, I hurt. Although he wasn't sure which hurt more, the pain in his rear or the pounding crush of his headache. Curling into a ball, Devlin winced as the sting in his bottom broke through his dream. He groaned, the dew on the rock beneath him sending shivers through his nude body.

What had happened? His mind caught the idea of a woman aiming a shotgun at him. Had he gotten shot? As if in answer, the throbbing increased in his butt.

Sunlight heated his back as he curled tighter, refusing to open his eyes, believing he'd be safe if he just stayed quiet. Undisturbed, he let his memory sort through the events of the previous night.

How could she have helped the hunter instead of coming to him? Didn't she realize who he was? She'd danced for him, right? Her call to the hunter rang through his head, giving him an ache of the — emotional kind.

The images changed as he saw himself nursing a beer, one of too many, and staring into the murky golden liquid. His friend's voice haunted him as he drifted backward in thought.

"Gee, Dev. So you're going to let some female you haven't even met mess up your mind?" Conrad downed his whiskey and popped another handful of nuts into his mouth. Now he remembered. He'd called Conrad for help. Devlin smiled, recalling how his buddy had rushed to meet him.

Aside from his rough exterior that had him looking more like a pirate with his long gray beard and hair, good old Conrad was the perfect right hand man.

After getting shot in the butt...which was hard enough to explain...he needed a change of clothing and someone to listen to him. Yet feeling the way he felt right now, maybe he should have stayed naked and mute.

"She's not just some female."

Hadn't Con listened to anything he'd told him? A vague recollection of Conrad laughing at his tale made him wince and roll over. Indistinguishable sounds filtered into his consciousness, but he ignored them, somehow knowing they meant trouble.

"Yeah, well, maybe. But if you ask me, they're all the same." Conrad growled what he considered a come-on to the girl who'd slipped up next to him at the bar. He shrugged when she'd taken off in fright, the corners of his mouth tipping upward. "So, Dev, old boy, how's the ass?"

"Never mind." Slugging back his drink, he squinted at his image in the mirror. When had everything gotten so fuzzy? He'd need another bandage soon, but his wound was the least of his worries. "I need to get out of this place. Go somewhere with trees. Somewhere with our kind."

Yeah, he and Conrad had gone somewhere all right. Somewhere he'd never have gone if he hadn't gotten drunk out of his mind. He remembered climbing fences, jumping over barricades, shifting, and planning to turn all the caged wolves loose. A plan they'd never fully executed. Where had Conrad gone to anyway?

The sounds outside his mind grew louder and he snarled, unwilling to allow them entry. Let the world go on without him.

"Hey, buddy. You all right?"

Aw, crap.

Devlin sent a skyward wish as a last resort. *Make the voice and the sounds go away.* All he wanted was to lie here and rest until his head deflated to normal size again.

"Did you call the police?"

"No. I called Tala instead."

"What the hell for? You should have called the cops like I told you to."

Will they just shut the fuck up? Devlin's lips pulled back, a snarl forming in defense. But he didn't, couldn't, and wouldn't move. Not yet.

The two voices argued for a bit longer while Devlin twisted into a tighter position. They could quarrel until the sun exploded for all he cared. That is, until a sharp pain hit his side. Something had poked him. And hard.

"Hey, dude. You're going to have to get up now." The younger voice seemed more agreeable than the older one, but Devlin didn't care.

"Move, man, or I'll move it for you." The owner of the older voice was definitely less friendly.

Another sting in his side left no doubt which voice did the prodding. Devlin flipped over onto his back, whipping his arm out, striking a hard object. The clang of metal hitting stone rewarded his effort. Peeking between puffy eyelids, he glimpsed two pairs of work boots, and squeezed his eyes shut.

Aw, double crap.

"Has he said anything yet?"

The sweet lilt wafted over Devlin's sore body, coaxing his eyes open again. Standing a few feet away was his female. His beautiful, golden woman.

"Nope. Not a thing." Surly-voice man wiped his nose on his sleeve. "But he did strike out at us."

"Only because you kept stabbing him with the prod." A younger man, his kind eyes meeting Devlin's, pointed at the metal pole lying on the ground near them. "Nothing I wouldn't do if someone poked at me."

"Ms. Wilde, we need to call the authorities. This guy's either wacko or waking up from an all-night binge." Surly leaned closer and sniffed. "From the stink of him, I'd say he's a drunk."

Ms. Wilde? What an ideal name for his mate. Would *she be wild?*

"I called you because I figured the zoo didn't need any more bad publicity." Kind Eyes continued even as Surly tried to butt in. "I mean, do we want to explain how this drunken man got over all the barriers and into a wolf pen? Remember the fuss when the little kid got into the chimpanzee cage? I say, we get him out of here before the zoo opens. Besides, he's injured."

Devlin stared up into her captivating blue eyes, his breath halting as he waited to hear her voice again. Had she come to help him?

For a moment, they gazed at each other, neither speaking nor moving. But with a slight jerk of her body, she stepped forward and knelt by his side.

"Who are you?

Devlin opened his mouth, ready to answer, but the best he could do was a croaking sound. Man, what he wouldn't give for a big, long glass of cool water.

Perfect eyebrows slid down toward a perfect, upturned nose, making him forget to respond. So she worked at the zoo. Although the thought was disturbing...her involved in caging wolves...he couldn't help but wonder what it would be like to have her take care of him.

"Do you want me to call a doctor?"

His hand flew to his butt, spreading blood onto his fingers. Shaking his head, he pushed up on his elbows and reached out for her.

She moved with quick ease, surprise more than fear highlighting her features. "Uh, here." She handed him a rag sticking out of her work overalls. "Tell me. Do you end up naked in a wolf's habitat every time you get drunk?"

Good. She has spirit. He grinned, thankful he'd swallowed the clog in his throat, allowing him to speak. "Not often. Just when I want to meet beautiful zookeepers."

Her chuckle warmed him more than clothes ever could have. "I haven't heard that pick-up line yet." Her lips curved at the edge in a natural way that could break a man's heart. She kept her eyes locked on him, a dare not quite hidden in the bright blue depths.

"Well, you know. A man does whatever works."

Her gaze slipped to his semi-erect shaft and rested there for several seconds. Faking a cough, he brought her attention back to his face as a flash of heat flickered on hers.

"Oh, my God."

He glanced at his now fully extended cock and back. "Yeah, I get that a lot from women. Impressive, huh?" He winked at her as she caught his joke, delighting in the blush flowing upward from her neck. "Thanks for noticing."

She blinked twice before lowering her voice, narrowing her eyes, and driving her statement home. "You have buckshot in you."

"Yeah." Devlin *humphed* and pushed himself into a cross-legged position, giving her an even better view of his jewels. He picked up a couple of the pellets finally working themselves out of his skin. "Damn weekend hunters. Makes a good argument for gun control."

Her mouth worked as if she'd tried to say something, but couldn't. At last, she tried again. "You're the man Bobby Lee saw outside the apartments, aren't you? You were there with a dog?"

"Are you asking or telling me?"

"Why?"

"Why what?"

"Why were you outside my home?"

How could she not know? He studied her and knew the answer. She hadn't called him. At least, not on purpose.

When he started to explain, she raised her hand and placed it against her chest. "No. I don't want to know. You stay away from me."

She bolted from him, wheeling toward the gate. Throwing one final confused look at him, she shouted orders at the two men left gawking at her. "Robert, get the man some clothes and show him out..." Her smirk parted her lips in unintended invitation, "...the *rear* entrance."

*****

Tala fought to keep awake. After spending the night wondering about the mysterious, not to mention, gorgeous man they'd found in the wolf pen, she'd had little time for sleep.

With her breakfast readied, she plopped onto a barstool in her tiny kitchen, took a bite of dry cereal, and flicked on the remote. The local news program she enjoyed every morning sprang to life and she took her second bite. Yet her mind couldn't focus on the newscaster's voice. Instead, her thoughts wandered back to the past two days and her mystifying visitor.

She'd moved to this complex, even though the rent stretched her budget to the limit, because of the neighborhood's safe reputation. Unlike the last part of town she'd lived in, where fights and robberies happened on a regular basis, the High Trail District boasted a spotless reputation for safety. Which made these past two days' events so unsettling.

Bobby Lee, once he'd calmed down enough to restore himself to coherent speech, related his story to Tala. While waiting for the police, she'd checked his injuries, tried to calm Caroline down, and listened to his description of the man he'd caught hanging from her balcony. Bobby Lee told her the voyeur had amber eyes and long, deadly teeth. And then the wolf had appeared.

Of course, she didn't believe Bobby Lee's story of the man changing into a wolf. Instead, she'd chalked his wild tale up to hysterics. The intruder must have had a dog with him. She frowned, remembering the creature she'd watched running into the woods.

But she wondered what had happened to the Peeping Tom. She'd seen the animal, but not the man. And when the animal's eyes had locked onto hers, she'd known she was looking at no ordinary canine.

Tala was shocked, not to mention embarrassed, by the idea of a voyeur watching her less-than-modest dance. Why had she opened the blinds in the first place? A knot grew in her stomach as she realized her lack of common sense. She'd never even considered someone watching her, spying on her. After all, it was well into the nighttime hours and most of her neighbors kept their own blinds closed. And with the woods directly behind her balcony, who'd have figured on a Peeping Tom slipping up at the exact moment she'd decided to be stupid?

"Shit. I thought I was safe here." Safe from crime, safe from dangerous neighbors, safe from weirdoes. She stared at the spoonful of cereal poised in mid-air.

The weatherman rambled on about high-pressure zones and the chance of rain, but Tala barely acknowledged the information. Instead, she took a spoonful of the cereal and let her mind wander again. This time, however, her thoughts took a more pleasant diversion.

If she had to have a Peeping Tom, then at least her Tom was a doozy. A hunk to the extreme. He was built without an ounce of body fat on him. Seeing him lying on the ground in the wolf habitat had stunned her, but not enough to keep her from taking stock of his remarkable physique. Once she'd laid eyes on that hunky bod of his, all her fear had evacuated her body, leaping out of the way of her fast-moving lust. His long, strong legs alone had caught her breath from her, nearly fainting from the sight of his ripped, toned body. And she wasn't the fainting type.

In fact, if the two other zookeepers hadn't been with her, she'd have given in to the heat coursing through her at the sight of his delicious form sprawled on the rocks. She shivered with delight as she imagined straddling him, the sun beating on her naked back as she rode him while the wild wolves looked on.

Tala groaned as she wiped the image from her mind. She should be worried instead of dreaming about having sex with a stranger. A stranger who'd found his way from her apartment to the zoo. Had he known she worked at the zoo?

Damn it all to hell and back, maybe she did need to get laid. She was sitting here fantasizing about a pervert. The girls would die laughing if she told them. Which, of course, she wouldn't dare.

After shoveling in a few more spoonfuls of the god-awful tasting cereal, Tala hit the "Off" button on the remote, snagged her coffee mug, and hopped off the barstool.

Crossing over to the glass door, she yanked open the blinds, flooding the apartment with sunlight. What she saw made her drop her mug, splashing coffee onto the window, the carpet, and her jeans, but even the burn from the coffee couldn't drag her eyes away from the figure lying on her lounge.

The man, her Peeping Tom, lay curled on his side, with his back to Tala. At first, the impressive distance between the tips of his shoulders caught her attention, and she swallowed against the tightness closing her throat. Long, black hair glistened in the morning light, and she held her breath, her fingers itching to touch the silkiness.

The denim shirt he wore lay open, half of the material draping over his back to expose the right side of his firm torso. His jeans, while cradling his ass, fell open at the top, exposing the top portion of his buttocks. One arm curled under his head for a pillow, while the other stretched out across his side.

My Peeping Tom is sleeping on my lounge. How cool is that? Perplexed at her ridiculous thought, she reached for the lock on the glass door and paused. Had he followed her home? This time she should call the police, right? Yet something rooted her to the spot.

He looks so peaceful. Loveable even. Like a puppy taking a nap. An incredibly sexy puppy taking a nap. A puppy with blood running down his tight butt.

She gasped, making her decision as she gazed at his wound, and unlocked the door. Why hadn't he gotten medical help yet? Sliding the door wide, she went to him, falling to her knees in front of him. She studied his tanned face; her eyes skimming over his slightly parted lips, and watched the steady rise and fall of his Herculean-muscled chest. *Wow, talk about a Greek god for Mel.*

For a second, she forgot about his wound, until he released a low moan. His moan galvanized her and she mentally ran through her first aid training. She shifted her body, leaning over his side to better examine him. Lifting his jeans, she examined the injured area, biting her lip to keep from making a sound. She'd need to remove his jeans to get a good look at his wound.

"Don't draw your own blood on my account. I think I've spilled enough for the both of us."

Startled, she jerked backward. His warm, brown eyes ran over her body, coming to rest on her face. Apprehension settled in her gut, yet her body wouldn't budge, providing time for her concern for him to overwhelm her fear for herself. "Are you all right?"

At his raised eyebrows, she coughed out a nervous titter, glanced at his injury, and returned to those beautiful eyes. "Sorry. Dumb question." Gazing into his eyes froze her brain, wiping it clean of any helpful ideas. "Uh...um..." He smiled, a slow, easy stretching of his mouth and she studied him, entranced by his rugged, square jaw. She tried to rise, shaken by the jolt racing through her body.

His large hand wrapped around her wrist, keeping her on her knees. "No. Don't be afraid."

She should be afraid. If he was here, she had a stalker. Yet fear couldn't raise its ugly head while her hormones raced like missiles through her body. She swore she could come any second now. "What are you doing here? Did you follow me home from the zoo?"

He closed his eyes, flattening his thick lashes against his bronze skin. When he opened them again, she could see the awkwardness he felt. "No, I already knew where you lived. Remember?" A frown creased his broad forehead. "But I didn't mean to spy on you the other night."

She cocked an eyebrow at him and inclined her head. "Uh, huh. Got some property in Brooklyn to sell me?"

His grin, a wide okay-you-caught-me grin, sent hot coals speeding to her stomach. "Okay, I did watch. But I couldn't help myself. I came by and I happened to see you. What man could resist watching a sexy woman dance?"

The man possessed a charm all his own. Besides being a hunk, he knew how to flatter. Should she believe him? God knows she'd yearned to hear those words from a handsome stranger. But *this* handsome stranger?

He winced and brought her attention back to his wound. Ashamed for allowing her mind to wander, she again tried to rise. Again, he stopped her.

"You need medical attention. Why didn't you get help before now? I'll get a towel or something to help stop the blood," she offered.

"No. I'm okay." He lifted up on his elbow and started to get off the lounge.

Shaking her head, she pushed on his chest, her hands sliding under his open shirt, and forced him down. "You're not going anywhere. You're—" The warmth of his skin shot a sizzle of desire up her arm to collide with the functioning of her brain. Her train of thought derailed in the crash. "Uh, you're—"

"I'm what?"

His tongue slipped over his upper lip, ratcheting up the burn between her thighs. She copied his gesture with her tongue while her fingers explored the sensation of smooth skin over hardened biceps. His jaw dropped, parting his mouth, and she fought the urge to thrust her tongue inside.

Raising a hand to cup the side of her face, his voice swept over her, making her breathe in deeply as if she could capture the richness of his tone by smell. Mesmerized, she watched his lips move again.

"I'm what?"

His thick eyebrows lifted in question, prompting her to break free of his spell. Snatching her hands away, she cleared her throat, and croaked out her answer. "Oh, uh, you're hurt. Wounded. Shot in the tail."

He blinked at her and dived those wonderfully masculine eyebrows toward his nose. "My tail?" Twisting to see his rear, he touched the bloodied area gingerly and turned to her. "No, I didn't. I got shot in the butt."

She stared at him, trying to understand the difference. "That's what I said."

The quizzical expression stayed on his face. "No, it isn't. You said I got shot in the tail. Trust me." Pointing at his bottom, he spoke in a clipped tone, punctuating each word as if she didn't understand English. "*This* is not my *tail*."

Tala glanced from his face, to his butt, and back to his face. What the hell did it matter what they called his rump? "Okay. Whatever you say. But your butt..." She added quotes for emphasis, "...has buckshot in it and requires a doctor's attention. So let me call for an ambulance."

Slapping away his hand, she rose and darted into her apartment. She'd reached the coffee table, scooped up her cell phone, and thumbed the number nine into the phone before his hand clamped over hers. "Hey!"

He tugged the phone from her and held up both hands above his head. "Please. Let me explain."

Alarm, cold and mean, sliced through her. In one swift motion, she scurried into the kitchen area, putting the counter between them. Her breathing quickened and she struggled to keep the panic at bay, allowing her to think. What the hell was the matter with her letting lust overtake common sense? Would he pull a psycho and slice her up? Not if she could help it, he wouldn't!

Wrenching open a drawer, she grabbed a paring knife and stretched out her arm, its small tip pointing at her hunk-turned-intruder. "Don't come any closer. I'll cut you. I swear I will."

His eyes twinkled at her and he chuckled. Lowering his hands, he nodded at the knife and spoke in a soft, placating tone. "Um, what do you think you're going to do with the cute, little knife? I'd think you'd have better luck if you called for Billy Bob instead."

"Bobby Lee."

"Whatever."

Irritation at the truth of his words tempered her fear, yet she wouldn't give in. "I'll gouge out your eyes if you come any closer. Stay away from me!" She jabbed the knife at him, hoping the gesture would make the knife appear more threatening. "And give me back my phone."

Yet when he attempted to move toward her, offering her the phone, she jumped and waved the knife again. "Stop! Don't get any closer!"

"I'm giving you the phone like you told me to do."

Again the truth of his words rankled her. Why the hell had she left the door open for him to follow her inside? Who knew he had the strength to follow her? "Never mind. Just put it down on the coffee table and get the hell out."

He put down the phone as she directed, but stayed rooted to his spot. "If you'll let me explain…"

"I told you to get out."

He sighed and flipped his sleek hair behind his ears. "I'll leave. But only after you promise to listen to me."

She fidgeted, unsure what she could do to force him out. How had she gotten into this mess? Trapped in her own apartment with a pervert. She ran through several crazy ideas of escape, none of which had a chance in hell of working, and finally gave in. "You'll leave once I've listened to you? You promise?"

Crap. Like a rapist would tell her the truth.

He drew himself to his full height and nodded. "I promise."

No one would come if she yelled. Her neighbors were all at work. And the likelihood of getting past him was slim to none. What else could she do except mollify him until she could figure a way out of this situation? "Go ahead."

He nodded and smiled at her. A smile, she--God help her--trusted.

"Let's start from the beginning. Okay? I'm Devlin Morgan."

She gaped at him and stammered until the words finally sorted themselves out in her mouth. "I don't want to know your name."

"Why not?"

When she didn't respond, he continued. "Okay, we'll do it your way. I told you the truth. I never planned on spying on you." He chuckled a deep, sexy sound. "I just got lucky."

She blew out a puff of air and tried to concentrate. But his broad shoulders beckoned to her, making her wish she could run her hands under his shirt again. Or maybe past his unbuttoned jeans? *What is friggin' wrong with me?*

"Nonetheless, I did watch you. I wish I could say I'm sorry I did, but I'd be lying. You're a gorgeous woman and I enjoyed watching you."

Although his declaration wetted a need she'd never filled, she couldn't let him get away with it. But he beat her to the punch.

Holding up one hand, he tipped his head in acknowledgement of her unspoken words. "I know, I know. I shouldn't have. Watch, I mean. I'm sorry. But I'll never say I'm sorry I enjoyed every minute of the show." When she glowered at him, he added, "But, hey, I got paid back. Annie Oakley from downstairs shot me." He sported his engaging grin and added, "In the butt."

Tala caught herself leaning on the counter, relaxing to the sound of his voice. She jolted up, renewing her defensive position. "Right. In the butt. We've established that fact. But since your wound doesn't appear life threatening, you can get out and leave me alone. Forget what I said about listening to you or helping you. I'm not helping some nut who gets so drunk he winds up in the wolf pen."

"Oh, come on. Like you've never gotten drunk and done something stupid?"

Her mind flashed to the night she'd gotten on all fours and howled in front of her friends. With pictures to prove it. "None of your business. Anyway, like I said. Forget I offered."

He swiveled, scaring her, making her jostle from foot to foot. "Don't move. Unless you're leaving."

He ignored her, crossing over to look at some of the pictures on her walls. "You like wolves." Turning in a slow circle, he stared at all the posters. "A lot."

She frowned, confused by this change of conversation. "Never mind my interests. The door's over there."

"Yeah, I know."

She watched him, readied herself to run, as he studied the poster of a wolf pack. Did he think he could get her to loosen up by commenting on her love for wolves? Was his interest real or fake? Lost in her thoughts, he caught her unprepared.

His eyes snared hers, drawing her into them. Holding her to him. Her chest tightened in trepidation, while her nipples rose in anticipation. Licking his lips, he ran both hands through his hair, opening his shirt to expose his rock-hard abs, and she waited for him to speak. Instead, he held up his head and howled, sending shivers sprinting down her spine.

She stepped back a couple of steps and gawked at him. "What the hell are you doing?"

His glorious grin, wolfish in quality, returned. "I'm howling for my mate."

Oh. My. God. The man may be the sexiest male she'd ever seen, but he was also the craziest. "You're howling for your mate? You mean, like a wolf?"

The image of her raising her head to the moon, howling until her throat hurt, flashed through her mind. She blushed, the heat coursing up her neck and into her cheeks. *No! This is not the same thing at all.*

"Right. Like a wolf." His gaze hammered into hers. "Ever done any howling?"

The blush deepened, but she shook her head, determined to never admit her part in the silliness of the other night. Especially not to a stranger. "Of course not."

"Oh, but I think you have."

How could he know? Her throat closed as if keeping her from an admission of guilt. "You're wrong." Tala swallowed and dropped her gaze. Her heart pounded against her chest, making her breathing more difficult. He couldn't know. Unless he'd seen her outside the bar. Terrified, she whipped her gaze to his and held on.

As if reading her mind, he answered her. "Don't worry. I'd never hurt you."

She had to get him out. Now. "I'm going to tell you one more time. Leave."

Ignoring her yet again, he pointed at a poster of a wolf and his mate. "Wolves mate for life, you know."

"What? What's that got to do with anything?" Thrown, she stammered, and tried to sort out the emotions whirling inside her. How did he keep her from yelling? Why isn't she screaming for help? Not that anyone would answer, but it was worth a try. Yet why was help the last thing she really wanted? She lifted the pitiful knife and slashed through the air. "Look. I'm warning you. One last time. Get the hell out."

As if answering her demands at long last, he turned toward the door, paused, and grinned at her. Right before he fell to the floor.

Chapter Four

What the hell?

Tala let out a cry as her intruder hit the floor with a resounding *thud*. She stepped forward out of instinct, wanting to help him, and then stopped, realizing the possibility of a trap. Instead, she bounced back and forth, undecided, on the balls of her feet. "Oh, damn. What do I do now?"

Eyeing her phone on the coffee table near him, she bit her lip, gathered her courage, and made a quick dash to retrieve it. With her phone in hand, she scampered behind the counter again. "Why do these things always happen to me?" She punched the first button on the phone, and paused when the man moaned. Something about the sound bothered her.

"What'd you say?" Setting the phone down, she leaned over the counter. "Devlin? Was that your name? Do you hear me?"

Of course he can't hear you, dimwit. He passed out.

The little voice in her head scolded her, phasing out some of the lingering fear. "Shut up. I know he can't hear me. Which is why I should call the cops and escape while I can." She paused, squinting at the lump on her floor as he rolled from his side onto his back. Relief flooded through her. "Good. At least he's moving. But why aren't I calling?"

Devlin moaned again and this time instinct sent her feet off and running before her brain could stop them. Crossing the distance in strides, she fell to the floor beside him, ignoring the warning shouts in her head. *Don't be a crazy woman. Don't be a stupid woman. Run, Tala.*

"Damn it all to hell and back. I don't know why I'm helping you. But right after I help you, I'm hiring the best psychiatrist in the city. For me."

What should she do? She searched her brain, trying yet again to recall the first aid information she'd learned. And came up empty. "I knew I should have paid more attention to that snotty instructor. She said I'd need this stuff sometime and she was right. Damn her to hell and back."

She reached out and placed the tips of her fingers alongside his throat. His eyelids fluttered a second when she did so, making her whip her hand away. Cursing under her breath, she reached out again and pressed harder against his jugular vein. "Good. His pulse is strong." Her hand slid down his neck as she'd done so many times before when comforting injured animals, while her eyes caught a good look at the bulge in his crotch. "Looks like something else is strong, too."

"Only because you touched me. Caught you looking again."

"Holy shit!" Tala threw herself backwards, landing on her bottom. Her nails dug into the carpet behind her as she supported herself on her palms. "Quit scaring me!" *Move, Tala. Now. Before he gets up.* But her body wouldn't respond. Not while entranced by those chocolate eyes.

Devlin's big eyes looked up at her and pulled her deeper inside. Her irritation melted away into their depths, soothed away by their soft gleam.

"Sorry. I didn't mean to." The gleam shifted into a wicked spark.

This man is dangerous. In good and bad ways. It ratcheted up her attraction to him to the next level.

"Yeah. Right." She wasn't certain if her remark was meant for his words or her thoughts. "You freaked me out when you fainted."

Devlin elbowed his back off the floor and let out a groan. "Men don't faint. Men pass out. Or better, get knocked out."

"Uh, sorry Mr. Macho. No one knocked you out. And call it what you will, but out like a light is out like a light."

He shook his head, his straight, black hair sifting over his shoulders. For a moment, Tala imagined his face transforming into the face in her dreams. His dancing dark eyes morphed into amber jewels, while his jaw changed, elongating, and his teeth grew longer. Somewhat afraid to, yet too curious not to, she sucked in a short breath and reached out.

The touch of Devlin's grip on her outstretched hand startled her out of her trance. His fingertips caressed hers, launching rockets of shivers through her hand and into her arm. Yet the shivers were nothing compared to the tremors he evoked when he laced his fingers through hers.

"Are you all right?"

His question was little more than a whisper, yet the concern in his tone blared in her ears. She tilted her head, and wondered how this stranger could cause so many reactions within her. She whispered in response, surprised to find her voice working. "Me? Sure. I'm not the one with buckshot in my ass. But are you?"

The expression in his eyes socked her in the gut with its sincerity. "I'm doing much better since I met you."

Damn it all to hell and back. The man knew how to lay it on. And she knew how to lap it up. Like a dog after a treat. Not that she'd ever let him know that.

"Okay, then. Since you're okay, you can leave." She rose and backpedaled away from him. He watched her as if not understanding her wariness, and pushed himself to a standing position.

His arm muscles flexed with his movement and she couldn't recall when she'd seen such a delectable sight. She swallowed, trying to push the image of him, naked in her bed, out of her mind. To her surprise, however, the expression on his face returned her to the present.

What was with this guy? His look, so sad yet determined, hurt yet forgiving, awakened all the yearning in her soul. Here was a kindred spirit. A man who knew what loneliness was. A man who ached for the touch of another of his own kind, to have that one special person beside him.

Get a grip, Tala. You're letting your own dreams run wild. And dreams rarely come true.

She'd just managed to convince herself of the truth behind her words when Devlin turned and started for the door. But her sigh, a mixture of relief and disappointment, died as he stumbled and clutched the end of her sofa to steady himself.

"Hey! You're definitely not okay." Seconds after his stumble, she was with him, tossing his arm over her shoulder and steering him toward her bedroom. "You need a doctor. You lie down and I'll call for an ambulance."

His head fell forward. "No. No ambulance. No doctor. You have to promise."

"But—"

"No! Promise. Or let me leave." He pivoted their bodies, weaving them away from the bedroom to the front door.

Tala shoved against him, at once keeping him upright and helping him stagger toward the bedroom. "No way. You need me." She grappled to hold his weight as she led him over to the bed. Shifting her body, she pushed him onto the bed. His weight catapulted her along with him, his strong hands gripping her, pulling her to him. Somehow, some way, they flipped, putting her under him as they landed on the soft mattress.

Their noses touched, reminding her of two canines greeting each other, as his body pinned hers to the bed. A sly grin lifted his mouth while he positioned his arms along the side of her head.

For a moment, she knew pure delight as the bulge in his pants pushed against the cleft in hers, fitting as if made for her. Only her. "Uh, I think you should get off of me."

His intense eyes changed, adding yellow flakes to their deep richness. "Can't."

"And why not?" She gritted her teeth, squelching her nervous laugh, as he nuzzled her neck, tickling her like a puppy playing with her.

"I wouldn't want to pass out again." At her quizzical expression, he added with a mock somber face, "You know. If I stood up too fast."

"I think we can risk it." Although a part of her wanted nothing more than to keep his hard body on top of hers. "Now get off of me." She grabbed him by the hair and pulled.

"Ow! Yes, ma'am." He lifted up on his forearms before pausing to stare at her. "But I need to do this first." With a spark of mischief in his eyes, he tilted his head and licked her.

She inhaled a quick breath as the rough texture of his tongue swiped along her collarbone. Yet instead of being disgusted by the gesture, hot juices burst unchecked between her legs, tremors racing from the moistness into her stomach. He'd made her come with just a lick!

With a low groan, he pushed away from her, falling onto his back against her bed. She stayed where she was for a second, unable to force her body to move. At last, common sense came back and she leapt up from the bed, pacing several feet away before daring to turn to him. "I don't let any hurt being, animal or man, go uncared for. So be quiet and lie there. Stay!" Why did she want to treat him like a dog? She cringed at the warning look he shot her before adding, "You know what I meant."

He ran shaky hands through the silky strands of hair covering his face, and then kept his arms stretched over his head. "Okay. Anything you say."

Narrowing her eyes at him, she studied his features for any telltale signs of deception and found none. "Good. I'll be right back."

Tala darted into the adjoining bathroom, opened the cabinet, and dug around for anything she could use to tend his wound. Why in the world had she let this stranger, this Peeping Tom, into her apartment? And to top it off, now he was in her bed!

Finding nothing useful in the cabinet, she flung the doors open on the storage area below the sink and sifted through the bottles, boxes, and other containers. She'd always rooted for the underdog but this time she'd gone too far. Who knew what this man really wanted? He could harm her or even kill her.

But I know he wouldn't. I know I'm safer with him than I've been with anyone else.

She stopped as the conviction of her thoughts smacked her in the chest, her hand coming to rest on top of a box of bandages. Grabbing a bottle of antiseptic and a couple of towels, she sprinted back into her bedroom.

"Oh. My. God." In the short span of time she'd spent in the bathroom, Devlin had pulled the covers down on the bed, and gotten undressed. He lay, with the comforter kicked to the foot of the bed, his hands folded on his chest, and his legs flung wide.

"What the hell are you doing?"

*****

"I'm ready for my physical."

If her mouth flapped any wider, he'd get a hook and reel her in. Determined not to laugh, Devlin cupped his hands behind his back and cocked his head at her. "What's wrong? Cat got your tongue? Mean, sneaky creatures, those felines."

"What?"

Someone needed to put her out of her misery. And who better than him? "Um, I figured you'd want to look at my wound, so I got undressed."

She finally managed to close her mouth. "You did?"

"Which are you asking about? Figuring you'd want to look at my wound? Or getting undressed?" The way she perused his body, he could almost see the smoke coming off her. She wanted him. Of that much he was certain. Her stare fell to his sizeable manhood and he had to bite the inside of his mouth to keep from grinning. Of course, a man had the right to have a little fun. Concentrating, he willed his dick to jerk.

"Oh. My. God."

"You sure say that a lot."

"Are you friggin' kidding me?

Funny she should say that, since he was. But he'd never admit it.

"About what?"

He saw the frustration flash through her and decided the time for jokes was over. "Never mind." He twisted onto his side to place his buttocks toward her, twisting to peek over his shoulder. "I'm hurting a lot. Do you think you could patch me up and get me something for the pain? Like maybe some liquor?"

Her body jumped in response as if startled out of a hard sleep. "Uh, I don't think so. In fact, I'm wondering why I'm not calling the police."

"You know you won't. Because you know I'm not a threat. Because you know something is going on between us."

"No, there's not."

He stared at her, intent on letting her know where he stood. "Are you sure?"

She returned his stare with her eyebrows diving toward her cute little nose. Her mouth moved to the side in an odd little quirk, but she remained quiet, soaking in his words. At last, she came toward him, unrolling the bandage as she walked.

Once she was by the bedside, she took the covers and lifted them over his legs. She paused for a moment when she reached his thigh and he caught her trying to get another look at his... *Oh boy*...When he snapped his fingers, she jolted back to attention., He took the sheet from her to pull over the front of his hips, leaving only his bottom exposed.

She coughed, a nervous, excited sound, and drew the chair closest to the bed toward her. Placing her materials on top of the sheet, she cleared her throat again and gingerly touched his wound.

"At least you aren't bleeding any longer."

"After seeing your clean, white sheets, I wouldn't dare." He'd have liked to watch her expression, but turned to the windows. No use in pressing his luck. "By the way, don't you think we should get introduced officially since you're going to cop a feel of my rock-hard butt?"

"It's more than obvious your ego wasn't injured. And my name's Tala."

"Tala. Yeah, I remember from the uh, wolf pen. Your name fits you. And your last name was…?" He knew her last name, but he wanted her to say it knowing it would sound sensual coming from her lips.

"Wilde."

He stretched around to grin at her. "Does your last name fit you, too?"

"What do you mean?"

Returning his gaze to the windows, he grinned, knowing she couldn't see him, and gave her some time to think about his meaning. She came to the correct understanding soon enough.

"None of your damn business."

"Hey, I just asked a simple question."

"Somehow I don't think any of your questions are 'simple.'"

He started to ask her what *she* meant when he heard the amazement in her voice. Instead, he sought out her pretty eyes again. Blue like the sky in the mountains.

"Okay, this is weird. You were bleeding on the patio. I know you were because I saw the blood. And, come to think of it, I don't remember any blood drops on my carpet. This wound is healing over."

Should he explain now? Or wait until after he'd finished explaining everything else first? "Um, yeah. I'm a fast healer."

"I'll say."

She flinched when she added the antiseptic to the injury, yet he didn't move. She'd flinched because she'd expected him to flinch. Which showed she had a lot to learn about him.

"So, you understand about the other night, right?" He held his breath, hoping he'd get the answer he wanted. Her hand grazed the skin around his wound perking up his nerve endings. Maybe she wasn't even aware of her action, but he'd bet all his claws she wanted to touch him. To absorb his texture. To enjoy the feel of his skin against her skin.

"I'm not sure. I guess so. But didn't you think watching me dance was a bit sick?"

"Sick? No. Not unless I'm not supposed to like women. Which I do. In fact, I love women. Ow!"

"Sorry. Guess I applied too much pressure. By accident, of course."

Yeah, right. Or had she done it because she didn't like what he'd said about loving women? Other women? "Besides, I thought your dance was for me." He heard a ripping sound as she tore off a piece of the tape. She continued to work with a quiet rhythm as he listened to the sounds behind him.

"Why would you think such a thing?"

"You mean it wasn't? You really didn't realize I was outside?" Again, her fingers played over his butt, sending a spark of heat rushing to his groin.

"How would I have known you were outside? Do you think I make a habit of dancing for voyeurs?"

She hadn't known he was there. Which meant she hadn't sensed him. But she'd called for him, right? Or had she? If not, how would he tell her the truth now?

She dabbed at his wound, bringing him out of his thoughts. "Trust me. I'm a zoologist. Not a stripper."

He gripped the sheet and grappled with the irritation flooding through him. First, she didn't realize he'd come for her and then he found out she was a zoologist? He'd hoped her job at the zoo was with people, not animals. What next? Medical research on wolves?

He growled the words through gritted teeth. "I didn't think you were." *A zoologist. In fact, I'd rather she was a stripper.*

"Good. Because I wouldn't put myself on display for men."

Best to get away from this subject before his irritation turned to anger. "So what do you do as a zookeeper?" God, he could barely spit out the word "zookeeper."

"Lots of different things. I deal with educating the public about the various animals. I take care of the animals, do tours with civic and school groups, and tape public service messages for the zoo."

He sighed a small measure of relief. At least it sounded like she didn't do anything distasteful working with the animals. "What about wolves?"

She pressed the bandage to his rear and applied tape to hold it in place. "What about wolves?"

Noticing her hand linger on the bandage, he tried to push away a hot flash of desire. But her touch on his skin was like a flame to kindling. "Do you do anything with the wolves at the zoo?"

Her hand slid along the curve of his buttocks in a gentle caress. Enjoying the sensation of her stroke, he flexed and imagined her hand stroking another part of his anatomy.

"Oh, sure. In fact, I helped design the wolf habitat you, uh, visited."

He grumbled at the thought of wolves being caged no matter what fancy term was used. "Habitat? Is that zookeeper lingo for cage?" She stopped and he twisted around to glare at her. "Well, is it?"

"Look. I love wolves. And we treat our wolves with the best care, love, and attention we can. What's your problem, anyway?"

Take it easy, Devlin. She doesn't understand. Not yet.

Turning his head away from her, he struggled to level his tone. "No problem. I just figured with all the wolf posters you have, you'd rather see wolves running free instead of cooped up in some manmade 'habitat.'" He tried, but he couldn't keep from sounding out invisible quotes around the nasty word.

"I would. But their home at the zoo is the next best thing. Besides, they're safe at the zoo. You know. Safe from hunters. And trespassing drunks."

"Safe, but not fully alive. Not able to live their lives as nature intended."

An edge to her tone carried her anger to him. In fact, he could almost see her lips thinning out, pressed tightly together. "The wolves at the zoo are happy."

"How do you know? Have you ever asked them?"

"Ask them? Now you're just being silly."

A rustling noise had him flipping over to see her gathering her materials and rising to her feet. "Hey, don't get mad. I'm carrying on a discussion, is all."

"I'm not mad." She stepped away a few feet, paused, and faced him. "Okay, maybe a little mad."

"Well, you shouldn't be."

Those big blue eyes grabbed hold of him and threatened to rip out his heart. Hugging the bandage roll, tape, and antiseptic against her breasts, she glowered at him. And he almost wished he'd kept his mouth closed about the wolves. Almost. "How about this? When I'm better, you promise to take me on a tour of the zoo. One on the *outside* of the pens." He leveled his best smile at her. "Convert me." *Or maybe the other way round.*

"Why don't you get some rest so you can be on your way soon." She blinked, started to shake her head, and blinked again. "Okay, I'll take you up on the tour if you promise to go with an open mind. Agreed?"

*****

"Do I hear the shower?" Tala peeked into the bedroom, expecting to see Devlin resting in her bed. Wanting to see Devlin in her bed.

When she saw the covers in disarray, she crossed over to the rumpled mess and smoothed out the sheets. Grasping the pillow, she picked up his scent and sniffed. *He smells like the forest, sunshine and testosterone. Or at least, what I think testosterone should smell like.*

She frowned and muttered to herself. "Holy crap. In a few short hours, I've taken in a voyeur, fixed his wound...a gunshot wound...and given him my bed. I've done some stupid things in the past, but this one tops them all. What the hell am I thinking?"

If she had a brain in her head, she'd call the police right this second. But how would she explain taking him in, fixing up his injury, and putting him in her bed? Not to mention the fact that they'd find him in her shower!

The sound of running water beckoned her. Answering the summons, she tiptoed to the bathroom door and froze.

Even with the clear glass of the shower stall fogged over, she could see enough to stun her into silence. *Could anyone ever get used to seeing such a magnificent piece of animal? Animal?* She wondered about her choice of word, but the sight of his bending over to scrub his legs, tossed the errant thought out of her brain. Although she knew she shouldn't stand there staring, she couldn't help but study him. Devlin *was* a damned Greek god. An Adonis comes to life. A capital M. A. N.

Strong, long legs, runner's legs, covered with dark hair drew her eyes upward to his groin. His shaft was extended, ready, as if knowing she would find him. Did this guy always have a hard-on?

Above the ramrod pole, a six-pack—*hell, an eight-pack*—abdomen rippled with every movement. And his chest. Good God, his chest overwhelmed her.

Mountain-like pecs dominated the broad expanse while his brown nipples stood guard on top. She moaned, an ache she didn't know opening wide, breaking free within her.

"Tala?"

She croaked out an answer, unsure if she could count on her voice. "Yeah."

The shower door slid open a few inches, letting the water splash onto the floor outside. "Come here."

Had any other man commanded her the same way, she would have blasted him with expletives as she threw him out the door. Yet the words this man, this stranger, this god, spoke to her didn't evoke such a reaction. Instead, her crotch grew wet, her pulse quickened, and her pelvic muscles tightened. Hell, yes, she'd come. In every way possible.

She moved without thinking about her actions, wanting to obey him, needing to obey him. And when her brain did start to object, she shut it down without a qualm. *Crazy?* Yes, what she was about to do was crazy. But she didn't care.

She couldn't *not* go to him. Not with his huge, beautiful cock calling to her. Not when all a woman's fantasies stood billowed in steam and hot water. She may be crazy to go to him, but she'd be crazier not to. She could almost hear her friends chanting, *"You go, girl!"*

Devlin held out his hand, dripping more water to the floor, and she reached out to place her palm in his. Spray from the showerhead hit her, soaking her hair and plastering her shirt to her breasts. The dusting of dark hair covering his chest drew her gaze and she lifted her hand to comb her fingers through it.

He groaned, cupped her breast in his big hand, and bent his head to her neck. His warm tongue slid along her neck until reaching her ear. Nibbling at her lobe, he slipped his fingers under her shirt and drew the soaked shirt over her head. Her bra followed her shirt to the shower floor, and she stepped on them. Arching her back, she welcomed his mouth on her tit. Somehow, she wasn't quite sure how or when, he'd managed to strip her jeans and panties away from her, too.

While his teeth nipped at the pebbled bud, his fingers slid between her folds to stroke her lower bud. Her arms slid around his neck, pulling him closer, sending him the signal of her desire. Another groan escaped him as he understood her silent request and knelt before her.

Tala's hands pushed against the side of the shower as he went to his knees. She watched in fascination as he feathered kisses along the soft mound of her stomach. Devlin slid his tongue in the crease between her leg and her crotch, and she lifted one leg to place it on the built-in shower seat.

He wrapped an arm under each leg, gripping her buttocks to bring her closer to him. Even though she knew he could never be close enough for her. She wanted him inside her. Part of her. Joined with her. Tala gasped as his tongue lavished her, sending shudders throughout her body.

Damn it all to hell and back, but he was great. Devlin knew how to please a woman. He knew exactly how long to lick. Exactly how long to bite. Exactly how long to devour.

With every orgasm, he increased his onslaught, attacking her swollen nub with renewed enthusiasm.

And each time, he brought her to an even higher zone of pleasure. Tala closed her eyes and allowed him to shoulder her weight. She had no choice. He'd taken all her strength. When he stopped, she looked down at his lust-filled face and smiled.

"Beats the hell out of my vibrator."

"I'd hope so." The wicked gleam in his eyes should have warned her, but she was too weak to focus. "And I'm not through yet."

Before she could utter a reply, he rose and grabbed her head, crushing her mouth with his. A small cry escaped her as her tongue wrestled with his, but the desire was too strong to fight. She could taste her own juices on his lips, and she sucked on his tongue. Dizzy with desire, she laced her fingers behind his head and held tight.

The kiss, however, ended too soon. He broke away and, tugging at the hair on the nape of her neck and turned her to face the shower wall. Her head fell forward to rest on the glass as his hands massaged her breasts, plying her nipples so they ached in pleasurable agony. But nothing compared to the delight of his cock rubbing the indent between her cheeks.

"Tala, tell me you want me to fuck you."

She growled, a sound similar to those he'd made, and answered the only way she could. "Yes. I want you to take me."

"You'd better tell me what you want me to do or I'll do it the way I want. And I want to fuck you rough."

A sliver of fear spiked somewhere deep inside her. Could she trust him not to hurt her? Could she trust herself not to let him? Her answer came to her, swift and certain. *Yes.* She could.

She moaned, long and hard. A moan of frustration, of lust, of heat. "I want you to fuck me the way you want. I want it rough."

He exhaled, a low, tortured sound that renewed her waves of hunger. "I want to take you from behind. I want to ram into you."

"Do it, Devlin."

He stepped back with her, pushing her between the shoulders so she'd place her hands on the tile ledge below the glass. Her buttocks opened for him as he ran a hand along the slit between her legs to find her throbbing. His shaft found its target and he rammed inside her, shocking her, thrilling her with the intensity of his move.

She moaned and bent lower, spreading her legs wider. With one, long push he shoved inside her again, bumping her against the shower wall. His resulting growl pleased her in some unknown way, and she rocked her body along with the pounding of his dick. Together their bodies moved, water cascading off them as if they were one form, the heat rising from their bodies mixing with the steam.

She'd wanted this from the moment she'd first seen him in the wolf habitat. From the second she'd laid eyes on him, she'd wanted him and she'd had to have him. No matter what.

Her panting breath echoed his while his hands held her up by holding onto her breasts. When his body tensed, she was ready and clenched the muscles of her cave together, dragging the last bit of manhood out of him.

"Argh. Tala."

Her release came when he called her name. Tremors rippled through her frame, traveling into his as he pulled away from her to roar his climax.

She swiveled to him again, wanting to see his face. A quiet satisfaction permeated him, and she smiled, knowing she'd given him that satisfaction. The water ran down their bodies, cleansing their juices from each other, as he pressed against her. Holding onto him, her sated body couldn't help but enjoy the quivers still moving along his arms and back. She slid her hands down the rugged surface of his torso, stopping to rest on his buttocks.

Her fingers skimmed down the curve of his ass, running over the smooth skin. Her heart gained speed with what she knew couldn't be true, yet she explored further, searching for his injury. *What happened to his wound?* The area where his rough wound should be was gone, replaced by smooth skin.

Chapter Five

"What happened to your wound?"

Devlin ran his hand along her jawline, while he licked around the rim of her ear. "Wound?" He sniffed, enjoying the intriguing scent of her skin mixed with the musky fragrance of their bodily fluids. Not to mention the soft sleekness of her toned body. She was his now even though he hadn't marked her yet.

She pushed him away, positioning him so he'd turn away from her. "Your wound! Your gunshot wound. It's different." She pointed at his bottom and it took a moment before he realized what she wanted.

He bowed his head, letting his wet hair fall in front of his face. How would he explain this to her? Was now the time to tell her everything? Or should he wait and tell her about his kind a little at a time?

She ran her hands over his buttocks again, making his dick twitch in response. But another session of lovemaking would have to wait. *Lovemaking.* A satisfied, happy glow flowed over him. As a healthy, strong male, he'd had lots of sex in his lifetime, but he'd never considered any of those encounters as making love.

"Your wound looks like it's healed. What the hell is going on?" She stared at him, and he tried to reply, but couldn't think of the right words to say.

Her eyes grew wide and she pivoted to push open the door. He clutched at her arm, but she jerked it out of his grasp as she stepped out of the shower and grabbed the towel.

"Tala, wait a sec." Devlin flipped off the water and followed Tala, but she'd already exited the bathroom. Without bothering to get another towel, he rushed after her.

He found her in the living room, the towel wrapped around her, pacing back and forth in front of the patio doors. She muttered a few choice words at him and slapped at his hands when he reached for her.

"This doesn't make sense. How could your wound heal so quickly?" She paused a moment, looking to him for an answer. "Well?"

Water dripped from him, dampening the carpet. "If you'll settle down, I'll try to explain."

Instead, she resumed her trek back and forth across the floor. "Explain what? Explain how?" Again, she stopped to stare at him.

"Yoo-hoo, Mr. Hung! Face this way so we can get a clear shot of your dong. In fact, come on out on the patio and pose for some pictures, okay?"

Tala and Devlin spun to the window to see a group of teenagers standing near the tree line behind the apartment house. The girl who'd called to them held up her camera phone.

"No fair, man. Tell the bitch to drop the towel so us guys can get some shots, too." A pimple-faced teen raised his phone, too.

"Shit! Why is everyone taking pictures of me nowadays?" Tala whirled and tugged the curtains closed to the caterwauling of the youths. "Go away, you little perverts." But the jeering didn't stop. Tala swung around to confront Devlin. "Explain how your wound can heal so fast."

"I can't." What could he tell her? Devlin jumped his eyebrows up, opening his eyes wide in innocence in a *beats-the-hell-outta-me* expression.

"What do you mean you can't?"

"Exactly what I said. I can't. Maybe the wound wasn't so bad to begin with. Maybe you're a good nurse. I don't know." He shivered as the air conditioner blew cold air on his wet body. Would she believe him?

Tala's frown deepened as she considered his lame explanations. She shook her head and he got ready for another barrage of questions. Yet none came.

"You're a really weird man." She narrowed her eyes at him, and he squirmed. He, Devlin, future leader of the Morgan Pack, squirmed under a woman's accusatory glare.

But what else could he say? "Guess so."

She gawked at him, thrown by his light-hearted answer, and laughed.

God, how he loved the sound of her. Goose bumps of desire popped out along his arms.

"Well, gee. As long as you admit it." She tossed him another exasperated expression. "You better go get dressed. At least then you won't be a naked weird man."

Flashing her a mischievous grin, he saluted her and marched toward the hallway. Yet before he left the room, he twisted back to look at her and caught her peering at his behind. "Hey, Tala. Like what you see?"

When she laughed harder this time, he bent over, shot her the moon, and wiggled his butt at her. A pillow hit him square in the rear as he dashed from the room.

*****

"Nice place. For a zoo."

Tala glanced at Devlin, searching his face for the sneer she'd heard in his voice. When she couldn't find any, she gave him the benefit of the doubt. "Yes, it is. I'm proud of our natural habitats for the animals. And, of course, our education department is top-notch." Maybe she shouldn't brag, but she wanted him know how much she loved her work and her accomplishments. Why she cared about his approval, she didn't know. But she did.

He pointed at one of her promotional photographs hanging on a wall. "And you're the poster child for the zoo and its good deeds?"

"Like I told you, I do some promotional spots for the zoo. Nothing big. Just local stuff."

The crease of his forehead left her wondering if he did approve. The thought of his possible disapproval tightened her neck muscles.

"One thing about the picture, Tala."

"What's that?" She planted her feet apart, adopting a firm stance, ready to defend her work.

"Doesn't do you justice."

His words flowed over her, erasing her suspicion, while giving her a major case of get-him-in-bed-right-now-itis. "Thanks."

She shifted her head to the side, trying to see Devlin's expression as he scanned the area around him. Yet she couldn't tell anything from what she saw. His features remained unmoving, transfixed in an emotionless, non-committal mask.

"Okay. Well, we've seen the giraffes, the predators, and the felines. Which, by your reaction, I gathered you don't like cats."

"You got that right."

She waited for more of an explanation, then continued when she didn't get one. "Okay, then. Let's move on into the arctic area. This is where we keep the arctic wolves."

She'd gone a yard or so ahead of him before she'd realized he'd stopped. "What, Devlin?" A strange expression flickered across his face, making her wish she could read his mind. But the look was soon gone and the unreadable mask fell back into place.

"Nothing. Let's go."

Tala sighed as they walked the path leading up to the wolf pack exhibit. An artic wilderness span out before them and she couldn't help but take pride in the layout. "See? I realize it's not as good as the real thing, but we've tried to create as close a natural environment for our arctic wolves as possible." She surveyed the area to locate the wolves and pointed when she found her favorite. "There's Shakan. See the big male sitting on top of the outcrop? Isn't he gorgeous?"

The pristine white of the male's fur struck a brilliant contrast to the dark gray of the rock. Lifting his head, Shakan sniffed the air, as if acknowledging their presence. His cold eyes noted Tala's existence, flicking over her in one, quick moment, to settle on Devlin, where his gaze stayed glued for several minutes.

Devlin's grunt brought her attention back to him. The disgust on Devlin's face was unmistakable. He loathed what he saw.

"What's the matter? Don't you like wolves?"

His answer came on the heels of a snarl. "Of course I do. But after seeing this, I'm wondering if *you* do."

Stunned, Tala whipped her eyes between Shakan and Devlin. "What're you talking about? I adore wolves. Can't you see how much I care in the home we've made for them?" The vexation rising up in her had her almost spitting saliva with her words. How dare he question her love of wolves? Of any animals. Including dumb human animals like him.

He remained still, arms folded across his chest, with repugnance oozing from every pore. "If you loved them, you'd want to set them free."

Tala coughed, a dry, sarcastic laugh. "They're here to help their species survive. They're here to help educate humans about them. They're here because I do care."

"If you say so."

For one brief moment, she thought about taking a swing at him. Damn it all to hell and back, how she'd love to wipe that sneer off his face. But she was smart enough to know her punch wouldn't faze him, much less change his opinion. Instead, she returned his glare with all the intensity she could muster. "Yeah. I do say so. I'm the expert here, remember?"

His dark eyes locked onto her and she froze. Something about the gleam in his eyes challenged her assertion. Almost as if he considered himself the expert and not her. Which, of course, was ridiculous. *Wasn't it?* "Devlin, you've never said what you do for a living."

The corners of his lips tipped upward, recognizing her probe. "I have various financial interests dealing with imports and exports."

"Anything to do with animals?"

"In my business dealings? Not the way you mean."

What had he meant by that?

He squinted at her and smiled a big, toothy grin. "But I've known some wolves in my time."

"Really? The four-legged or two-legged variety?"

His throaty laugh rang out, and a few of the wolves moved together to stand staring at him. "Both."

What did he mean now? She searched his face and saw the humor there. "Oh, I get it. Two-legged variety as in womanizers. Is that what you are, Devlin?"

This time he faced her before laughing. "I'm both." Spinning on his heel, he strode away from her before she could respond to his strange answer.

"Wait a sec." She sprinted after him, catching him by the arm to twirl him around. "How can you be both?"

"Remind me to show you sometime."

She started to complain about his cryptic answer when he grabbed her arms, his head whipping around to scan the area. His grip tightened on her, causing her to cry out. "Ow! What's wrong?"

Devlin's features scrunched together as he let her go to swivel toward the small building adjacent to the wolf exhibit. "Do you hear her?"

Tala did a one-eighty, trying to spot something out of the ordinary. But the crowd around them kept on walking, laughing, and enjoying the zoo. "Hear who?"

Devlin took off down the path leading to the small building. Tala ran after him, trying to keep up with the speeding Devlin. Following on his heels, she burst into the building to find George Groggins, a new employee, standing outside a small holding cage, beating an injured wolf with a large metal pole. With a wounded leg, the animal was trapped, unable to move, defenseless against the attack.

"George!" Her shout brought the stubby man around, his gleeful face freezing in place. Recognizing his boss, his features came together to show the affable exterior she'd come to expect from him.

George opened his mouth to speak, but choked on his words as Devlin's hands wrapped around his throat.

*****

The gurgling sounds coming from George's mouth encouraged Devlin to squeeze harder. Placing what little of his hands he could get around Devlin's large wrists, the rotund man fought for his life. Devlin could hear Tala shout at him to let go, but he ignored her. Instead, instinct kicked in and his primary thought was to destroy the enemy of the injured she-wolf. His lips spread wider as the animal within him took over.

George's eyes bugged open, silently beseeching her, as Tala seized one of Devlin's arms and pulled at him with every bit of strength in her. But Devlin's hands remained locked firmly around George's throat. Tala was a mere afterthought. He wouldn't let this slime ball of a human hurt any wolf if he could stop him. And he could definitely stop him. For good, if necessary.

Lifting her legs, Tala hung from Devlin's arm like a kid hanging on a massive oak tree branch. Still, he didn't, wouldn't let go. His focus stayed on George as his power grew stronger with each second.

Landing on her feet, Tala left them and, although he wanted to see where she'd gone, Devlin kept his eyes on his prey. She'd return. He was sure of it. And then, once he'd dealt with this bastard, he'd explain everything to her.

"Let him go, Devlin!"

She stood behind him and tugged on his shoulders. He heard the plea, the panic in Tala's voice, yet wouldn't let her dissuade him. "No. This hyena should pay for what he did."

"He will, Devlin. I promise. Let him go now."

Shaking his head, Devlin opened his mouth wider, exposing his long, sharp fangs. His warm brown eyes altered, feeling the conversion take place. George, unable to cry, managed a strangled whimper and kicked his feet wildly, trying to break Devlin's hold on him. To stop George's kicking, Devlin bent his head to him, and laid the points of his teeth against the man's neck, pressing just hard enough to make an indentation, but not enough to draw blood.

Pain hit him between his shoulder blades, zapping his transformation back to full human form. Loosening his grip on George, he whirled toward Tala.

"Shit!" His angry glare fell to the iron rod in Tala's hand and disbelief flowed through him like cold water through an icy creek. "You struck me?" Shudders racked his body, but he managed to stay upright even while George's limp body slumped to the floor beside him. "Were you trying to hurt me?"

She lowered the rod, her mouth dropping open. "Wow. Most guys would have dropped like a sack of dog food. But you're still standing. Amazing."

"Not that I care for the comparison, but thanks a lot. Wanna try another whack? Maybe this time you can take my head off."

"Don't be so dramatic. I only hit you a little." At his probing glare, she changed her tune. "Okay, maybe more than a little. But you're a big, tough guy and can take it. Obviously. Don't be such a wuss."

He took a shaky step toward her, but stopped when she pointed at George.

"Oh, shit, Devlin. I think you killed him."

With the ache between his shoulders starting to ebb, Devlin bent to examine his victim. "No, I didn't. The little coward passed out, is all." Snarling his disgust, he pivoted and strode over to the cage where the she-wolf lay unmoving on her side.

His stomach rolled over as he turned to see Tala holding George's head in her lap. "He doesn't deserve your sympathy. She does." A caustic laugh brought his true feelings out. "Hell, I do for hitting me."

Tala stared at him, her face unreadable. But Devlin didn't have time to sort out her emotions. "Key. Where's the key to this cage?"

Without saying a word, Tala nodded to a pegboard on the wall closest to him. He returned her nod and retrieved the key. Turning the lock, he opened the door and stepped into the cage.

"Devlin, no! You can't go in there. She's wounded and possibly dangerous."

A great sadness crept over Devlin when he looked at Tala. Could she not see that the man she comforted was the dangerous one? Stupid brutality was always much more dangerous than the instinct of self-defense. Yet, instead of speaking his thoughts out loud, he chose a different method of teaching her. "No, I don't think so. Trust me."

Kneeling beside the female arctic wolf, Devlin ran his hands over her long, muscled body. He blew out a breath of relief when he didn't find any broken bones, other than her bandaged leg. Placing both hands on her, he gently stroked her, giving her the best form of treatment he knew how to give. "The asshole didn't break any of her bones. But he beat her up a lot. She'll have bruises on most of her body."

George groaned and Tala laid his head on the floor to move away from him. "That's incredible. She must be injured big time to let a human run his hands all over her. And without sedation." She continued to stare at Devlin as he glanced at her from time to time.

"Call the police." George's croak had both Devlin and Tala crooking their heads in his direction. Even the wolf tried to lift her head at the sound of his voice. "Call the police."

"What for, George?"

Devlin, elated at the vehemence in Tala's tone, grinned up at her as she turned toward George, struggling to a sitting position.

George pulled his shirt away from his neck. "That freak bit me."

"I don't see any bite marks. Or blood." Still, Tala checked with Devlin. And although a smile covered her features, he noticed the glint of worry, distrust, and confusion in her eyes. "You bit him?"

Devlin puffed a bit of air out the side of his mouth and rolled his eyes. "Of course not. The man's an idiot as well as an animal abuser. The only person I'd ever bite is you."

He swallowed a chuckle as the pink zipped up her neck and into her cheeks. Coughing, she confronted George. "Okay, George. I'll call the police. When they get here, you tell them Devlin bit you and I'll tell them about your mistreatment of the animals." At his surprised expression, she added, "Yeah, that's right. I've had my suspicions before now. More than one animal has turned up with bruises. So, Georgie. Still want me to call the police?"

Cursing at them, George scrambled to his feet and staggered to the door. "Your boyfriend's a freak or something. You'd better watch out."

"I'll do that, George. Oh, and Georgie?"

When she had his full attention, she let him have it. "You're fired. Get the hell outta my zoo."

Devlin watched as George tossed more threats and curses at them, and stumbled outside. "Way to go, Tala. Although I'd like to have finished him off for good."

"I was afraid you had. I'll call the police later, but if I report George now, then he'll report you for attacking him."

Tala crossed over to him and knelt on the other side of the wolf. "How is she?"

He raised his head to gaze into her worried eyes. "She'll be fine."

Tala nodded and reached out to touch her. But when her hand got close, the she-wolf raised her head, bared her fangs, and growled. "Easy, girl. I won't hurt you. I guess she doesn't let just anyone touch her. But you certainly have a way with her. Or is that true for all females?" Tala's blue eyes twinkled at him, her next question reaching her eyes well before it reached her lips. "You're really something with her. So tell me. Why do you have the magic touch?"

He chuckled, wanting to keep his answer as far from the truth as possible. "I guess she realizes I'm her knight in not-so-shining armor."

She smiled, although a frown creased her forehead as she considered the description. "I guess we can consider your helping her as passing your luck on."

He tilted his head at her, questioning her statement. "Huh?"

"You know. I helped you. Now you're helping her. Passing it on."

Understanding, he nodded and drew his hand over the wolf's head. The tired animal closed her eyes, giving total control over to Devlin.

"Just incredible. If you ever want a job at the zoo, just let me know."

He knew she'd meant the offer as a compliment, but he didn't care. "No thanks. I'd rather be an animal than take care of one."

"Oh, you're an animal, all right. The perfect mix of man and beast." Retrieving her cell phone from her pocket, she flipped it opened and punched a number. "Floyd? It's Tala. Send doc over to check out the she-wolf in the containment building, will you? Oh, and call personnel to tell them I just fired George Groggins."

Devlin took a deep breath and relaxed. He'd dodged a bullet from any further questions about wolves. Or so he thought until Tala spoke again.

"Devlin? How'd you know she was a female? Even before you came into the building?"

*****

What the hell went on in there? Mickale watched from a safe distance, his body hidden by the bushes and trees surrounding the area around the wolf habitat, as a short, balding man stumbled from the building. Although the chubby man didn't appear injured, the choice words he used about Devlin left no doubt he'd run into his brother. After following Devlin and the female his brother had called Tala around the zoo most of the morning, Mickale figured he'd be in for a boring day. So much for boring.

When the cry of a she-wolf ripped through the air, Mickale had watched as Devlin charged into a small building. What was with his brother? Just because some bitch yelled for help didn't mean he had to answer her call, did it? Who knew what kind of mess Devlin found?

After a lot of commotion, the man had left, and Devlin and Tala had remained inside. What could they be doing? Why didn't they come out? After all, the she-wolf's call was more out of alarm than pain and he hadn't heard anything from her in awhile. Which meant she was either okay or dead.

Mickale lifted his nose to sniff the air, and resisted the urge to shift to wolf form. The way his luck ran lately, he'd get snatched up by some industrious zoo employee and thrown in the habitat with those other poor bastards. Or worse, a wolf-shifters' nightmare, by the dogcatcher. No, better to wait and see.

He'd waited all these years for his father to name him as his successor. And when his father had betrayed him, he'd kept his cool, knowing disagreement wouldn't change anything. Instead, he'd come up with his own scheme to become leader. Mickale Morgan would be leader of the Morgan Pack, of that he was certain.

Mickale growled to relieve the irritation of having to wait, and to rethink his plan. The plan was a simple one since simple plans always worked better than elaborate ones. He'd keep Devlin from taking his mate. Maybe by turning her against him. Or him against her. Hell, he'd even consider mating with her to keep her out of Devlin's life. Devlin would never marry if his intended female were already mated with another. Especially if she were already mated to his own brother. And if Devlin didn't mate, then Devlin couldn't rule. A simple, yet effective plan.

The first part of the plan, following Devlin to the city, had proven easy. Devlin, being of a one-track mind, led him straight to his woman. Mickale licked his lips at the image of the blonde beauty dancing in her apartment, the lights casting a luminous glow around her sensual, alluring body. He repositioned his shaft, as it grew thicker with the image playing in his mind's eye. He'd enjoy taking Devlin's mate as his own. And, of course, he wouldn't let having a mate keep him from playing around. Not this wolf, anyway.

Where were they? Should he take a chance and sneak over to the building's windows for a look inside? The crowd had thinned out, making hiding in their numbers more difficult. Or should he sit tight and wait them out?

Mickale's stomach rumbled, reminding him of his last meal over twelve hours ago. He sniffed, this time not hunting for the she-wolf's or Devlin's scent, but for food. Wishing he could follow the tempting smells coming from the antelope habitat, he scanned the area for man-made food. A hot dog vendor sat several paces away and he frowned. What a crude name for a food. But it would be better than nothing.

Mickale started to part the bushes and step through when another scent hit him so hard, he had to grip the branches to steady himself. An odor, so disgusting and repulsive it caused his empty stomach to roll over, assaulted his nostrils. Something foul was close. Very close.

Ducking back behind the bushes, Mickale allowed a partial transformation. His eyes shifted, narrowed and changed. Sliding his gaze around the open area in front of him, Mickale searched for the owner of the stench. And found it.

A disheveled man scratched himself and motioned to three other men. Although the sightseeing public didn't see the difference between themselves and these men, Mickale did. The way the men held their bodies…alert, tense and ready to spring into action…shot warning signals through Mickale. The walkie-talkies fastened to their belts blinked on and off. And if Mickale knew anything at all about these men, he knew they secreted weapons of various descriptions on their bodies. Each man studied their surroundings, checking out both visitor and zoo employee.

Mickale shifted a little more, careful to contain his instinct to shift all the way. One tiny step too far into wolf, and he'd be in danger. In full wolf mode, these men could pick up his scent. But as a human, Mickale could hide. Still, he allowed his ears to change, wanting to pick up the men's conversation.

"Shit. I know I smelled werewolf a moment ago." The tallest of the four men kept turning, scoping out everything around him. "It was here for a good five minutes before I lost it."

The burly, box-shaped man nodded. "I know, Carl. I got the same impression. A shifter is near, men, so keep on the alert."

The two other men grunted and pulled away from Carl and the burly man. One of them walked up to the arctic wolf exhibit, raised his hands with an imaginary rifle and pretended to shoot the big male snarling at him from the rocks.

"Skanland, we're close. Damn it, I want another shifter. A year's too long to go without a kill."

Skanland shook his head at Carl. "Yeah, I know. But remember, I want some fun with this one first. We capture one and *then* we kill it."

Mickale ground his teeth together, refraining from snarling and drawing their attention. *Shifter hunters! Curse their kind.* But he guessed their appearance was about due. These scumbags crawled out of their holes every year around this time. While werewolves were unknown to the general population, a group of semi-humans knew about the shifters and made it their mission in life to eradicate them. Thankfully, the hunters' skills were limited and they rarely found a shifter. But sometimes, like a year ago when they'd run across Jimmy Chow of the Chow Pack, they killed.

Mickale stooped lower into the bushes. Too bad he couldn't go into a full shift and rid the earth of a few of them right here and now. But how would Devlin and the woman get past the hunters? Did they know the hunters were around?

The hair on Mickale's neck stood at attention. He'd have to do something to help Devlin. Sabotaging his brother's mating was one thing. But Devlin was his brother and, no matter how strained their relationship might get as a result of their father's decision to put Devlin in leadership, he'd protect his brother with his life. As soon as Devlin exited the building, the hunters would pick up his scent. Mickale couldn't let the hunters get Devlin or the female. But what could he do?

Chapter Six

Mickale stretched out his neck, hoping to hear more of the hunters' conversation. Maybe, just maybe, if he found out what they had planned, he could come up with a way to help Devlin and Tala without his ending up as a trophy mounted over their fireplace.

A man dressed in khaki pants and shirt emblazoned with the zoo's insignia, passed by the hunters, heading for the small building beside the wolf habitat. Switching the black satchel he carried from his right to his left hand, he pushed open the door of the building and called to those inside. "Tala, what's the problem?" The rest of his words drifted away as the door slammed shut behind him.

Carl, the hunter closest to the building, whipped his head toward the opening. "In there, Skanland. I smelled shifter coming from in there. Faint, but there."

Skanland nodded and moved closer, dropping his voice as he drew near. "Yeah, I smelled it, too. Like one of them went into wolf mode and then back real fast."

Carl motioned to the other two men who'd moved toward the building along with Skanland. "About time. Let's go get him." He slid his hand underneath his shirt and lumbered forward until Skanland's grip on his arm brought him up short.

"No. I told you. I want this one alive." Glancing at the visitors swarming around them, he added, "Besides, it's too busy here. We wouldn't want to make a scene." His grin sported discolored teeth made even uglier by the shine of a golden tooth.

"So what'll we do?"

Crooking his finger at the others, Skanland brought them into a huddle. "We wait. He's gotta come out sooner or later. Plus, this way, we can make sure how many we're dealing with. From the smell, I figure it's only one, but a big one. Or maybe two. But you never know until you see their hairy asses."

The other hunters chuckled their agreement and followed as Skanland led them to a nearby picnic shelter. Too far away for Mickale's sensitive hearing to pick up their words, but still close enough to watch them.

Should he try and make it inside the building to warn Devlin?   No, then they'd all be trapped. Mickale's lip curled in disgust. Why couldn't these sub-humans leave them alone? As far as he knew, no shifter had ever done them any harm...except in self-defense. But that didn't seem to matter to the hunters. He couldn't remember a time when the hunters hadn't wanted shifters dead.

Could he take all four of them? Mickale sized up the men and decided he might have a chance. Four against one wasn't the best odds, but he'd had worse. Still, he considered himself a lover and not a fighter.

Hunters were a predictable bunch, which is why Mickale never expected them to do what they did. Forming a tight group, the hunters strode away from the building and their intended prey.   Mickale frowned, unable to figure out their actions. And try as he might, he couldn't believe their departure was a good thing. Something was up.

Devlin and the female exited the building at the same moment Mickale made his decision. He guessed they'd known nothing about the hunters from the daffy smile on Devlin's face. "Shit. He's already panting after her. Talk about a dog in heat."

Mickale ducked as Devlin's eyes drifted toward the bushes he hid behind. If Devlin had already marked her, claiming her as his mate would prove almost impossible. So he'd have to break them up. He shook his head, unhappy at the thought, but deepened his resolve. He'd do anything to rule Morgan Pack. An image of Blair, batting his eyes at him, shot shudders through him. Well, almost anything. Every wolf has his limits.

Mickale kept low to the shrubs lining the path Devlin and Tala followed that led away from the wolf area. He stayed a few yards behind the couple and paused whenever Devlin turned around to scan his surroundings. He knew Devlin could sense his presence, yet Mickale was sure he hadn't seen him. He'd tail Devlin and Tala until he found out where she lived.

As they left the park, the sun started to set beyond the horizon. Purple and blues painted the sky as Devlin and Tala walked through the parking lot. Mickale ducked behind cars as he trailed behind them, keeping them within earshot.

"You can't find your own car?"

"Not a word, Devlin. I don't normally park in the public parking lot. I did today so you could see the entrance to the park. My reserved space is in the employee parking lot, so I'm not used to hunting for my car."

Devlin's soft chuckle matched Mickale's. *She's a spirited one, all right.*

A dark shadow darted by him. Whipping to his right, Mickale searched the rows of vehicles, while the hair on his neck stood erect with warning. Another dark shape stumbled between a van and a motorcycle, bumped into a fender, and plopped onto his rump with a grunt.

Hunters! But clumsy ones. This could be fun, after all.

Mickale ducked as Devlin spun around at the hunter's groan. Both Mickale and the bumbling hunter froze until Tala pulled Devlin along with her.

Psst!

The hunter jolted, startled at Mickale's hiss, his mouth falling wide as he gawked at him. Wiggling his fingers in a small wave, Mickale closed his hand, leaving his middle finger extended. The hunter, dumbfounded, continued to stare at him.

"Aw, hell. Looks like I didn't get the brightest one of the bunch. And that's saying a lot."

Deciding the man needed more coaxing, he snarled and quickly discarded his clothing. Still the man remained motionless.

"What do you not get about a naked man, dude?"

When the possible misunderstanding of his question struck him, Mickale cringed, hastening to clarify. *Thank God Blair wasn't around.* "Now hold up. It's not what you're thinking. I meant…a naked man about to shift, you idiot." Without hesitating, Mickale dropped to all fours and shifted. Black hair covered his body while his ears elongated and claws scraped blacktop. Growling, he tensed his legs and flung his body at the not-so-bright hunter.

*****

A nerve-splitting howl startled Tala, sending her spinning toward the sound. "What the hell?" Two shapes rolled against the tires of a jeep, setting off its alarm system, striking with a force strong enough to dislodge the hubcap and propel the sphere straight toward her.

Devlin grabbed her arm and yanked, pulling her out of the way of the vehicle's airborne missile, and into his arms. His eyes, a strange mix of brown and gold, held her with him until another cry...human this time...pivoted them toward the noise. One of the dark shapes scampered underneath a car and Tala bent over hoping to see where it'd gone. "Did you see that?"

Had she really seen what she thought she'd seen? She bent lower to get a clearer view, but the shape was gone.

She straightened up just as two kaki-clad men raced in pursuit of the fleeing form, pausing to grab the first man, haul him to his feet, and question him.

"Why'd you let him get away?"

The first man shook them loose. "It ain't my fault. I ain't used to seeing another man get naked."

Tala crooked her head, wondering if she'd heard him correctly. *A naked man? In the zoo parking lot?* She glanced at Devlin, wanting to make sure he was near her. After all, he'd ended up in the zoo, naked, once before.

Devlin caught her suspicious glance to check his whereabouts and rolled his eyes. "Oh, come on. Tell me you didn't think they were talking about me."

She made a face and turned back to the men as they dashed between the rows of cars. Several yards away, one of the men stopped and turned to stare at Devlin as if only now noticing the pair watching them.

His mouth dropped open and he pointed at Devlin, but before he could say anything, the others reversed their course to snatch him along with them.

"Come on. We need to get out of here." Devlin jerked on her arm, breaking for the opposite direction.

She wrenched her arm free and whirled on him. "No! I want to see what's going on. Don't you?" She stared at him, confused by his lack of curiosity. Devlin's face twisted, almost as if his jaw extended before her eyes. *Must be the excitement.* She shook her head, denying her eyes, and clearing her head of the sight. "I want to know what I saw. 'Cause if I didn't know better, I'd swear I saw a wolf. I saw a man wrestling with a wolf." *But if the man had wrestled a wolf, why had he mentioned a naked man instead of the wolf?*

Devlin glanced in the direction they'd run and shook his head. "Doesn't matter now. They're long gone."

"But I need to tell zoo security about this." Tala turned back toward the zoo.

"Tala!"

She twisted around and found herself held in his gaze. His eyes, more yellow than brown now, trapped her, sealing her feet to the ground. Her breath shortened, quickening to match the pace of her pounding heartbeats. "Yes?"

Again he stretched out his hand to her. And this time, she took it.

Leading her, Devlin sprinted away, weaving in and out between the rows of cars. Tala fought to keep up, her long legs lengthening to match his stride as her breath scratched through her throat.

With unerring accuracy, Devlin brought them to her sports car, took the keys from her and punched the button to unlock the doors. Swinging her into the passenger's seat, he jogged to the driver's side and slid into place. After shooting her a disgruntled look, he turned the ignition and pulled out of the parking spot without another glance at her.

"I don't understand you. Why didn't you want to find out what was going on? Especially with a wolf involved. And why didn't you tell me you knew where my car was?"

Devlin grunted and kept his eyes on the road, swiveling his head back and forth as he scanned the lot. "Don't care. Not our problem." He tossed her a smirk. "Didn't ask."

"What's with the stilted speech? 'Don't care.' Me, Jane. You, Tarzan?"

He shook his head, tipped up the corner of his lip, and kept his sight glued to the outside. "Home, Tala. Now." Bowing his head at her, he raised both his eyebrows, and added, "Clear enough?"

"Yeah, clear. Very bossy but clear. And, by the way, I don't take well to anyone bossing—"

Tala flew forward as Devlin stomped on the brakes. Her hands, held up to protect her, rammed against the dashboard as her attention locked onto the hood of her car. A very large black wolf crouched on the shiny red surface.

Tala's mouth fell open and she grabbed Devlin by the arm. Even while she tugged on him, Devlin ignored her, gaping at the wolf. She gawked as the wolf and Devlin stared at each other. Then, in the same moment, both Devlin and the wolf cocked their heads at each other, each lifting one eyebrow in a *what-the-hell-are-you-doing-here* gesture.

Tala whispered, unable to believe what she'd seen. "Did you see him? He copied you. You two did the same gesture."

But again, Devlin didn't answer. Man and wolf concentrated on each other for a full minute more before the wolf tensed, muscles rippling in preparation. Baring his fangs, the wolf growled at Devlin, and flicked his tail in a defiant gesture.

"Go home. Now."

Tala's head swiveled to Devlin. "Go home? Are you kidding? He's not someone's pet, you know. You might as well ask him to fetch your slippers." Yet she'd swear she saw understanding in the wolf's eyes.

"Get them!"

Devlin, Tala, and the wolf turned in sync to see the three men joined by a fourth. All of them rushed through a line of vehicles as they headed toward their car, weapons drawn and ready.

Tala's adrenalin kicked into high gear, sending her into flight mode. Devlin was right. This was no time to ask questions. At least, not until she understood what this was about. As if reading her thoughts, the black wolf sprang away from the car, raking claw marks across her hood, and landing on the roof of a nearby sedan.

"Hey, my car!"

The damage on her car was forgotten when the wolf lifted a front paw to cover his mouth. Almost as if saying, "Oops. Sorry." Tala blinked, squinted at him but by then, he'd lowered his paw and hunkered down into low crouch. The sedan's roof bent under its weight, creaking in protest when the wolf bounded to yet another vehicle. Straining to follow the wolf's path, Tala lurched against the seat as Devlin rammed the accelerator to the floor.

She checked the side mirror to see the men stop in their tracks, shout angry slurs at them, and rotate as a group to continue the way the wolf had gone.

"Oh. My. God. I told you I saw a wolf." Tala reached into her pocket, flipped open her cell phone, and dialed. "He's not one of ours, either. So huge. So amazing. God, he was beautiful."

"I wouldn't call him 'beautiful.' Average, maybe."

What'd he say? She stared at Devlin, not believing the tone in his voice. "Shit, Devlin. You actually sound jealous. Of a wolf." Whether it was about a wolf or not, his being jealous was hot. And making her hotter by the second.

Devlin ignored her as he wheeled around the exit causing Tala to grapple for the strap above her as the car swerved, barely missing a collision with the parked vehicles on each row. A low rumble sounded from deep inside Devlin and the warmth flowing between her legs doubled in intensity.

"Damn it all to hell and back, Devlin. Watch where you're going!"

"I am."

The strain in his voice shot her in the gut with apprehension, cooling the burn in her abdomen. He hadn't appeared this nervous before they'd gotten in the car when the men were almost upon them. So why now?

After several rings, she heard a man's voice on the other end of the line, and pressed her phone to her ear. "Jim, it's Tala. You're never going to believe this.

There's a wolf. A big, beautiful, black wolf in the parking lot." She laughed; astounded she could do so. "No, I'm not kidding. He's huge and gorgeous. Get some men out to the lot, but not before you notify the authorities. Some jackasses are trying to hunt him down and I got the impression they're not selective on who might get hurt in the process."

She listened to the disbelief in Jim's argument, but didn't let him finish. "I don't know where he came from, Jim. Maybe someone's pet got too big. Or more likely, he's down from the mountains." She clutched the door's armrest as Devlin yanked the car to the left, inches from a head-on crash with a lamppost. "Shit, Devlin!"

Devlin fixed her with an expression loaded with worry. "No, he's not someone's pet."

"I'm talking about your driving, you maniac." She covered the phone to question him. "How do you know that, anyway?"

"I just do. Trust me on this one."

"What? Yeah, Jim. I'm here. Huh? No. Just a friend. Now get going." She clicked off the phone as another swerve swept her against the door.

Devlin whooped as he saw the exit and whipped the car out of the lot and onto the side road leading to the zoo. The car banked off the side of the road, spinning its wheels in the gravel, and rocking Tala against the door. "Hey, come on! Are you trying to kill us? Slow down."

Devlin looked down at this foot to ease up on the gas pedal. A truck's horn blared, jerking both of their heads up to see the oncoming eight-wheeler.

"Shit! Devlin!" Tala fell sideways and grabbed the steering wheel. Cranking the wheel toward her, the car careened to the right and onto the shoulder of the road. Gravel, dirt and debris struck the car and windshield as a cry tore from her throat. "Hit the brake!"

Instead, Devlin slammed his boot down on the accelerator sending the car fishtailing along the side of the road. She screamed, loosing her grip on the steering wheel.

"The brake, Devlin. The brake. The other one!" Tala bounced in her seat, and gritted her teeth against an unavoidable accident.

Devlin's jaw slammed tight as he thrust his foot onto the brake. Lurching forward, Tala's head jerked back and forth, with her tongue getting caught between her teeth. Blood squirted into her mouth, but she held fast to the dashboard and handgrip. When the car settled to a stop, she turned to Devlin, anger struggling to break through the fear.

"Where'd you learn to drive? The Indy 500?"

His teeth clenched together, as he grumbled at her. "I'm doing the best I can. Considering."

"Considering what?"

"Considering I've never driven a car before."

Tala didn't know whether to laugh or to cry at Devlin's declaration. But for damn sure, she'd get him out from behind the wheel. They'd gotten lucky this time. Usually the road leading to the zoo was filled with motorists, but today, only a few cars had spun by them, honking their horns in warning.

"You never driven before?"

Devlin, in typical macho-male style, glared at her, and returned to staring out at the road. "Not officially. Never had a need to drive."

"How can you not have a need to drive?" Who *was* this guy? First he howls like a wolf, then he comforts a wild wolf and, to top it off, ends up driving her car when he doesn't know how. Tala ran the possible scenarios through her mind. Was he from another country? One where owning and driving a car wasn't the norm? Was he Amish? Was he independently wealthy with a chauffeur? Various ideas ran through her mind and she checked them off one by one.

"But you managed to get us on the road. You almost killed us a few times, but you knew enough to get us out of the parking lot."

"I watched you drive to the zoo. It didn't look too difficult."

Tala tilted her head to gawk at him and wondered if the day could get any stranger. "Oh, right. It's a cinch. No need for any actual instruction."

"Look. Don't make this a big deal. You can drive now if you want." Devlin swung open the driver's door, pushed his massive body out of the car and strode to the passenger's side.

Blowing out a huge breath of relief, Tala climbed over the console and into the driver's seat. "Gee, thanks. I believe I will."

Waiting a bit longer for her hands to stop shaking, Tala switched on the engine and pulled onto the road. Picking up her ringing phone, she answered, hoping her jangled nerves wouldn't show in her voice. "Tala here."

Devlin kept his head averted, looking out the window, as she glanced over at him from time to time. Listening to Jim on the other end did nothing to soothe her uneasiness. "You didn't find anything? No wolf?

No men? But how?" She listened to Jim's answer, noting the disbelief registering in his words. "And nobody else saw or heard anything?"

After Jim's explanation, Tala shut her phone off and slid it back into her pocket. Even though Devlin didn't act interested, she decided he needed to hear the news. "Jim, my assistant, said they canvassed the entire lot and came up empty. No men and no wolf. Only a couple of dented and scratched cars. They're continuing to check out the rest of the zoo, but nothing so far."

Again, she checked for a reaction from Devlin. But he kept his head turned away from her. "Well, I have the claw marks on my hood to prove I'm not insane. And you, of course." *As evidence. But on the other...*

Devlin twisted to face her. An odd expression covered his features. "You're not insane." He shot her a rueful expression, as if he'd heard her thoughts. "And neither am I."

Now it was her turn to avoid a face-to-face talk. She kept her eyes on the road before them, fighting to keep from asking him questions.

"Still, I wouldn't go spreading the story around if I were you. Those marks on your hood are just that. Scratches, not necessarily claw marks."

Tala stretched her neck to get a better look at the long lines running the length of her hood. "Yeah, I guess I can't prove they came from wolf claws. Or claws of any kind." She wouldn't want any reporters to get wind of the story, anyway. "The media would have a field day with a large wolf who can mimic people's gestures. Besides, I wouldn't want anyone to panic over this. Visitors might stay away from the zoo."

Devlin slumped, the stress oozing out of his body in waves. Why would he worry about this? Tala made a mental note to call Jim once they were home. She needed to make sure the authorities kept an eye out for the animal. Not to mention the strange men.

*****

They arrived at her apartment after a quiet, yet tense, ride home. Tala stalked around her car, noting the damage to the hood as well as other scratches and dents, and the after-effects of Devlin's first driving experience. Devlin, wanting to distance himself from her curse-filled outbursts, left her beside her car while he waited at the foot of the stairs leading up to her apartment. He decided the best course of action was to keep his mouth shut until she finished her tirade. He didn't blame her, of course, but he didn't see the need to be close enough to get singed from her hot wrath. Instead, he waited for her to finish and silently followed her up the steps into her apartment.

"I could use something to eat."

Tala shot him a you've-got-some-nerve look, but headed into the small kitchen anyway. In rapid-fire motion, she dove into the cupboards and refrigerator, putting a loaf of bread and sandwich meat onto the counter beside him.

"Just so you'll understand. I'm not your waitress or your cook." She stopped, hands on her hips, ready for action. "In fact, I'm not sure what I am. Or what we are. Or even what *you* are."

Figuring silence was beneficial to his health; Devlin shrugged, quickly made two sandwiches, and shoved one of the sandwiches into his mouth. Maybe if he kept his mouth full she wouldn't expect him to answer. If he were lucky, her hurricane rant would blow itself out soon.

"I have this problem of taking in strays. Especially injured strays." She eyed him, suspicion oozing from her. "But you're well enough. In fact, I still haven't figured out how you healed so fast. So why are you still hanging around? And why am I letting you?"

Devlin lowered his head, letting his hair fall in front of his face. Next to her dropping the subject, he hoped his passive behavior kept her talking without expecting any responses. Fortunately for him, it did.

"Because I'm a sap, that's why. A grade-A, prime beef, stupid ass sap. A sucker for a hurt soul and a helluva great—"

At her abrupt end, Devlin glanced up and caught the expression on her face. Grinning, he finished the sentence for her. "A helluva great lover?"

She blushed. This tough, independent, liberated, sexually free woman blushed. And he loved the color on her.

"Never mind. And don't go finishing my sentences for me."

She tried to move past him, but he caught her around the waist and pulled her to him. "I don't think you want me to 'never mind.' In fact, I think you want me to mind a lot." He nuzzled her earlobe and she rewarded him with a shuddering sigh.

Slipping his tongue inside her ear, he ran his hand along her spine to slide under the clasps of her bra. He copied the gesture with his other hand, moving up the front, and pulling her t-shirt along. In one smooth motion, shirt and bra fell to the floor.

"Devlin."

"Don't tell me to stop."

Her head leaned to one side as his mouth traveled from her ear to her throat. His hand fondled her breast, playing with the firm tip of her nipple as the heat from her radiated into his palm.

"Devlin."

He nipped at her throat, making a small red mark on her skin, and smiled. Soon he'd mark her. Soon she'd be his and the entire world would know it. "What, Tala?"

Her hand took his, breaking his grip on her as she pivoted away from him. "Bedroom. Now."

"Whatever you say."

Following her to the bed, he thrust her around to face him, and dove at her breast with his mouth. Sucking her tit into his mouth, he played his tongue over the strong softness there, while his hands worked to strip her of her jeans.

A different kind of force surged through him. Not the power of a shift, but a strength he'd never experienced. A drive so much greater than any other. A yearning so much more consuming. An intensity he could only get from Tala.

One final tug sent her jeans and thong to the floor. While he fondled her bottom, her hands made quick work of his clothes, and soon they stood together, naked in the dimming light filtering through the curtains on the window.

He growled and lifted her in both arms. Throwing her to the bed, she laughed in delight as he fell on top of her. Both hands supported her breasts as he stuck his head between their fullness. Eyes closed, he allowed the soft fullness of her to hold him, and he soaked in the musky aroma of her warm skin.

Tala laced her fingers in his hair, encouraging him to stay between her voluptuous globes. She moaned as his thumbs caressed both nubs and she spread her legs wide for him, widening his desire for her.

"Take me, Devlin."

He raised his head to gaze into her eyes, and struggled to keep the animal inside from showing. "I'm going to make you scream, Tala. I want you to scream my name."

The heat in her face drove his own higher and he thrust his hands into her long hair, securing her head in place. His tongue attacked her mouth, wanting to possess all her tastes, all her essence. A raw rumble rolled in his throat and he reached down to rub against her, luxuriating in the touch of her. As he rubbed, she whimpered, a whimper of need and urgency, pushing him to the edge. Positioning himself, he moved his hand back to her head.

"Ready to scream, Tala?"

Her eyes narrowed, but she nodded, her panted breaths making her breasts bounce to their rhythm. "We'll see who screams first."

Grabbing her hands, he pulled her arms above her head and held them with one hand. She paused, motionless, as a flicker of alarm crossed her face.

"Tala. You know you can trust me."

An answering challenge gleamed in her eyes and she twisted, trying to break free of his hold. The harder she fought, the tighter he held her, the brighter the shine in her eyes became. "Yeah, but can you trust me?"

An amused delight pumped his blood faster as he understood her meaning. "So you want to play rough?"

She gritted her teeth and bucked, trying to throw him from her, a grin spreading on her determined face. At the sight of her, sweating and fighting against him, the power within him rose up, threatening his tenuous hold. Fangs grew and he battled to keep from shifting. "Damn, woman, you're strong."

"Not sure you can handle me? Come on, Devlin. Show me what you've got."

Devlin renewed his hold on her hands and, using his other hand, guided his shaft into her folds. As he slammed into her, he pushed one leg higher and she followed his direction, wrapping both legs around him. His teeth found her nipple again and sucked as he pounded into her.

"Scream my name, Tala. Scream it so everyone will hear you."

"Devlin."

"Louder. Don't just say my name. Scream it."

With her head thrown back, she called his name. "Devlin."

Devlin rammed into her and she grunted as the force of his thrust scooted her body toward the headboard, bumping her head. "God, that's a beautiful sound. But scream louder, Tala."

She screamed his name, digging her nails into his back, fixing his body to hers. "*Devlin!*"

The exhilaration flowing through him found its way to his heart and he couldn't resist any longer. He gave into his release with a howl ripping from his throat. Fighting temptation no longer, he lowered his head, opened his jaws, and sank his fangs into her shoulder.

Chapter Seven

"Ow! Shit!"

The strength she'd shown earlier was nothing in comparison to the strength she used to toss him off of her. Scrambling from the bed, she stumbled backwards until her back struck the dresser. She sunk to the floor and leaned her throbbing shoulder against the solid oak. "Ow! Damn it all to hell and back. You bit me!"

Devlin rose up on one elbow, blinked at her for a moment as if trying to focus, and swung off the bed. "Tala, let me explain."

Tala gripped her shoulder, blood oozing onto her hand. "Are you nuts? What do you think you are? Some kind of animal? You bit me!" She grabbed an old t-shirt from the dresser and stuck it on top of her wound.

"You said that twice."

She scowled at him, his remark stoking the volcano threatening to erupt from within her.

Seeing her unveiled warning, he winced and continued, "I know. I'm sorry. I didn't mean to." Devlin held out his hands to her and tried to move closer.

"Get away from me." She attempted to calm the mix of pain, shock and, God help her, lust trying to overwhelm her brain, but couldn't. "Why the hell did you bite me?"

"I didn't mean to. I got carried away in the moment." Pushing his hair away from his tormented face, he beseeched her. "Tala, please."

Devlin inched nearer until she thrust out a hand to stop him. "Please, what? Please let me go for the jugular this time? You want me to lie still while you finish the job?" Keeping her eyes glued on him, she grasped the furniture and hauled herself to her feet. She couldn't believe this. This guy bit her! With her teeth gritting at the pain, she wheeled around, snatching up her robe in the process, and headed for the bathroom.

Devlin started to follow her, and she spun to confront him. "You stay where you are. Or get out. But don't you dare follow me." She thrust out her finger in a threatening jab and stalked into the bathroom, slamming the door behind her.

Tala fell against the door, and tried to catch both her breath and her sanity. What had happened? One minute, she's getting laid and laid good. Okay, laid great. And the next, she's got a teeth marks in her. She crossed over to the sink to check her wound in the small oval mirror above the basin. With two fingers, she gently removed the robe and blood-reddened shirt to examine the injured area. Two major holes flanked a row of smaller indentations with similar marks in another semi-circle below. *Looks like a wolf's bite.*

Reaching for a washcloth, she wetted the soft cotton under the faucet and gingerly dabbed at the gashes. She cringed as the sting shot down her shoulder and into her arm.

"Tala? Are you all right?"

"Never mind. I'll take care of myself."

Tala continued cleaning the area, until the bleeding finally began to slow down. She fumbled through her medicine cabinet, located the alcohol, and turned the top onto the cloth. Inhaling a long one, she held her breath, and placed the alcohol-soaked material on her shoulder. A quick yelp escaped before she could stop herself.

"Tala, please. Let me help you."

She ignored Devlin's knock on the door as well as his words. As tears came to her eyes, she stuffed the other side of her bathrobe's collar into her mouth to stifle her cry. Gripping her robe with all her strength, she waited for the pain to lessen.

"Tala, are you all right? Answer me or I'm going to break down the door."

She'd thought she was angry before. But the fury boiling over in her now, put her previous ire to shame. How dare he threaten her! First, he tears up her car, then he bites her like some caveman…more like a Saber tooth tiger…and now he has the nerve to threaten to break down her door?

"Devlin, you back off right now or I'm going to bite your balls off." *Crap, would he think that sounds as sexy as I do?* Her mind was on sex when she'd just been bitten? Was she as crazy as he was? She threw the blood-soaked cloth to the floor, grabbed the bandages from the medicine cabinet, and plastered on a quick bandage.

"I'm worried about you, babe."

Even as the red stain on the bandage grew, she pivoted and swung open the door.

She registered Devlin's surprised expression as she charged at him, relishing the fact that he moved as fast as he could to get away from her. He'd gotten dressed in the meantime, and his shirt flew open in his attempt to get out of her way. But though he tried to get away, she kept at him, punching her finger into the middle of his solid chest.

"I told you to back off and I meant what I said. And don't call me 'babe.' I'm no one's 'babe.' Especially not yours."

Devlin's startled look transformed into deep furrows on his brow. "Will you stop acting like I beat you up? I realize I screwed up but, after all, it's only a bite." He widened his stance, a fortified front to withstand her furious attack.

"A bite? *Only* a bite?" Tala laid one hand on her bandage and the other fisted on her hips. "You drew blood. Who the hell draws blood while having sex? When I wanted to play rough in the sack I didn't have bloodshed in mind."

The gleam in Devlin's eye slowed her down, and uneasiness rippled through her shaking frame. How could he stand there, with the corners of his mouth slightly crooked, and act like what he'd done was no big deal? Even if he did look sexy as hell. Even if part of her wanted to jump his bones right now. Tala sucked in a big gasp of air and tried to steady herself.

"I didn't mean to bite you. Besides, we were making love. Not having sex."

Man, how she'd love to smack his shitty, smug smirk off his face. Making love? Is that what he thought? "Love hurts. Is that what you think?"

"No. But I wasn't the only one wanting the rough stuff. You did, too."

She ground her teeth together, and resolved to keep his butt on the line. "Don't try to change the subject."

Devlin's big, brown eyes met hers and his eyebrows, such masculine, heart-stopping eyebrows, lifted in an imploring manner. Almost the way the she-wolf had looked at him earlier. As if asking for help. As if asking for understanding from a kindred soul. An "ah" went down from her brain and straight into her heart. Why was she such a pushover for this guy?

Devlin reached around her and tried to draw her into his arms. For a second, the temptation to snuggle against his broad chest almost broke her determination, but she stepped back, keeping clear of him.

"I don't think it was an accident." She peered at him, knowing in her gut something else was at the bottom of his bite.

He let his arms fall to his side, not following her as she moved away from him. "Okay. You want the truth? Well, here it is. I wanted to mark you."

"Mark me?" What the hell did he mean? "Like branding a cow?"

Devlin stammered, opened his mouth several times as if to speak and then closed his mouth, his lips a tight line across his face. Had he started to tell her something? The real, whole truth? She studied his face, searching for some meaning behind his actions, and saw him mentally shut down.

"Uh, of course not. I wanted to mark you as in..."

"As in what?" She took a step closer to him, hoping he'd come out and say what he found so difficult to say. "Just tell me."

"As in giving you a hickey."

Tala's head jerked in stunned response. "A hickey? You bit me trying to give me a hickey?"

Devlin tucked his head, averting his face from hers. "Yeah, I know. It was a stupid thing to do. I guess I just lost control when I started to give you a, you know, and got a little too excited."

She couldn't help it. She had to laugh. "What are you? Fifteen? Since when do grown men give hickeys?"

He shot her an exasperated expression, one filled with anger, embarrassment, and frustration. "Can we get off this subject now?"

"No. If you're going to give me a hickey like some high school kid, then I want to know we're going steady."

"Steady? So, like, does that mean you'll go to the prom with me?"

Devlin's expression was priceless, taking some of her steam away. But not enough of it. "It was a joke. Where the hell were you raised, Devlin? You've never driven a car, you still give hickeys and you have an uncanny way with wolves. Were you raised by a pack of wolves or something? By nature-loving hippies? Where?"

The twinkle in his eye vanished as his features hardened, and he spit his words out at her. "Okay, I've had enough. I messed up and I apologized. Now get over it."

The volcano boiling within her let loose, exploding in rage. "Get out, Devlin. Get out now."

His jaw worked and he glowered at her, but he didn't budge an inch. "You're making a bigger deal out of this than you should. Grow up, Tala."

"You're telling *me* to grow up?" Whirling, she left the bedroom and marched to her front door. As she knew he would, Devlin followed on her heels. Thrusting the door wide open, she shouted at him, and pointed out into the hallway. "Get the hell out of my home!"

Devlin snarled at her…a snarl that weakened her knees…and strode out into the hallway, scaring elderly Mrs. Puwoty as he stormed by her. The elderly woman screeched in fright, clutching her hands to her chest in her bumbling attempt to sidestep him.

The instant he'd left, an ache greater than Tala had ever known, assaulted her, leaving her chest tight and her body shaking in the aftermath. Trying to put on a brave front for Mrs. Puwoty, Tala smiled a small, tight smile, nodded at the older woman, and closed the door.

*****

Devlin walked for several blocks, ignoring the people and sounds around him, before the rage inside him calmed to a low simmer. He couldn't figure out who made him the angriest. Tala or himself.

He let the tension roll out of him with a low growl and sent a young woman carrying an infant scurrying to the other side of the street as her baby let out a plaintive wail. *Great. First old ladies, and now I can add scaring young mothers and babies to my list of achievements. What next, Dev, terrorizing school kids?*

How had he lost control of the situation? Should he have told Tala the truth? Should he have told her he marked her as his mate? He shook his head, started to growl again, but stopped when he caught the anxious expression of an old man who stood, rooted to one spot, warily watching him. Instead, he spread his lips in what he hoped passed for a reassuring smile and waved. *Crap. Add giving old men heart attacks to my list.*

Had Tala thrown him out for good? If so, how would he get back into her life? Although anger permeated his body, another more dangerous feeling lay just below the surface. *Heartache.* His heart was in pain. He'd never experienced this kind of internal pain before. This kind of emotional hurt made getting physically injured seem like a skinned knee.

"Devlin."

The familiar voice of his brother brought Devlin to a standstill. *Mickale.* Sweeping the darkening street around him, he picked out a black shape resting against a light pole. Striding over to his brother, he grabbed him, enveloping him in a bear hug.

"Thank God you're okay." He put Mickale at arm's length and ran his gaze up and down his brother's body, checking for anything out of place. "I see you escaped the hunters in one piece."

Mickale's echoing grin dropped at the question. "Well, duh. Since when are four inept hunters a match for Mickale Morgan? In fact, I had a great time playing with them."

"Just as long as you're okay." Devlin cupped Mickale's cheek in his palm and nodded. He kept nodding as he drew back his arm and socked his brother in the nose, knocking him to the ground.

"What're you doing in the city, Mickale?"

The few people left on the street scurried away from the two large men. Mickale hollered after them, acting as though they were worried for his safety, instead of fleeing for their own lives. "No, no, everyone. Everything's fine." He pushed himself to his feet, calling to the onlookers. "Just a family squabble is all. No problem."

"I asked you why you're here." Devlin's pitch was deep and threatening, even though he put on a pleasant facade for the few people daring to linger and stare at them.

Mickale took Devlin, hooked his arm around his shoulder and started walking, leading him toward a hole-in-the-wall bar. "I'm here to keep you out of trouble. Which I've already done. Those hunters, my dear bro, were after you."

Devlin started to pause, but Mickale held on to drag him into the bar. The awful combination of tobacco, human body odors, and liquor hit Devlin's sensitive nose and he coughed, trying to rid himself of the stench. "Me? It looked like they were after your sorry butt. Not mine."

"Ah, well mine would make the more handsome trophy. But that's where you're wrong." Mickale slid onto a barstool and motioned for Devlin to do the same. "Those scumbags wanted to ambush you and your lady friend. Fortunately for both of you, I sidetracked them." He stuck out his chin to draw the bartender's attention. "Two draft beers."

Devlin waited for the bartender to set their drinks in front of them before questioning his brother. "So the hunters were after me. How'd they pick up my tail? Er, trail?"

Mickale choked on his laugh, sending beer splattering onto the counter. When the bartender shot him a dirty look, he added, "Don't get your panties in a bunch, dude. It's only a little spit." He used his sleeve to wipe up the mess. "How do they ever pick up a trail? Sheer luck most of the time. But the point is, they know we're here. Both of us." Mickale dragged a long swig from his glass, winked at a neon-red haired girl sitting at the edge of the counter, and nudged Devlin. "Talk about picking up some tail..."

Devlin sipped his drink, running his thoughts through his mouth as they came into his head. "Yeah, I guess. The trail, not the tail. Which explains their presence, but what about you? Why are you here? And how did you know where to find me?"

Mickale raised his glass at the girl, who was joined by two girlfriends. "Don't look now, bro, but there's a trio of honeys at three o'clock."

Devlin glanced at the girls, noted the caked-on makeup as a failed attempt to look more sophisticated and attractive, and grimaced at their skimpy outfits. Hookers? He studied them better, coming to a different conclusion. Nope, not hookers. Worse. Barflies on the prowl. He darted his attention elsewhere before he accidentally made eye contact. Besides, after Tala why would he want anyone else? "Answer my questions, Mick."

Mickale puffed out an exaggerated sigh and turned to face Devlin. "No biggie. I figured someone needed to keep an eye on you, and it's a good thing I did, too. Big brother to the rescue."

"Maybe so. But something tells me there's more to your reasons than simple brotherly protection." Devlin eyed his brother hard enough to force Mickale to avoid him by swiveling around to the bartender.

The young woman, red hair sticking out at all angles, waved at Devlin as she ran her tongue over her even redder lips. Yep, all he needed was some bar bimbo after him. Devlin groaned, wished he were with

Tala, and confronted Mickale again. "So you followed me?"

"Hey, a brother's got to do what a brother's got to do." Mickale's grin grew wider as the redhead cupped her boobs and jiggled them at him. "Besides, if the mopey expression on your face is any indication, you could use your older brother right now. What's up? Your female kick you out already?"

Mickale's quick assessment of his situation dropped his mood another ten notches. "Sort of." He frowned, annoyed at the glimmer of delight in his brother's eyes. "But it's only temporary. Once she calms down, she'll forget all about my, um, mistake."

"Um, mistake?" Mickale scooped up a handful of complimentary peanuts from the bowl on the bar and tossed them into his mouth. "Oooh, sounds interesting. You must have fucked up big time for her to boot you to the curb. I mean, you two looked rather chummy strolling around the zoo. Like two little puppies in love."

Devlin sputtered into his drink. "Just how long have you been following me? All the way from the mountains?"

Not fazed by Devlin's reaction, Mickale shrugged off Devlin's question and his surprise. "What'd you do to piss off Tala? You break into the zoo butt-naked again and hit on the elephants? I know how you like big bottoms on your females."

Now how had Mick found out about his drunken escapade in the wolf pen? Devlin decided he'd better leave well enough alone and tried a diversion. Devlin set his drink down on the bar, rattling Mickale's glass in the tremors from the blow. "What are you? An intelligence-gathering agent from the CIA? How'd you learn her name? And she doesn't have a big ass, either."

Lifting his chin, Mickale barked out a sound resembling a cross between a howl and a loud chuckle. The girls perked up and giggled along with Mickale's hysterical outburst even though they weren't close enough to hear the brothers' conversation. "Nowadays, bro, the words Central Intelligence Agency and intelligence gathering are rarely used in the same sentence. Unless you're talking screw-ups."

Devlin shifted in his seat and put his nose within inches of Mickale's. "I'm not kidding. How do you know Tala's name?"

A flash of irritation zipped over Mickale's features before the mask of calmness settled over him again. "Take it easy, bro. I've got sensitive ears, remember? I heard you two talking at the zoo. Right before you raced off to play wolf-in-shining-fur at the call of some she-wolf."

Devlin relaxed, and unclenched his fists. Fists he hadn't realized were primed to punch his brother's lights out. "Well, okay. I guess."

"Besides, her picture's hanging all over the zoo. She's a local celebrity."

"She helps teach hu — uh, the public about the animals. Her work helps animals." He'd almost said the word "human" within earshot of the bartender, but knew his brother would pick up on his meaning anyway.

Mickale shrugged again. "Goodie for her." He downed the last of his beer and ordered another one. "Is that what you did wrong? You say something bad about the zoo? I'd imagine she wouldn't like you dissing her work very much."

"Dissing?

Mickale shrugged. "I heard some kids using the word. I think it means 'disagreeing,' or 'disliking,' or something bad."

Devlin frowned. "Well, anyway, no. I got a little too aggressive in bed. So when I accidentally bit her—"

"You bit her?" Mickale's jovial attitude disappeared in a flash. "Did you mark her?"

The abrupt change in Mickale's attitude sent warning flares up and down Devlin's spine. He knew his brother didn't want him to become leader. Yet, hadn't Mickale expected Devlin to mark his mate? He stared at Mickale, watching as he struggled to keep a composed appearance. But Devlin could tell Mickale wasn't happy about what he'd heard. "No, I didn't mark her. I started to, but I restrained myself. Just in time." *No need for him to know the truth just yet.*

The relief flooding Mickale's face didn't help Devlin's mood any. *So I'm right. Mickale doesn't want Tala marked.* Would he try and keep him from marking Tala? All in hope of gaining leadership? Devlin swallowed a gulp of beer, reflecting on the irony of his situation. Here he'd gotten what Mickale wanted, but he'd trade places with his brother in a second if he could. Maybe he should tell Mickale about his business? Maybe together they could change things?

Like someone switching on a light, the concern vanished from Mickale and the happy-go-lucky grin was back in place. Cupping his hand around Devlin's neck, Mickale drew his brother closer and whispered to him. "How about we have a little fun tonight? You know. Before you go getting hooked up with one female for the rest of your life." Mickale pointed with his chin at the slutty trio and winked at Devlin. "Better live while you can."

Devlin sneaked another peek at the girls with the wild hair and tight clothes. Maybe before he'd met Tala...but not now. He cringed as the chunky blonde blew a kiss at him. "No thanks. But if you want to, don't mind me."

Mickale slid off the bar, and Devlin caught him by the arm to stop him in his tracks. "Remember, don't involve me. Understood?"

"Sure, bro. No problem." Mickale flashed him a wicked sneer and tugged his arm free. He'd taken a couple of steps, sauntering toward the women, when he stopped and turned around. Wrinkling his nose, he sniffed the air. "Damn, Dev. Do you smell something rotten?"

A shadow came out of the crowd, heading straight for Mickale. Devlin's warning growl came too late as the hunter smashed a bottle over Mickale's head, buckling his knees, and sending him crashing to the floor. Devlin howled and threw himself at the hunter standing over his brother with a jagged bottle in his hand as the other patrons scattered to the corners of the room.

"Argh!" The hunter scrambled backwards, trying to elude Devlin's attack, and tripped over his own feet. Landing on his back, he flipped onto his hands and knees, and tried to scramble out of reach. Devlin ripped his shirt as he clutched his collar, and flung the man against the bar. The man passed out, one hand still holding the broken bottle and his head lolling to the side.

"Get them!"

Devlin roared above the screams of the crowd as two more hunters ran toward him. Letting a small part of his power loose, he grabbed each of the men by the neck and lifted them into the air.

"Kill 'em, Sweetie!"

Devlin pivoted, holding the men high, to see the Bar Bitch Trio jumping up and down, clapping and cheering. He bashed the hunters' heads together, delighting in the *crack* reverberating around the room. Reveling in the force coursing through him, he bobbed a short bow and saluted his fans.

The bartender, apparently used to brawls, stood, arms crossed in a patient, easy manner. He scowled at Devlin, but didn't say a word.

"Don't look now, bro, but another one's headed this way."

Mickale, recovered and standing beside him, patted Devlin on the shoulder as he rubbed the back of his head. "Shit of an asshole. He really whacked me."

"Good thing you don't use your head for anything   important,   huh?"

"Very funny, bro. Ha, ha." Mickale rolled his eyes at Devlin before he pointed at the hunter winding his way through the throng of bar patrons rushing for the door. "Damn. This one's carrying something more deadly than a bottle."

A squat, box-shaped hunter neared them, with his hand stuck inside his leather jacket. His lips curled in a snarl, accenting the thick scar running along the side of his neck. As the hunter drew close, he pulled out a large handgun and pointed it at Mickale.

Devlin lurched forward, but the hunter darted away. "Don't try it, shifter, or your canine crony here is road kill."

The power surged through Devlin, begging for release, as he scanned the room around him. Too many eyes would witness a transformation if he shifted. Yet he couldn't stop his fangs from lengthening as he opened his jaws in a challenge. "Hunter, you pull the trigger and I'll rip out your bowels." A sneer lifted his lips at the flicker of fear in the hunter's eyes. "I haven't had dinner yet."

"Now, boys, what's the problem?" Mickale snaked his arm around his brother's waist. "My sugar daddy here and I were having a little drinkie-poo together when your friends," Mickale wiggled his wrist to flap his fingers at the unconscious hunters. "...decided to break up our little tête-à-tête. Wasn't that just plain rude?" Sliding away from Devlin, Mickale sashayed a few feet closer to the hunter. "Oh, I get it. Do you want to get it on with us, too? Huh, Sweet Thang?" Mickale puckered his lips, pouting his lips at the man.

"Mick. Be careful." Devlin's eyes widened, shooting him an unmistakable signal. "His finger's already twitching."

The squat hunter took a step back, revulsion written on his face. "What the crap? Keep your queer paws off me, you limp-wristed dogface."

Mickale feigned a shocked expression, clamping his hands over his mouth before puffing up in fake indignation. "I can not believe you just said those mean, horrible things to me. You are a bad, bad, little man."

"Mick, don't push it. I've heard Skanland's stupid, but not that stupid."

Skanland darted his gaze between the brothers. "Never thought there could be anything worse than a shifter. Now I know there is. A fag shifter."

Mickale *tisked* at him and shook his index finger. "We prefer the word 'homosexual,' you, uncouth pig. How very un-PC of you."

Devlin shrugged at his brother's *see-I-told-you-so* expression. "Then again, maybe I'm wrong." He couldn't help but add, "Word of advice, Mick? You might think about spending less time around Blair."

The hunter pressed the muzzle of the gun to Mickale's forehead, pointing his chin at Devlin. "So you know my name, huh? Good. You should know who's going to wipe out you and all the other mongrels." He glared at Devlin. "Listen to your brother, Dog Breath. When my associates wake up, we're all going to take a little walk outside to my van for a party at my house. You're gonna love our party favors."

Mickale jumped up and down, clapping his hands together. "Yippee! A party. Oh, but wait. I forgot. We've already made plans for the evening."

Devlin caught the direction of Mickale's glance and nodded his understanding. "He's right, friend. No offense, but we'd rather party with them." Jerking his chin out, he indicated the person standing behind Skanland.

"Come on, you think I'd fall for that old trick? I ain't stupid, you know." Skanland rolled his upper lip in scorn at Devlin's unspoken disbelief. "I ain't!"

Devlin tilted his head and shrugged. "If you say so. But my daddy always told me. You shouldn't ignore a lady with a stun gun."

Skanland's body convulsed as the red-haired barfly rammed the weapon against his neck. Spasms jerked his body around as he hit the floor face first.

Chapter Eight

"Talk about in the neck of time." Mickale cocked his head at the redhead, aiming his glorious smile at her. "Get it? Neck of time? You, sweetheart, are a life saver."

The redhead saluted him and kicked the hunter's gun under the bar. "No problem. I can't stand to see anyone picked on by bullies. Especially not yummy-looking hunks."

Devlin blew out air he hadn't realized he'd held in check. "And I'm glad you did. Thanks for the assistance."

"No problem." Red's fire engine lips spread wide and Devlin couldn't help comparing her to the Tasmanian She-Devil. He swallowed, forcing the image from his head.

"She can't take all the credit. The stun gun's mine." The big-breasted blonde standing next to Red batted her eyes first at Mickale and then Devlin.

"Yeah, Betty, but I taught her how to use it." The last of the trio, a skinny brunette, pushed her way between her friends. "All you did was let Roxy try it out on you."

Betty blinked twice, opened her mouth to speak and came up empty.

What we have here is a lack of brain function. Devlin couldn't believe the absurdity of their conversation. Roxy, aka Red, had used Betty Big Breasts as her guinea pig for stun gun training? "Then we should thank all of you."

"Devlin, my brother, is right. We should thank you. With ev-er-ee-thing we have to offer." Mickale drew out the word 'everything,' making it sound like three words instead of one.

Sometimes Mickale could charm a worm out of an apple. Although Devlin figured he wouldn't need much to charm this group. Clean breath would charm these girls.

"How about we get out of here?" Mickale opened his arms as the redhead and her overweight blonde friend slid into his welcoming embrace. "I don't want to be around when those guys come to."

"Skinny" pouted and gave Devlin a give-me-a-hug face. Succumbing to the moment, Devlin wrapped his arm around her and followed Mickale and her friends to the front door. The girls' giggles echoed around the room as Mickale's hands dropped to squeeze both of their butts.

Slinging the bar door open, Mickale and the girls didn't hesitate, but made a straight arrow to a multi-colored, convertible Volkswagen Beetle. Devlin tried to release his hold on the other girl, but she kept a death-grip on his waist.

Red hopped into the back seat and motioned for Mickale to do the same. "Come on, man. Let's head on over to our place and keep the good times going."

Betty clapped her hands in delight and hopped up and down, turning her huge mammary glands into quivering mountains of flesh. "Ooh, goodie. Playtime with men." She climbed into the back seat, squashing next to Mickale, and tossed the keys to Devlin's human attachment. "You drive, Trixie. I don't want to miss a minute with my new man." Licking her lips like a fox in a henhouse, she ran her gaze up and down Mickale's body. "And I bet he's got a long, hard one just ready to make me all hot and happy."

Red wasn't about to give up an inch. Especially not an inch of Mickale. "Hey, who said he's yours? I'm the one who saved his cute ass tonight. So I should have dibs on him first."

Mickale wiggled his eyebrows at Devlin as he ate up the attention from the two complaining women. "Now, girls, there's no need to fuss. Trust me. I have more than enough to satisfy both of you. One at a time or, my preference, all at once." He pulled Red to him and planted a quick kiss on her ruby lips.

"Hey!" Betty stuck out her lower lip until Mickale laid a smack on her, too.

"Dev, bro? You coming?"

The girl hanging onto Devlin tugged at him. "Yeah, Devvy. Come on. Let's go. You can ride shotgun for me."

Devlin's mind flew into high gear, visualizing a shotgun in the hands of Trixie's backwoods' father. The image shook him, racing a shudder along his spine to tingle in his feet. No way would he risk another load of buckshot in the butt. Taking her arms, he gently pried her away from him. "Sorry, sweetheart. I'll have to pass.

"There they are!"

Devlin whirled to see the hunters exiting the bar and storming, albeit it on wobbly legs, toward them. Impressive speeds for men recovering from a serious bruising. Of course, hunters were notoriously hardheaded and resilient. Snarling, he pushed a protesting Trixie around the front of the car and into the driver's seat. "Girls, I suggest you hit the road."

"Get in, bro. This is no time to hang around here." Mickale lifted up to reach for Devlin, but Red and Betty dragged him back down onto the seat again.

Devlin snarled at the men moving closer to the car, and slammed the car door after Trixie. "Damn it all to hell and back." Hurdling over the car door, Devlin landed in the passenger's chair just as Trixie turned over the engine.

"Where'd you pick up that phrase?"

But Devlin didn't have time to answer. Trixie shouted at the top of her lungs, soon joined by Red and Betty, and stomped her foot to the gas pedal. Gravel shot in the air and rained down on the angry men running behind them.

"Zero to sixty, sugar. Zero to sixty." Trixie laughed, her ratted hair holding as hard as a rock in the wind as the crowded Bug flew into traffic. Horns blared and drivers cursed as Devlin held onto the handle and prepared to die. And Tala thought his driving was bad!

Thirty minutes later, after twelve near collisions, a couple of incidents of road rage, and one fender bumping incident, Trixie pulled into a run-down apartment building's parking lot and swung into a space beneath a metal carport. Shoving the gear into "P," the girls piled out of the car, pulling the brothers along with them.

"Woo-hoo! Testosterone time!"

*****

Tala surveyed the area behind her apartment and chewed on her bottom lip. *Damn him to hell and back. Damn that Devlin.* Why did she get involved with the all the offbeat men of the world?

"Crap." She swiveled and headed to the kitchen for one last cup of coffee. Just like the last five cups she'd called "the last one." But she'd known she wouldn't get any sleep tonight. Not with her stomach as messed up as her heart.

"Where the hell can he be?" She scowled at her reflection in the microwave as she heated up the coffee. "Well, what do you care, anyway? You're the one who threw him out. Argh!"

Picking up her cup with care...even though she felt more like throwing it...she traced her steps back to the sliding glass door. Leave it to her to get hung up on a man she'd just met. A man she knew nothing about. Or was the mystery part of his attraction?

The moon rose above the horizon as she peered into the woods around her home. To top it off, he had her wishing he were out there, snooping on her again. "You are one sick, sick woman, Tala."

She sipped the hot brew and let her mind wander. What if he's hurt again? "No, he's fine. Better than fine." She reached up to rub the marks on her neck. "He bit me. How strange is a man who bites a woman? Even if it did turn me on. And stranger yet, who heals as fast as he did?"

How *had* Devlin healed so fast? Had she thought the injury was worse than it really was? She'd seen enough wounds on animals at the zoo to know his injury wasn't a scratch. Yet, without proper medical help, the wound had closed up and starting scarring over within hours.

So the man heals fast. So what? Healing quickly isn't a bad thing, after all. Unusual, maybe. But biting people? A man who bites while making love? Tala smiled as she remembered Devlin's insistence on the term "making love" instead of "having sex." Lots of people do kinky stuff in bed and by some people's standards, biting was pretty tame.

But what if he's like Mark? Was his aggression lurking under the surface of his handsome exterior? Tala paced to the sink to dump the rest of her coffee down the drain.

No way could she let herself fall into another abusive relationship again. She stared into the pool of brown liquid at the bottom of her sink as if trying to find the answer in the murky darkness. She'd gone to hell and come out the other side with Mark. Didn't her recognizing Devlin's aggressiveness right away mean something? She was in control, right?

Then why do you want him back? The voice in her head shouted for her to beware. Cried for her to think with her head and not her soul.

Tala moved her hand along her neck, massaging out the rigidity in her muscles. "Besides, what kind of stupid woman takes a man like that inside her home? Not to mention into her bed?" Yet the memory of Devlin's tongue on her body sent renewed goose bumps along her arms. "But damn it all to hell and back. He's the best lover I've ever had."

Wanting him as a lover was one thing. Yet a deeper, stronger urge ripping her heart apart took hold and held on. Devlin was more than just a good lay. Something about him called to her, making her want to throw all logic aside and follow him anywhere. Even to hell and back.

She renewed her stance at the window. Could she take him in again? Would she let him in her bed again? And more important, should she let him in her heart forever?

*****

At this point, Devlin was unsure if the Bar Bitch Trio were more of a danger than the hunters. As Trixie held onto his arm and pulled him toward her apartment, Devlin's gut twisted into a tighter knot.

He protested each step of the way, but she dismissed each of his polite arguments, and ignored his not-so-subtle attempts to break free of her. As they drew closer to her apartment door, he gave up the pretense of civility and jerked his arm out of her grasp. "Look! I'm sorry!"

Mickale, flanked by Betty and Red, swiveled around, and all the girls gaped at his outburst. Cocking his head, Mickale shot him a warning *don't-blow-this-for-me* expression. "Problem, bro?"

"Yeah, problem." The low pitch of his voice challenged Mickale, drawing an invisible line in the sand.

The foursome glared at him, ready to meet his dare. Red spoke up, ice dripping from her tone. "So what's your problem? Is Trixie not good enough for you?"

Hunters, where are you when I need you? Right now he wouldn't mind getting shot and mounted on one of their walls. "Uh, sure, she is." He smiled at Trixie, the picture of Daddy's Little Girl Gone Wrong with confusion, anger, and hope somehow managing to show up under all the heavy makeup. "But I can't be with any woman."

A stunned silence followed his statement. What they thought was plain enough for a blind man to see.

Red turned to each of her friends before narrowing her eyes at him. "But wasn't the gay thing a gag for the bully?" She stepped back from Mickale, skimming her eyes up and down his body. "Are you telling me you two really are together? And I mean, together, together." Making a circle with her thumb and middle finger of one hand, she poked her other index finger through the hole.

Devlin couldn't wait to correct her. "No, wait. You don't understand."

Trixie stepped up to him, pressing her skinny frame against him. "No, we understand good. And I'm sorry if we dragged you along for nothing. We didn't know you were really gay. If we had, we'd have left you alone. Unless you don't want to be gay?"

Red gave Trixie a slap on the shoulder. "Don't be dumb, bitch."

Trixie, however, couldn't give up the dream without a fight. "Are you sure? I mean, I could try and change you. You know. Bring you back to the straight and narrow. I mean, I like a dick as good as the next person, but if you try pussy, you might find out you like it a whole lot better. Have you ever been with a woman?"

Measuring his shaft against a giant's couldn't have delivered a bigger blow to his self-esteem. "No. Yes. I mean, you've got me all wrong." Devlin bounced his gaze from one girl to the next. Mickale rolled his lips inward, trying to suffocate his laugh. "I swear. I love women. All kinds of women."

Red scoffed, "Well, sure you do. Most homos do. You know, to go shopping with. Queers love gal pals."

Mickale fell against the wall and clamped a hand over his mouth. But he couldn't stop his body from shaking with humor.

Devlin fought to maintain some spark of dignity. "You're not getting this right. I like women. I like fucking women." He stood up straighter, trying to puff up his chest as well as his image. "And I've fucked my share of females, let me tell you."

All three women paused, considering his claims. Ever the brilliant one, Trixie asked the question Devlin could almost see chugging through their tiny brains. "Then I don't get it. If you like women and I'm good enough, then why won't you come inside and get it on?"

Bluntness, thy name is Trixie. "I'd love to, hon. Except for one thing."

"Yeah? Like what?" Trixie's eyes filled with tears.

"I belong to one woman and one woman alone."

To his utter relief, all three women let out a group "Ah." Tears streamed down Trixie's relieved face while the other two gathered him into their arms.

"Wow. A one-woman man. I ain't never met one of those." Red's astonishment at his declaration floored him.

"This is so special. We won't try to take you from her." All three women shook their heads, fervent in their commitment, with Betty furiously nodding her head.

Devlin raised a questioning eyebrow at Betty. *Seems Betty Big Boobs has a Big Heart, too.* "Even though we could, you know." *But not as big as her ego.* Devlin adopted a pious look and nodded as he extricated himself from their clutches. "I'm glad you understand." He caught Mickale's eye and shot him a silent message. "But my brother, on the other hand, is a lady's dream come true."

The women dropped Devlin's arms faster than lead weights off the side of a punctured hot air balloon as they scooted over to Mickale. Grabbing and pulling him toward the door with the sign "Hottie Hangout" emblazoned on the front, Red shoved her friends off him. "Back off, bitches. I saw him first."

Yet Betty wouldn't let Red get away with anything. Much less Mickale. "Don't care. He likes blondes best, don't ya?"

"But can't we all play with him?" Trixie opened the door and wiggled her fingers at Devlin. "By-ee, Devvy."

"Ladies, ladies. As I said before. I can satisfy all of you. No need to fight over me." Mickale allowed himself to get dragged inside the building without another glance at Devlin. "Unless you'd like to go a few rounds of wrestling. Winner takes all?"

"Good luck, brother. You're going to need it." Devlin chuckled, turned on his heels and slipped into the night.

*****

After leaving the Terrible Trio with Mickale, he'd wandered for an hour, giving Tala more time to cool off and him a chance to explore. Too often his infrequent trips to the city consisted of business and no time for anything else.

He passed through many residential areas, none of which appeared too different from all the other neighborhoods. How did humans stand living in these tiny boxes? Traveling on, he entered the business area of town. Storefronts adorned with neon lights and outrageous displays astounded him, causing him to stop more than once to gawk at the sights before him.

Did people actually dress the way these mannequins looked? He glanced around and got his answer. People dressed in outlandish outfits, exposing inch after inch of skin. Devlin frowned at a young man sauntering by him. What would cause a person to puncture his skin so many times with various metal objects? The youth caught Devlin staring at him and stretched his face into a grimace, exposing yet another metal object impaled in his tongue. Devlin continued to gape, too mesmerized by the sight to tear away his eyes.

A horn blared behind him, sending him into a whirling crouch to confront the streams of cars zigzagging along the road. Shaking off the curious stares of the people around him, he jerked to a standing position to find a group of six teenagers surrounding him. All of the boys wore similar outfits of black along with hair reminding him of Red's own spiked top. Tattoos adorned their exposed arms and necks, and Devlin bent his head to try and read the elaborate lettering on one boy's arm.

The tallest of them snorted, taking a leadership stance. "What's your problem, man? You never seen cars before?"

Devlin glanced at the traffic then back to the gang. "No problem. I'm not used to the noise yet."

Another teen spit on the ground at his feet. "How come? You just get out?"

Get out? Out of the mountains? Devlin tilted his head, wondering how the boy could know. The youth didn't smell. Well, he did, but not like a shifter.

Tall-Boy edged closer, his attitude growing more menacing. "You got money, dude?"

Following their leader, the rest of the group formed a tight circle around Devlin as the people around them hurried away. His internal alarm went off, launching his instincts into orbit. Adrenalin surged through him as he sensed his body starting to shift. Fangs lengthened and fingernails grew, curving while they sharpened into razor-edged weapons. Devlin thrust his hands in his pockets and tucked his head to his chin.

Aw, crap. Not this. Not after everything else today. "No. I don't have any money." He avoided their faces, instead focusing on the timbre of their voices. He had to stay human. Shifting on a public street would cause a panic and complicating problems.

"You got card?"

Card? Social security card? Baseball card? Credit card? He carried only one credit card, the one he always used for his business, but he wasn't about to give it to them.

A hard shove sent Devlin stepping toward the street. He struggled to keep the wolf inside him controlled. After all, he knew he could handle these punks without shifting.

"That's bullshit. Everyone has cards. Gimme your ATM card, man."

Another shove propelled him closer to the street and he stumbled to stay upright. "No, I don't." Sensing the atmosphere change around him, Devlin lifted his head and saw the blind hatred on the faces of the teens. These boys didn't care about money as much as they wanted to spill blood. His blood. "Boys, I don't have any money or any cards. And even if I did, I wouldn't give them to you."

Curses assailed him, but he stood his ground, ready for their next move. Tall-Boy drew a knife and his companions jostled for a better position. "Give me your wallet, man."

A burn seared its way upward from Devlin's gut and into his chest. "I told you. I don't have any money."

Tall-Boy and his gang pressed closer to Devlin. "You lie, asshole. Now give me your money or I'll give you this." He held up the knife and twirled it in his hand, letting the glow from the city lights glint on its shiny surface.

Damn, sometimes life doesn't give you a choice. While holding a full transformation in check, Devlin's lips stretched wide, exposing his two longest teeth at the sides of his mouth. Tall-Boy's forehead creased and he stared at Devlin's face. "Whoa. Are those real? Who are you? The Big Bad Wolf?"

"So you aren't as dumb as you look." Devlin opened and closed his mouth, making chomping motions. "They're real and sharp, and all the better to eat you with, my dear."

Exclamations ranging from bewilderment to outright fear jumped among the youths, yet Tall-Boy stood his ground. While the others retreated, Tall-Boy appeared unable to move his feet. Devlin bent his lips upward; exposing all his teeth in what he knew was a frightful sight. Pulling one hand from his jeans, he raised his hand, flexed his long, sharp claws and swiped the air right in front of Tall-Boy's face. "Let me fill you in on a little known truth. In the real story, Little Red Riding Hood made a tasty entrée after Grandma's appetizer."

"Shit!"

"Oh, holy crap."

The band of boys bumped into each other as they wheeled around and fled. Tall-Boy, eyes wide with terror remained unmoving.

Running his tongue over his fangs, Devlin reached out and plucked the knife out of Tall-Boy's hand. "Little boys shouldn't play with sharp objects." When the teen still didn't move, Devlin pressed his face inches from the boy's face and whispered, "Woof."

Horror splintered the youth's shocked expression. With a shout of dread, Tall-Boy turned, fell, scrambled to his feet again, and ran down the adjacent dark alley.

Devlin called after the gang members. "Hey, don't go! Was it something I said?"

*****

"This part of the city has changed. And not for the better."

Devlin kept up his rapid pace as he strode past the late-night street crowd. After his encounter with the teenage gang, he needed to go somewhere different. Somewhere calmer. Quieter. Darker. More like home. Remembering a park he he'd passed along the way to Tala's apartment, Devlin broadened his stride and tried to ignore all the discordant, over-powering sights and sounds around him.

Taking a short cut through alleys had provided him with images he'd rather forget. Yet that route had given him quicker access to the park. He puffed out a breath of relief as he came near the darkness and comforting silence of the park. He couldn't wait to go home to the mountains. Especially with Tala along as his mate.

Running off the hard concrete of the street and over the park's roped perimeter, he paused to breathe in the aroma of trees and grass. He closed his eyes to enjoy the comforting fragrance. "Nothing better than the smell of trees. Nothing except the smell of Tala's—"

He staggered as something rammed into his legs. Startled, he opened his eyes as he reached down to grab the object.

"Let go of me!"

A young boy struggled against Devlin, yanking himself away to try and break free of Devlin's grip. Two more boys dashed by Devlin, hurling curses at him. Watching the others sprint out of the park, Devlin let go of the boy, allowing him to rush off with his friends. But not before he flipped Devlin the finger.

"Don't humans ever keep their kids home at night?" Devlin glared at the boys who ran off down the street, shouting and shoving each other along the way. He followed their progress until they disappeared into the blackness of the streets.

Pushing through the bushes along a dirt-packed trail, Devlin continued until he entered a clearing, an oasis of tranquility. He jogged over to a bench, sat down, and pulled off his boots. Wiggling his toes in the damp softness of the lawn, Devlin relaxed against the bumpy wood of the bench and let his guard down for a second.

He'd never understand how anyone could stand living in the racket and dirt of the city. What possessed a reasonable creature to choose such harshness to the relaxing comfort of nature? But at least the city offered this little patch of sanity. Devlin rested against the bench and let out a low moan.

An answering sound snapped him to attention and he scanned the area around him. The moan, more of a whimper now, came again. Rising, he moved over to a group of prickly-leaf bushes and, drawing the shrubbery aside, peeked around, searching for whatever had made the sound.

The round, black eyes of a snow-white poodle gazed up at him. Devlin frowned as he sensed the vibrations of fear and pain radiating from the small dog. She struggled in an attempt to flee, but couldn't as she was held fast by the thorny branches. Shivering, she whimpered again and stared unblinking into Devlin's eyes.

"Hey, little one. Do you need help?" Devlin murmured to the poodle, careful to appear as non-threatening as possible.

The pooch whined again, but stopped struggling to get free. A tiny pink tongue fell out of her mouth, panting in nervous fright.

Devlin shushed the female and reached down, sending reassuring thoughts to her. Keeping his fingers away from her pointed little teeth, he cupped her under her soft belly and extricated her from the prickly undergrowth. "Shh. Don't worry. I won't hurt you. You'll be all right in a minute."

Although he tried to lift her as gently as possible, the poodle yelped in distress, bringing Devlin's attention to the remaining problem. Thorny leaves matted her curly fur as she struggled whenever a thorn poked her tender body.

"Damn, little one, how did you get in such a mess?" He raised the poodle in one hand, taking a good look at the predicament. "Did someone throw you in the bushes?" As she answered him with her turbulent thoughts, anger, fresh and strong, set his jaw and he smoothed the female's fur. "Whoever did this ought to have the same thing done to them. But it's okay. I'll take care of you."

An image of the young boys crept into his mind and a short growl escaped him. The poodle, frightened by his growl, shuddered until Devlin held her close to his chest and clucked his tongue in a soothing manner. Why were humans so cruel?

Taking care to not jostle the animal any more than necessary, Devlin returned to the bench. Uttering calming noises, he set the small animal on the bench and put on his boots. "Don't move. You're only making the problem worse." The poodle crouched into a ball, shuddered, and whimpered again. But when she stared at him this time, Devlin knew she'd understood him.

"Officer! Officer! Over here!"

Devlin's head jerked up to see a very large woman puffing her way to him. Sweat dripped from her round, red face as she slammed to a stop in front of him. Scooping up the poodle, she cradled the tiny animal against her massive chest and lifted the poodle's face to hers.

"Oh, Cuddles! I'm so gwad I found you. Mommy thought she'd wost you forever." Fat drops fell onto the poodle's head as "Mommy" let loose with a flood of tears. "Mommy thought you'd run away. Ouch!" She held Cuddles at arms' length and examined her. "You're sticking Mommy and you're a horrid, dirty sight!"

As fast as they'd come, the tears evaporated. Arching one eyebrow, she cast Devlin a superior look that had him disliking her intensely. "What are *you* doing with my little Cuddles?"

Amazing how the word 'you' could sound so evil. Devlin opened his mouth to speak just as a uniformed policeman burst through the bushes. "Ma'am, is this your missing dog?"

"Oh, my baby! My poor widdle darwing. Look at her, Officer Petry." She could turn on the baby talk as easily as she could the waterworks, as she held up the squealing dog toward the officer. "Look what this beast did to my poor widdle Cuddles."

She twirled to confront Devlin again, a wicked snarl curling her upper lip. "This is the thief who took her when I turned my head for a moment. Here's your dog thief. And an animal abuser, no less."

Devlin jumped to his feet as realization of her words sunk in. She thought *he'd* hurt her dog? How could anyone think he'd ever hurt a defenseless little animal? "Hold up. I didn't do anything to her."

Officer Petry's disgusted expression turned on Devlin. "What are you doing with Mrs. Skylard's dog? Never mind. Just be quiet and cooperate."

Devlin gaped at the cop, fighting to force the right words off his tongue. How could he convince them he hadn't done anything? Why should he have to explain anything? "You've got this all wrong. I didn't take her and I didn't throw her in the bushes, either."

Mrs. Skylard's tears erupted again as she held the poodle at arm's length. "Oh, precious me. She's getting stuck and she's in pain." A quick glance at the dirt and debris covering Cuddles' white coat had her handing over the dog to Petry. "Take her."

The officer shook his head. "No, ma'am. She's yours to care for. You keep her. I'll take care of the perpetrator." Renewing his glare at Devlin, he reached behind him and withdrew a pair of handcuffs. "Dog-napping and animal abuse. What a joke. Sir, you're under arrest for…"

Devlin's didn't hear anything after he'd heard the words "under arrest." This could not have happened to him. Devlin, a shifter, a friend of all canines, arrested for animal abuse?

Chapter Nine

Devlin protested all the way to the police station. Officer Petry, however, wouldn't listen to Devlin's declarations of innocence. Instead, the policeman kept advising Devlin to "shut up until you contact your attorney." At long last, Devlin took his advice and quit trying.

The booking was a humiliation Devlin wouldn't have wished on his worst enemy. Even a hunter deserved more respect than he got as he was jostled from one booking station to another, processing him into the system. From the mug shot to the fingerprinting, Devlin stood stone-faced and somber, amazed at how he'd ended up in jail. Various degrees of humans passed by him, some smelling worse than anything he'd ever smelled in the mountains, but Devlin held on to the hope of someone listening and recognizing the truth.

"Sit here." Captain Winters, the officer who'd processed Devlin, pointed at a chair next to one of the many identical desks in the station room. "Stay put or I'll have to handcuff you to the chair."

Devlin nodded, trying to appear as cooperative as possible. After all, once they'd finished with all the procedural necessities, someone would let him tell his side of the story. Or, at least, he hoped they would. Captain Winters shot him a stern look and ambled over to the file cabinet at the side of the room.

Devlin scanned the room around him, taking in the busy scene as police officers, male and female, went about answering phones, interrogating people, and doing paperwork. So many people with so many problems. Listening in on the conversations surrounding him, he learned about one garishly dressed woman's arrest for prostitution, an older man's detainment for drunk driving, and another man's refusal to give his name or any other vital information.

At least Devlin had something in common with the unidentified man. Neither of them had any identification on them. Although Devlin could and did give his name and age, he'd stumbled on telling his home address. After all, he couldn't very well say "in the den in the northwest portion of the mountains to the west." And he didn't want to give his business' address or contact any business associates, either. He cringed to think how Conrad would ride him about this latest fiasco. So when Tala's name popped into his head, hers was the name he'd given the frustrated officer as the friend he'd stayed with in town. Still, he'd had to confess he wasn't sure about the address.

Devlin frowned and closed his eyes against the headache pounding at his temples, trying to block out all the noise. A warm moistness brushed against his hand as warmer air tickled his palm. Glancing down, he stared at a large German Shepherd police dog sitting on his haunches, staring at him, beckoning him. In the moment their eyes met, Devlin knew what the dog needed.

"No. Go away." Devlin waved his hand at the dog. "Who do you think I am, Dr. Doolittle? Go away. I'm not helping anyone else tonight."

The dog made a sound similar to a groan and laid his jaw on the arm of the chair. Raising sad, pained eyes to Devlin's, he stared some more, imploring Devlin to respond. When Devlin continued to ignore him, he pushed against his arm with his nose

"No, I said. Didn't you hear me? No more. Look where helping one of your kind's already gotten me."

The dog moaned at him again, laid down on Devlin's feet and then flopped over onto its back in submission. His head rolled to the side to lick Devlin's leg.

What did this dog think? That he was like all these other humans and easily swayed by a show of affection? Pulease. Devlin scowled at the dog, and shuffled his feet, hoping to scoot out from under the dog. "Don't give me the sad eye routine. I'm not your master. Shoo."

The dog blinked at Devlin as if pretending not to understand. "No way. Won't work. Don't try your fake we-don't-talk-the-same-language routine. Get off of me."

"What's the matter with you? Don't you like dogs?" A young policeman kneeled beside the dog and patted his neck. "God knows why, but Davey must like you."

"I don't like him." *Lie, Devlin. Lie.* "Get him away from me."

'Hey, Ray. Your dog's a bad judge of character. That creep's in for stealing some rich lady's pedigree pooch and abusing the pup."

Ray pivoted to Captain Winters and back to Devlin. "Is that right?" He scratched Davey behind the ears and studied Devlin. "Davey usually has a good sense about people. But I think he's been sick for a few days, so maybe he's off this time. Come on, boy. You don't want to mess with this guy." Ray rose and clipped a leash to Davey's collar. Turning, he led the dog toward the nearest door.

As he followed his master, Davey crooked his head around several times to stare at Devlin. All at once, Davey pulled against his leash, spun in a circle and squatted on his haunches. He wouldn't budge an inch no matter how much Ray tugged on his leash. "What's the matter with you, boy?" Ray knelt down, pulling Davey's head to look at him. "What's wrong with you?"

Davey moaned again, barked at Devlin, and plopped onto his side. Ray and all the people in the room gaped at the dog and then turned their attention to Devlin.

Damn dogs. Devlin sighed. He didn't want to get involved. Not again. Yet when Davey's soulful eyes caught him in their grip one last time, he couldn't resist.

"He's hurting."

Ray gawked at Devlin as if he'd spoken an alien language. "What'd you say?"

"He's hurting. Down here." Devlin rotated his hands in a circle over his abdomen.

Ray moved closer to Devlin. "And how the hell would you know? You a vet?"

"Yeah, right. A vet in for animal abuse." Captain Winters chuckled and leaned against the file cabinet to watch. "No, wait! I've got it. He must be a dog psychic."

"You're a true comic, Captain." The cold glitter in Ray's eyes reinforced the steel in his voice. "How would a scumbag like you know what's wrong with my dog?"

Devlin gritted his teeth against his frustration. How easy it would be to shift and tear all these idiots apart with his claws and teeth. But even though the urge was there, he knew he'd never do anything to harm a human. At least, not an innocent human. "I didn't do anything to the lady's dog. I just found her in the thorn bush. Wouldn't surprise me if the dog jumped in the bush to get away from the prickly, old broad."

Ray caught his insinuation and the tension lined in his face eased. "Right." He cocked his head to the side and studied Devlin closer. "And now you're telling   me   Davey   is   sick?"

"*You* said he didn't feel well. I'm telling you why."

Ray stepped a bit closer to Devlin. "In his gut?"

"Right. He's hurting. And he has a hard time pissing."

"And you know that how?" Laughter echoed around the room as Captain Winters mocked Devlin. "You go to the john with him? Or did you two meet at a fire hydrant."

In sync, Devlin and Davey fixed onto the captain and growled, sending the roomful of people into jeers. Ignoring everyone else, Devlin focused on Ray, determined to say his piece now that he'd gotten involved. "Trust me on this. For Davey's sake, check it out. If I'm wrong, then no harm done. But if I'm right…"

Ray paused as he considered Devlin's remarks. "Yeah, maybe." Wheeling around, he pulled Davey up and started to lead him from the room. Davey, however, had other ideas, pulling on his leash to get closer to Captain Winters. Wheeling around and straining at the leash, Davey hunched over and answered Nature's call, dumping a load of dog poop onto the floor at the captain's feet.

The room burst into chaos as those around them caught wind of the dog's deposit. Policemen took off in several directions to get away from the stink.

"Damn it, Ray!"

"Shit, man, take him outside."

"You have got to be kidding me!"

Ray grimaced and scowled at Devlin. "I thought you said he was having a hard time doing his business?"

Devlin couldn't help but grin as he shrugged and caught Captain Winters' eye. "Nope. I said he was having a hard time pissing. Obviously, he can take a dump just fine. And as a dog psychic, I'd say he's trying to tell the captain something."

*****

"Ms. Wilde?"

The voice on the other end wasn't the one Tala wanted to hear. She'd hoped it was Devlin with his rich, deep timbre to soothe her. So much for hoping. Tala slumped onto the couch as her stomach dropped to the floor. "Yes. This is she."

"This is Officer Ray Williams at the downtown county jail."

Jail? Why would a policeman call her? Her stomach bounced up from the floor and landed in her throat. "Yes? Is something wrong?"

"We've got a friend of yours down here. He says his name is Devlin Morgan. Do you know him?"

Tala shut her eyes as apprehension crept along her spine. "Uh, yes. Yes, I do. Is he all right?"

"Yes, ma'am, he is."

Happiness shot through her and she smiled into the phone. "Thank God. He's been gone for hours. I thought something might have happened to him."

"Something did. He's been arrested."

Tala hopped to her feet and paced the floor. Her heart pressed against her chest, as if pushing its way to the outside. *Devlin arrested?* "For what?"

"For stealing a dog. And animal abuse, ma'am."

She dropped to the couch again as her knees gave out from under her. "What? Animal abuse? You're kidding, right?"

"No, I'm not. But Ms. Wilde?"

The roar in her head almost drowned out his next words. Devlin, an animal abuser? *Damn, I do know how to pick 'em, don't I?*

"Ms. Wilde? This is off the record, but I don't believe he hurt the animal."

Cradling the phone as close to her ear as she could get it, Tala whispered her question and held her breath for the right answer. "Why not?"

"Because of what he did to help my dog, Davey. He told me Davey was in trouble, hurting, sick, and I had him checked out. Davey was sick. He had bladder stones tearing up his stomach and they kept him from, uh, doing his business. Or at least, number one of his business."

"And Devlin told you all this?"

"He did. Just by looking at Davey. So you see, I figured I'd help him out and give you a call. I don't know the man or anything, but I get the impression he's too embarrassed to call you himself."

Tala's mind tumbled with questions. Devlin helped another animal? Like he'd done with the she-wolf? Yet he'd gotten arrested for animal abuse? She knew in her soul he'd never hurt an animal. "Officer? Can I bail Devlin out?"

A low chuckle wafted into her ear. "I think he'd appreciate it. Last time I checked, he looked like a caged lion pacing his cage. I've seen people who can't stand getting locked up and this guy takes the prize. You'd better get him out before he loses control."

"Okay. Tell me what to do." Tala dashed for a pad and pencil to jot down the information. "Got it. Thank you, Officer."

Hanging up, she grabbed her keys and purse, and dashed out the door, taking the steps down to the parking lot two at a time. She muttered as she slid into her car, threw the vehicle into reverse, and raced out of the parking lot.

Due to the late night hour, traffic was light, tempting Tala to break several speed limits on her way downtown. As she whipped her car into a space adjacent to the jail's front door, she took a moment to stop and consider the situation.

How did she know Devlin was innocent? After all, her instincts weren't the greatest. Hadn't she proven her bad judgment about men with Mark? And what if he had done such a foul act? What would her superiors at the zoo say if they found out she'd paid the bail for an animal abuser?

Tala caught her reflection in the rearview mirror. "Alleged animal abuser. Everyone's innocent until proven guilty no matter how odd they seem at times."

Tala bit her lower lip and slumped down in her seat. Nonetheless, maybe she should forget she'd ever met him. But could she? She closed her eyes and thought about Devlin. In only a few hours, she'd gotten involved with a total stranger. One she'd caught peeping into her home, no less. And in that short time, she'd had sex with him and grown to care for him. Somehow, without her wanting to, she'd committed more than her body to Devlin. She'd given him her heart as well.

"Damn it all to hell and back, Tala. What have you gotten yourself into?"

*****

"Man, you don't look so good."

Sitting on the bottom mattress of the holding cell's bunk bed, Devlin lifted his head to glare at the man sitting cross-legged with his shoulders resting against the opposite wall. "You don't say."

"Yeah, I do say." His cellmate spat a load of spit onto the filthy floor. "You look like shit."

Devlin groaned, allowing the knot inside his chest to loosen a bit. Figures he wouldn't get a private cell.

Working his head in a circle, he tried to keep the ton of bricks resting on his shoulders from breaking his neck. Nothing was worse than being confined. Although he didn't mind small places, the mere thought that he couldn't open the door and walk out twisted his guts into a petrified ball of spaghetti. The sliver of uneasiness he'd experienced earlier in the processing room exploded into outright anxiety. If he didn't get out of this cage soon, he'd go crazy.

He wished he could have stayed in the precinct booking room. At least there he'd had people to keep him company. Instead of this animal.

As impossible as it seemed, the man's appearance was worse than his smell. His long, greasy hair hung around his thick, grimy neck. If the stub between his head and shoulders could be called a neck. His blackened half-grin, half-sneer showed the man preferred chewing tobacco over cigarettes. Devlin cringed as the man sniffed, then rubbed the back of his hand under his nose to catch the drip the sniff hadn't gotten.

Locked in a tiny cage with a foul-smelling beast of a man. Will this night ever end? Could things get any worse? Hell, yes, they could. Could and would if my deeper instincts take over.

Although Devlin feared nothing from this walking, talking waste of human flesh, he decided his best course was to keep silent and hope the man took the hint. But he should have known the scumbag wasn't intelligent enough to catch subtlety.

"Ain't you gonna talk?" The man rose to his feet and stepped away from the wall. "What's the matter? You scared of something? Or are you some kind of idjit?"

For a second, Devlin pondered the definition of the word "idjit" and how ironic it was for the man to use the term. If anyone was an "idjit," it was this sorry excuse for a man.

The power, aching for release, surged through Devlin. A lot of time had gone by since Devlin had unleashed his full power and he knew to do so now would send his spirit soaring. Yet he also knew to shift here would make more trouble than he already had.

Hang on, Devlin. You've got to stay in control. In normal circumstances, keeping his other side at bay was easy. But this situation tested his endurance. His self-control. Perhaps beyond its limits.

The man inched nearer to Devlin. "Oh, I know what's buggin' you. You're afraid of the boogey man. Ain't ya?"

Devlin smiled at the question. *If he only knew. Boogey man, witches, and werewolves. All real.*

The unexpected burst of instinct sent Devlin's brain reeling in its intensity. His jaw lengthened as his fangs grew, while he watched his fingernails grow and change, tuffs of hair forming on his knuckles. Tucking his head again, he scrunched his features together and shut his eyes, willing himself not to shift.

"Answer me."

I can't. You wouldn't like my answer.

Without looking, Devlin gauged the distance between himself and the scumbag. What was with the human population these days? He'd suffered enough in his confrontations tonight, and didn't know if he could stand another one. If it weren't for Tala, he'd think everyone was a belligerent "idjit."

Tala. How he'd love to curl up next to her right now. Next to her soft curves, her firm butt, her generous breasts. Devlin sighed, wishing his desire could zap himself out of this cell and into Tala's arms. Instead, his desire fueled his shaft, making him hard in seconds.

Ah, hell. This is definitely not a good time for a hard-on.

His hands slid to his groin, hoping he could cover his erection without his cellmate noticing. "Leave me alone." Devlin forced out the words, trying to keep his tone level and non-threatening. Yet, some of his frustration leaked through, anyway.

"Don't you go telling me what to do. I don't like people telling me what to do."

Devlin's erection stiffened as his face shifted a little more. He could tell his nose, his eyes, and his mouth were different than a moment earlier. *Oh, crap.*

"Hey. What's with you? Your face looks weird."

Devlin shook his head, pulling his hair as far in front of his face as he could. He wrestled with the power boiling inside him and won a temporary victory. He could sense the man crossing the small cell, bending over, and trying to inspect his face.

"Something about you ain't right, man. I'd swear I saw something different about your face."

Thankful he'd resisted a complete transformation...for now...Devlin tilted his head at the man and arched an eyebrow. "You're seeing things."

His cellmate's thick forehead creased, giving him the appearance of an old hound dog. "Naw. I ain't. I done sobered up awhile ago." His frown deepened as he narrowed his eyes at Devlin. "You're sick, ain't ya? You better tell old Roscoe the truth."

"No. I'm not sick. But maybe you are. Sick in the head."

"Shut the fuck up!"

A shove at Devlin's shoulders rocked him back onto the cot. Devlin twisted, trying to hide the instant changes rippling across his features, but wasn't quick enough.

"Holy shit! What the hell?" Yet, as horrified as the man was, his terror grew greater as his gaze fell on the bulge in Devlin's pants. "No way. I don't go for no homo shit. Especially with no sick bastard."

Devlin snarled, an irrepressible growl rumbling from his throat, and pushed to the head of the cot to wedge his back against the corner of the wall. How much had the man seen? Could he explain his transformation away? Maybe his hard-on would prove useful, after all. A much-needed distraction.

Devlin peered out from the shadows and watched as the man shuffled backward until he hit the other side of the cell. From the mix of disgust and fear on his face, he'd seen too much.

Maybe he should shift all the way and give his body, his natural instincts a release? Especially since he'd gone so long without shifting. *Maybe just this once? After all, who'd believe this creep anyway?*

As soon as his mind opened a crack to the possibility of shifting, Devlin's body lurched into high speed. His jaw thrust out, elongating his face as silky hair bristled into coarse fur. His chest expanded as his heart beat against his spreading ribcage. The buttons on his shirt popped off at the widening of his torso, and a pain stabbed his crotch as his jeans fought against the burgeoning muscles in his thighs and legs.

Devlin tore at his clothes, yanking them away from his body before his transformation shredded them. His eyes, even more sensitive than before, zeroed in on the man as he moved out of the relative darkness of the bunk.

"Noooo!" His cellmate flattened his body to the wall, his hands scratching at the cement block as if he could dig his way out. "No. No. No. Not you again."

Again?

Devlin stopped in his tracks and tried to remember meeting him before today. No, he was positive he hadn't.

"Stay away from me. You're supposed to stay in my dreams." Roscoe thrust out his arms, averting his head while his terrified gaze locked onto Devlin. "Nightmares ain't real. Monsters ain't real."

He thinks I'm a creature from his nightmares. Drunken nightmares. Devlin sneered and reached out to watch the man jerk away in fear.

Roscoe's eyes bulged out of his face as he ducked his head under his arms, only to pop up for a quick peek. He shivered, while spittle dribbled down his chin.

Devlin threw back his head and howled. "Who's afraid of the boogey man now?"

Roscoe whimpered, a tight, strangled sound, a sound similar to the one Cuddles had made. Devlin stopped and stared at the absolute shock in the other's face. His scrunched up, tortured expression reminded Devlin of the look on Tala's face when he'd bitten her.

Devlin turned and dashed back into the darkness of his bunk. His cellmate huddled at the opposite end of the cell, mumbling incoherently as shudders racked his body.

Had Tala been afraid of him, like this? No, she'd been furious, not frightened. After learning about her troubles with her ex-boyfriend, no wonder she'd gone ballistic when he'd bitten her. Who wouldn't have?

Growling in frustration at himself, Devlin closed his eyes and concentrated on returning to human form. In quick succession, his jaw morphed, replacing the black, short hair with an after-five shadow. Claws and fangs withdrew, sinking into his adjusting skin. Rolling his head to the side, he mourned for the freedom of his alternate self. Naked and trembling from the rapid transformation, Devlin scooted off the bed and prepared to confront the crumbling mass of man.

As Devlin moved toward him, the man unwrapped his arms from around his head, and lurched to a standing position. Rattling the bars with both hands, he found his voice. "Help! Someone help me!" He cried as tremors shook his body, but continued his high-pitched scream. "Get me outta here!"

Devlin reached out to Roscoe, which sent the poor wretch into a greater state of panic. Backing off, Devlin tracked his fingers through his hair, and searched for some way to comfort him. Short of actually touching the man, of course. No way would he make physical contact.

"Quiet down in there!" Ray, the policeman who'd taken care of the dog, Davey, yanked open the door leading to the holding cell area, and strode toward their cell. "What's all the racket about?"

When he saw Devlin, he skidded to a stop and surveyed the scene before him. A smirk curved his lips while both eyebrows arched upward. "Uh, maybe I misunderstood what all the hollering was about. You fellas having fun getting acquainted? Should I leave you two alone?" His gaze rode up and down Devlin's nude body and over to Roscoe who reached through the bars as if salvation lay with the cop.

Devlin glanced down, remembered his current state of undress, and whirled to gather his clothes on the cot. In seconds, he'd dressed and stood holding his shirt together. "Was this guy arrested for drugs? 'Cause he started freaking out for nothing at all."

Ray nodded slowly as if trying to believe the unbelievable. "Right. You don't think maybe he's freaking because you're naked?"

"No. And I'm not anymore, but he's still freaking." Devlin tried to maintain what little dignity he still possessed.

Ray motioned with his chin. "And what happened to the buttons on your shirt?"

"Oh. They were loose." *Shit. I'm a crappy liar.*

"Uh, huh. All of them fell off at the same time. Jeez, I hate when that happens." Ray walked over to the still trembling Roscoe who pressed against the bars as if trying to squeeze through them. "Take it easy, buddy. If you don't want to be friends with Devlin, then that's your choice. No one's," Ray sent Devlin a pointed look. "...going to make you do anything you don't want to do."

Devlin blew out his disgust and sneered at Ray. "Are you friggin' kidding me? I wouldn't touch him if you gave me a reward."

"Get me outta here, will ya?" With trembling hands reaching out for help, Roscoe pleaded with Ray. "Put me in isolation. Put me in a hole. Anywhere. I don't care. Just get me the hell away from him."

Ray nodded at him, clamping a hand on his shaking shoulder. "Calm down. Don't worry about him. His girlfriend's on her way to bail him out. She should be here any second now."

"Tala's coming?"

"Yeah. Ms. Wilde." Ray tucked his head a bit, giving Devlin another onceover. "I figured I owed you one after you helped Davey. So when I checked your file and found her name, I called her and told her what you did to help my dog." He shrugged and narrowed his eyes at Devlin. "Besides, you don't strike me as an animal abuser."

Devlin grinned at Ray; thankful he'd helped the dog. But really thankful he was now dressed. After the cop's implication of his activities with his cellmate, he wouldn't want Ray seeing the stone-hard erection he'd gotten at the mention of Tala's name.

Chapter Ten

"I appreciate you paying my bail, Tala."

Although her legs weren't a match for Devlin's long stride, her anger at him propelled her several feet ahead of him as she led the way to her car. "Yeah, sure. My pleasure." She heard his groan as he recognized the sarcasm in her voice. She smiled an evil smile. He deserved a heavy dose of guilt as far as she was concerned. "Yep, bailing her lover out of jail is every woman's dream of a fantasy come true."

"Her lover, Tala? Or her love?"

She slowed her pace, started to turn around, and decided against the idea. No use in letting him know he'd gotten to her. "Lover. One-night stand. Sexual playmate. Don't do the semantics game with me. Got it, Devlin?" *Love. Shit. She couldn't, wouldn't love this guy.* Now all she had to do was convince herself. But the pain in her chest told her she was already too late.

"Whatever you say, babe."

This time she did wheel on him. "Do. Not. Call. Me. 'Babe.' I am nobody's 'babe.' Especially not yours." Yet when he smiled and looked at her with those big, fudge-colored eyes she almost took back her words. *Stand firm, Tala.* "Humph!" Spinning away from him, she stomped toward her car.

"Hey, Tala?"

"What?" She flung the word over her shoulder, not trusting herself to turn around. She punched the "Open" button on her car's remote a second before grasping the door's handle.

"Want me to drive?"

A giggle bubbled over even though she tried to clamp her mouth shut to keep it inside. She was mad at him and planned to stay mad. But the guy was funny. She'd give him that. And she loved funny men.

In answer, she slipped into her car, waited for him to get into the passenger's seat, and headed home. Halfway there, he tried to strike up another conversation, but she clammed up and gave him the silent treatment. Too bad the silent treatment didn't extend to her brain. Questions battled with confusion and irritation as she tussled with the reason behind his arrest. Could he have done what they said he'd done? Her mind tried to persuade her it was possible, but her heart kept rejecting the idea.

As they neared her apartment, she took a chance to glance over at him. And caught him staring at her. "Knock it off, Devlin."

"What'd I do?"

"You're staring at me."

His chuckle rushed heat over her body, dimming her frustration at him. She remembered that chuckle. He'd made the same chuckle while lodged between her legs. Skidding the car to a halt in front of her building, she shoved open the car door, and raced toward the stairs.

"What's the rush?"

Ignoring him, she dashed into the living room, leaving the door wide open for him to follow. Flinging her purse on the couch, she whirled to confront him. "Okay, I kept my mouth shut about this all the way home. But animal abuse? Something about a poor, little poodle? Can you explain?"

She saw the flash in his eyes a second before his face hardened. "I didn't hurt Cuddles. I helped her. Someone else threw her in those thorn bushes. I'd never hurt an animal like Cuddles. You know I wouldn't."

"I do?" She crossed her arms, trying to maintain a stern exterior. "How do I know?"

"After seeing first hand how I helped the she-wolf? After hearing about the police dog? Does that sound like someone who'd torture a poodle?"

The truth of his words seeped through her as her gaze landed on one of her wolf posters. An image of Devlin, cradling the she-wolf's head in his lap came to her, breaking the ice-cold reserve she'd tried so hard to keep. No way would he have hurt the poodle. "No, it doesn't."

She released pent-up air and unfolded her arms as he crossed to her. An ache for him lashed through her abdomen, shooting her libido into overdrive. His hands, warm and comforting, rested on her arms. Following her desire, she leaned into him and rested her head on his strong chest. "But then why did they arrest you?"

"Wrong time, wrong place."

Her head moved with his shrug and she slipped her arms around his waist. His body next to hers felt so good, so right, easing the tightness in her chest so she could breathe easier.

"The whole thing is a misunderstanding. I pulled Cuddles out of the bushes right before her owner and the cop showed up. I guess from their perspective, my actions seemed suspicious."

He hugged her closer and ran his hand down her torso, stopping right above her buttocks. The corners of her mouth tilted upward as she slid her hand along his body to rest in the same place above his rear. *Move lower, Devlin.* "So why didn't you explain it to them?"

"I did.   But they wouldn't listen.   I think Cuddle's owner is some sort of high society lady they needed to pacify."

"Oh."   The tighter he held her, the less she cared about the reason for his arrest. Memories of their lovemaking sent shivers through her and all other thoughts fled her brain. Lust, hot and fluid, ripped through her body, making her throb in anticipation.

Devlin moved his hands into her hair, bringing her gaze to his. "Tala. You believe me, don't you?"

She nodded, sure of her answer. "Yes."

"I wouldn't hurt any animal for no reason." His gaze dove into hers, imploring her, commanding her to believe. "Like I'd never hurt you."

She inhaled a quick breath as tears stung her eyes. Did he understand the pain she'd suffered in the past? Could any man truly understand? She searched his face and found the answer she'd dreamed of. Still...

"But you did hurt me."

She caught the quick flash of regret on his face and held him to her. *Tell me what I want to hear.*

"I'm sorry. It won't happen again."   Diving into her being, he searched inside her for the truth. "Unless you want me to."

Taking his hand in hers, she led him to the bedroom. Once they'd reached the bed, she turned to him, took his face between her hands, and brought her mouth to his. Her tongue slipped between his lips, seeking his, finding his. As their tongues played, she snaked her hands around his ribcage, bringing the shirt along with her. He shook it off and let the material pile at his feet.

Nibbling at his bottom lip, she flipped open his jeans, pushing down the zipper by pulling the flaps apart. Devlin copied her with her jeans, tugging them off her hips so she could step away from them. The rest of her clothes soon joined her jeans as she shrugged them to the floor.

Tala pushed him to a sitting position on the bed and dropped to her knees. His excited groan thrilled her almost as much as her eye-level view of his enlarged cock. Wrapping her palms around him, she licked the underside of his shaft, gliding her tongue along the thick trunk until she reached the tip. Devlin grabbed her hair to keep her close, but she resisted, pushing against the bed for support.

With slow precision, she twirled her tongue over his tip until he had to let go of her hair to fall back on the bed. He moaned a tortured, happy sound. Smiling, she paused, removing her mouth from him.

"No, don't stop."

Pleased by the thickness in his voice, she deep-throated him, driving him as far into her mouth as she could do. He gasped and clutched at the bedspread.

"Tala. Oh, shit, Tala."

"Do you like it, Devlin?"

He growled and reached for her, but she weaved out of his reach. "Uh, uh, uh. This is my turn." Again, she dove onto him, pulling and sucking as she watched the ecstasy flow over his face.

He was hers. As she worked with her hands and her mouth, her mind rejoiced at the thought. Giving head to any other man would have felt wrong, dirty, even submissive to her. But not with Devlin. With this act, she'd claim him as her own. For good or bad. Forever.

As she sighed, her warm breath cascaded over her hands and his shaft. He uttered another, louder growl. Pumping with her hands matching the rhythm of her mouth, she gave her man all the love she held inside her.

At last, he yelled, sat up, and dragged her into the bed. "You're torturing me, woman."

Tala giggled and squeezed him to her. "Woman, huh?" She arched an eyebrow and shot him an I-don't-know-about-that look. "I guess 'woman' is better than 'babe.' But not by much."

He buried his face in the curve of her neck, his chuckle tickling her skin. "Would you prefer 'My Queen'? How about 'Beautiful'?"

"Nope. I have a name. Use it. And be careful, bud. No more biting. Got it?"

In answer, he slid his tongue along her collarbone and the tiny scar remaining from her wound, and made his way across her chest. She laughed as his mouth latched onto her breast, sucking at her tit like a starving man. Spreading her legs, she guided him to her. "I need you, Devlin. Big time." Wiggling her eyebrows at him, she added, "And I do mean 'big' time."

He growled again. Why did he growl so often? Not that she minded. In fact, she loved his growl. Yet the question went unanswered as his cock thrust into her. Her legs locked around his hips as he pounded into her, his raw growl washing over her, exciting her, driving her need higher. She slammed back into him, wanting to drive him farther inside. "Oh, Devlin."

She met each of his thrusts with her own, pulling him to her with her arms and her vagina. Heat, uncontained, roared inside her as her release escalated, soaring to the sky. Throwing back her head, she let loose with an animal-like scream in the same instant Devlin turned his head to the side and howled.

*****

"I have never tasted anything so good in my life." Devlin licked the fingers on one hand while balancing the take-out box on his other. "Well, almost never." His wicked grin left a small fire burning in Tala's abdomen. "I'm telling you, if Mankind never did anything more than invent pizza, he'd have fulfilled his purpose in this world."

Tala laughed and punched the button on her car's remote. "So forget about world peace, just keep the pizza coming?"

"Give everyone in the world free pizza and you'd have world peace. And solve world hunger at the same time."

They crossed the restaurant parking lot together with the late afternoon sun warming their backs. Tala giggled, comfortable in the Devlin's company. *Who'd have thought so much could come in such a short time?* After a relaxing day spent together, she looked forward to another night of bliss wrapped in Devlin's arms. She slipped her arm in his and greeted his smile with one of her own.

Whether the smell or the flash of movement out of the corner of her eye made her stop, she wasn't sure. Maybe it was both. Yet when she looked at the bushes, she saw nothing out of the ordinary. However, she couldn't mistake the familiar stench.

"I know that smell."

She glanced at Devlin, not surprised he'd caught the odor, too. "Yeah. I'm trying to place it, but—Oh, crap."

"What?" Devlin folded her into his arms, and scanned the foliage around the pizza parlor's lot. "Did you see something?"

"I thought I did. But I remember what...or who...makes that stink. It's George Groggins' aftershave."

"Who?"

She pulled away from Devlin to search for the ex-employee. "You know. The man who harmed the she-wolf. He must be somewhere close by."

"Not for long."

Was that Devlin's voice? Tala turned to Devlin. His tone was lower than she'd ever heard, meaner, like controlled chaos ready to break free. She'd expected him to react, but was unprepared for what she saw.

Devlin inhaled a quick, sharp breath and, without warning, his face changed, contorted, until he didn't look like himself. His jaw twisted, shooting outward. His mouth opened, forced wide by his rapidly growing teeth.

Holy shit.

Tala stared at Devlin. *Are those fangs?* Falling backwards, she continued to gawk at Devlin as she forgot all about George. *How did any man, anyone, have teeth like that?* Amazed, yet strangely drawn to the sight, she gaped at Devlin, trying to match what she saw with anything logical. She bit down, surprised to find that her own teeth felt too big for her mouth. *I'm losing it. Maybe someone put drugs in the pizza?* She gritted her teeth again, but this time her teeth seemed normal. *Am I tripping?*

A growl rumbled through Devlin as he stalked in a circle, checking out the surrounding vehicles. "Do you see him anywhere?"

"What? Who?"

Devlin, the normal-looking Devlin, met her gaze and in his eyes she saw recognition, acknowledgement. What now? Why couldn't she find Mr. Nice and Normal? "Why do I get the impression you're hiding something from me? You changed a second ago. So spit it out, Devlin. I'd rather know now than find out later." *But was it already too late?*

He inhaled deeply and licked his lips. "You saw, didn't you?"

No. Maybe she didn't want to go there. "I don't know what you mean."

Devlin tilted his head and arched an eyebrow. "Yes, you do. You saw my fangs."

He'd said the words. Out loud so he couldn't take them back. "I, uh, I don't know. Maybe. But no. I'm sure I imagined everything." She blurted out a short laugh, hoping to make a joke of what she'd seen. What she thought she'd seen. She grasped at straws. "I'm thinking the pizza was doped."

"No, you didn't imagine anything." He stared at her, molding his gaze to hers. "Tala, I need to tell you about me. All about me."

Damn it all to hell and back. I'm successful. I'm strong. I've got everything going on in my life. Except Mr. Right. Damn, I'd take Mr. Not A Weirdo right now.

Her breathing quickened as the air around her became heavier, denser, harder to suck into her lungs. She didn't want this conversation to go on. If it did, they couldn't stay like they were, and everything she'd hoped for might end up lost. "I don't want to hear this, Devlin. L-Let's just go home." She wheeled around and started for her car. "And no, you can't drive."

His hand on her arm brought her around until she stood close to him. The blood rushing through her veins picked up speed and her heart thudded against her ribcage. "Let me go." Yet his eyes of warm chocolate melted into hers, leaving her unable to break free.

"Tala, I know this will be hard to understand and accept. But if you look into your heart, you'll find I'm telling you the truth."

"No." She looked around her and then down at the ground. "I'd rather not. Let's go back to thirty minutes earlier when you crammed two slices of pizza into your mouth. Hell, let me cram two slices in your mouth."

"I'm what people call a werewolf. But we prefer to call ourselves shifters."

She didn't know what she'd expected. But not this.

She couldn't help herself. She had to let it out. Nothing could control her reaction.

She laughed. Full out, full throated, hold-the-belly-cause-it-hurts laughed.

In fact, she couldn't stop laughing. "You're kidding me, right? A werewolf? Holy shit, Devlin, are you saying you change into a wolf during a full moon?"

His features hardened as he clenched his jaw. "I'm serious, Tala."

"You're telling me you're the Wolf Man?" She wrapped her arms around her waist as the tears streamed down her face. But she couldn't stop laughing. "So you grow fur and everything? Don't you know most women don't like hairy men?"

"Tala, stop."

He reached for her, but she weaved out of his grasp. Whistling, she snapped her fingers. "Here, boy. Oh, wait. I guess wolves don't heel like dogs do, right?"

Wrapping her arms around her waist, she continued to giggle. Yet, her chest tightened as if her heart couldn't pump the blood fast enough through its arteries. "And what, Devlin? Were you going to bite me and change me into a werewolf, too? Recruit another werewolf for the pack?"

Devlin locked onto her, his face a cold mask. "I'm serious."

She'd be very worried if this weren't so funny. Or was it? A nervous knot formed in her belly and wouldn't let go. No matter how loudly she laughed. "Oh, crap. You did bite me." She whirled around, looking at her bottom. "Am I going to grow a tail when the moon comes out? Will I chase my tail? Oh, shit. I just did!" She stopped spinning and dropped her mouth open in feigned delight. "Does this mean instead of children, I'll have puppies? A litter?"

"We need to talk about this, Tala."

"Too bad, Devlin. I don't think there's a full moon tonight, so we'll have to wait a few days for a romp under the stars. But, hey, in the meantime, you can pick out which brand of dog food you'd like me to feed you. Or does your appetite run to steaks?" Her voice pitched higher, hysterics pushing aside her restraint. "But here's the good news. We don't even have to cook them. Werewolves prefer their meat rare, right?"

"Tala, don't mock me."

"Then don't feed me a crock of shit."

He grabbed her hand in his and yanked her forward. "I'm not. You need to know who I am. What I am."

"I do know you. And you are one funny man. But the joke's over, okay?"

Devlin growled, frustration echoing through the grumble.

"And what's with all the growling, Devlin? Part of your act?"

He brought her to him before she could react, his mouth slamming against hers, his tongue driving into her mouth with hurricane force. Strong arms held her to him and she struggled, making a vain attempt to get away. Yet, although she told herself she wanted to run, her body responded to him, heating up in seconds as he pressed against her.

Devlin's kisses traveled down her neck as his hand pulled aside her shirt. His teeth nipped at her skin and she tilted her head to give him easier access. Giving up the pretense, she slid her arms around his broad chest and under his arms to grip his shirt from behind. She clung to him for a minute before taking his hand from the hollow above her bottom, and placing it over her breast.

Bending his head, his mouth sought out her nipple and bit through the fabric covering the firm bud. "Tala, I have to tell you all of it. You have to know."

The warmth in her panties increased as she grew wet with desire. She didn't want to know. All she understood was how much she wanted him, lusted for him. "Shut up, Devlin, and let's go home."

The shock of him pushing her away left her dazed and unsteady on her feet. "No. Don't stop." Why couldn't he just do as she asked?

Cupping her face between his hands, he forced her to look at him. His hard gaze trapped her, snaring her like a rabbit in a noose. "You have to listen to me."

Afraid to say anything, afraid to move, she waited, knowing she had no choice but to listen. Her pulse quickened to an impossible rate as fear ran an even race with longing.

"I'm a shifter."

"No." She reached for his hands and averted her gaze from his face.

He gripped her harder, forcing her eyes back to his. "I'm Devlin Morgan of the Morgan Pack. We've lived in this area for generations, both in the city and in the hills."

"You've got a problem if you think I'm going for this wolfman thing." She silently begged him, wanting him to tell her everything was a joke. Better that than a mental illness. "It's a joke, right? I mean, what I saw…" His bark sounded more canine than a human. Yet, still she wouldn't, couldn't believe.

"Tala, I came to the city to find my mate." He kissed her, lightly, lovingly. "I came to find you."

What had he said? Stunned, she waited, hoping she'd misunderstood him. She was his 'mate'? How far would he take this joke?

"I'm telling you the truth. You're my mate, Tala."

He's serious. Oh. My. God.

Tala broke free and stumbled from him. Whether she'd dredged up enough strength at long last, or he'd loosened his hold on her, she didn't know. And didn't care. Her soul ripped apart as the scariest thought of all sunk in. *I love him.*

She backed away from him, her heart pounding not from all he'd told her, but from the truth no longer hidden within her. "I—I need some time. Give me time." Without giving him a chance to speak, she spun around and headed for her car.

*****

"A werewolf. A shifter. The man thinks he's some kind of an animal."

She clicked to shut down the Internet connection and snapped the laptop closed. Glancing at the front door, she again wondered where Devlin was, but pushed the anxiety from her. She'd asked him to give her time and stay clear of her until she'd calmed down, hadn't she? And he'd return later, no doubt. At least, she hoped he'd return. Didn't she?

Two hours of scouring the Web and she'd learned a lot about werewolves. More than she'd ever wanted to know. Yet the information she'd obtained didn't help her much. Just fantasy and old folk tales. Nothing about the real possibility of werewolves.

As if. She *humphed,* angry with herself for wasting time on something that couldn't be real. No matter how much Devlin claimed it was.

But you saw him. Don't you believe your own eyes?

The nagging thoughts dug at her, making her search a little deeper, a little longer. Her love for him couldn't have let her do anything less.

Damn it all to hell and back. I do love him.

She frowned, and then smiled. She'd found him at last, her wolf-like man. Gazing at the poster of a pack of wolves, her mind wandered, allowing her to believe the unbelievable.

The wolves in the picture moved as she saw herself as the female. Pups surrounded her, while the large wolf...Devlin, of course...stood watch over their romping youngsters. Sighing, Tala let the cozy family image play in her mind. Pups. Would she and Devlin have lots of—?

"Pups? I'm thinking of having puppies?" What in the world was the matter with her? "I've gone crazy. Pups instead of children. Or would they be both?" She glanced at the poster again. One of the pups put on a doggy smile, waved, and called to her. "Hi, Mom!"

Tala fell against the back of her couch and shoved a pillow over her face to bury her scream. Yelling for a full minute helped ease the stress building inside her. Slowly, she dared to peek above the cushion, squinting at the poster again. Thankfully, the poster had returned to normal with no moving animals. "You've got to get a grip, Tala."

She threw the pillow against the wall, striking the poster of the male wolf and his mate. Maybe she deserved this? Was her attraction, her love of wolves driving her over the edge? Hadn't she imagined her own teeth morphing into fangs?

"This cannot be happening."

She tunneled her fingers through her hair and scanned the room around her. Wolf pictures, knickknacks, and figurines were everywhere. Could Devlin be playing on her obsession? She shook her head. No, he'd been sincere in his declaration. Frustration brought the tears and she growled at her lack of control.

Growled? Now I'm growling, too? Like Devlin.

She spotted her grandfather's picture and paused as a memory floated through her mind. Her grandfather shared her passion with wolves, particularly the wolves around this area.

Rising to go to the mantel to pick up the photo of the small, gray-haired man, Tala worked to recall the story her grandfather, Ross Wilde, had told her during her childhood visits to his home outside the city. Hadn't the story included wolves? Wolves as part of a family? Maybe her family? As hard as she tried, she couldn't fit the pieces of the tale into place. Too many years had passed since she'd last heard the story.

"I think it's time to pay Gramps a visit." Reaching for her cell phone, she punched in the numbers, and waited for him to pick up. After several minutes, he answered, his voice bringing a tender glow to her heart.

"Gramps? It's Tala." She smiled into the receiver. A visit was long overdue, no matter what the reason.

"Tala? Hi, honey. How ya doing, Cookie?"

Her grin stretched wider at the affectionate nickname he'd always used for her. "Fine, Gramps." God, how she loved him. She'd forgotten just how much until she'd heard his voice. "Gees. I'd almost forgotten what you used to call me. Only you could get away with giving me such a cutesy name. I used to sock anyone else who tried."

He chuckled, his tone vibrant and full of life. "Hey, grandfathers can get away with all kinds of shit."

Tala laughed and mimicked her late grandmother. "Watch your mouth, old man. Knock off the swearing, damn you."

He hooted, delighted at her imitation. "Your grandmother could cuss with the best of them. Much to your mother's distress. I never did understand how such an uptight lady came from your Granny and me."

Tala couldn't respond. Not with her throat swelling up with emotion.

"Your grandmother would be proud to know you're keeping me in my place. So how's the zoo? I see you all the time on television. You remind me of your mother, you know. Not the uptight part, of course. The pretty and smart part. She'd be real proud of you, too, Cookie."

Tala eyes watered at the mention of her deceased mother. The car accident claiming both her parents' lives was years ago, but the heartache lived on. "Thanks, Gramps."

A moment's silence passed between them as Tala thought about her parents. Lost in thought, she caught only a part of her grandfather's next words.

"...calling about? Not that I'm not happy to hear from you. You should call me more often and drop by sometime."

"Funny you should say so because I thought I'd come out for a visit. You know, to catch up on things." *And to ask you about my werewolf lover, Gramps.*

"Hey, terrific! When you coming?"

"No time like the present. If you're not busy." She pictured him, sitting around the big kitchen table with his friends. The smoke from the cigars he'd refused to give up would fill the room while potato chips and beer littered the counters around them. "Got a game going later, Gramps?"

"Naw. I wiped the boys out last night. Any time's fine."

The "boys" consisted of five men, Gramps' closest friends who were all about the same eighty years of age and from the same neighborhood in the city. They'd managed to remain close throughout the years. Closer than most people ever got. Tala frowned, remembering her grandmother's name for Gramps and his friends. She'd called them "The Pack." *Like Devlin's pack?*

"Tala? You there?"

Pulling her mind back to the present, she answered in a voice not as steady as she'd have liked. "Uh, yeah. I'm here." Snatching up her purse, she was out the door and down the stairs to her car. "And I'll be there before you know it." She was out of the parking lot, heading for the highway almost before he managed to answer.

"See ya soon, Cookie."

Tala disconnected the call and dropped the phone on the seat beside her. Dodging traffic, she wound along the thoroughfare until she spotted the exit leading to her grandfather's home.

"I hope this isn't a mistake."

Following roads she'd not traveled in a long time, Tala left the busy avenues behind and drove into the quiet neighborhood. One last turn brought her to the curb in front of his ranch-style home. She slid out of the car seconds after throwing the gearshift into place.

She paused, noting the lights Gramps had left on for her. "Okay, Tala. Time for some answers. Whether you like them or not." Lengthening her stride, she took the route over the yard, straight to the steps, and up to the front door already opening for her.

"Hey, Cookie. You're looking hot."

Tala shot Gramps a you-are-such-a-flirt look. "Watch it, old man. You're too old for me."

He laughed and pushed the door wider for her, giving her a chance to glance around, noting how little had changed in the neat, small house. Granted, the neighborhood had grown when the city had expanded to include the outlying areas, but Gramps had resisted selling any of his five acres. Now his house sat on the cul-de-sac, surrounded by newer, bigger homes.

"Ah, leave it to you, Gramps." Tala strode over to the coffee table and picked up one of the boxed cookies sitting on the coffee table. "Chocolate Chip. My favorite. You always had these ready for me whenever I visited."

"Sorry they aren't homemade like your grandmother's."

She hugged him as he came over. Sitting with him on the couch, she kept her head down, not yet ready to ask the tough questions.

"So, Cookie. What's up? What's bugging you?"

She looked up to find him eyeing her. "I never could hide anything from you."

He ran a hand over her shoulder, comforting her with his touch, sending waves of reassurance flooding through her. "Don't even try."

Taking in a large breath, she decided to dive right in. She couldn't put it off any longer. "Do you remember the story you used to tell me when I was a kid? You know. The one about wolves?"

His hand slid from her shoulder at the same moment his smile slid from his face. "Sure. Why?"

"I can't really remember it all. Did it have something to do with...?"

"With what?"

"I know this will sound stupid, Gramps. But did it have something to do with werewolves?"

Gramps' eyes met hers and a trickle of apprehension ran down her spine. *Oh, shit, he's going to tell me something I'm not going to like.* "Cookie, the story isn't just a story. It's about your family. It's about the pack."

Chapter Eleven

The pack? The butterflies filling her stomach turned into bats. Big, bad, ugly bats. "What do you mean?" Did she really want to hear this? A part of her shouted for her to run. But she couldn't. She was stuck to the couch.

"The pack's just a name Grandmom called your poker buddies." She shoved the cookie into her mouth. *Stop talking. Stop asking questions and get the hell outta here.* Yet, she knew she couldn't, wouldn't leave until she knew the truth. Indeed, if she were honest with herself, the idea of a pack was intriguing.

"Yeah, it was. But those buddies were also part of our lives. Part of our heritage." He gave her a comforting smile. "The members of the pack are our kind of people."

"I don't understand. What are you saying?" *You know what he's saying.*

"Do you remember me telling you about your special ancestors? Remember how I told you they had a gift, a power most other humans didn't have?"

Fear constricted her breathing, but she pressed on. "Yeah, I remember. I sort of chalked the gift thing up to your tendency to exaggerate. So what? Gramps, get to the point, okay? You're scaring me."

Reaching out, he took her hands in his and leaned forward. "I don't mean to scare you. In fact, I think this should make you happy. Besides, I should have told you long ago. I would have, too, if your mother hadn't been so dead set against you knowing."

She saw the excitement building inside him. And felt it churning inside her. A spark glittered in his eyes as he continued.

"You're going to find this hard to believe, but I swear it's the truth. A long, long time ago, your ancestors were part of a group of unique individuals." He squeezed her hands, his bushy eyebrows arching at her. "Cookie, you have shifter blood in you."

She gasped as the world tipped at an odd angle and her vision doubled. Needing strength in the connection to a sane world, a world of reality, she gripped his hands and held on. "What? Do you mean werewolves?"

A frowned creased his brow. "We're not fond of that word but, yes, werewolves are what most people call our kind."

"Gramps, you're making this up. Tell me you're making this up."

He shook his head, a strange, sad expression flitting across his features. "No, Cookie. I'm not. You should be proud of your heritage. You come from shifter blood."

An idea came to her. A way to disprove all this nonsense. "Then why haven't I ever seen anyone change into a wolf? I've never known anything, anyone remotely odd." She squeezed his hands, hoping to get him to admit his joke. "At least, not odd in a supernatural kind of way."

"First of all, we aren't 'odd.' The reason you've never known is because our blood has gotten mixed and diluted with human blood for many years. Most of us have lost the ability to shift."

Hope filled her as she grasped at another straw. If she had to buy into this nonsense, then she'd find another way out. "So we don't have enough of this so-called shifter blood in us to do us any harm?"

Gramps shook his head and released her hands. "Harm? To shift was a gift, not something bad. Your great-great-grandfather was the last one who had the ability to shift."

"Did you ever see him change?"

"It's called shifting. And no, I never did."

Tala rose and paced to the other side of the room. Her grandmother smiled at her from a brass picture frame, making her wonder how the matriarch would have approached this situation. "Then you don't know if this is for real and not just a family legend, do you?"

Gramps straightened, making his posture more rigid and commanding. Stronger. "Rumors are often more truth than fantasy. I know if you'll search your heart, you'll realize I'm telling you the facts. Be proud of your heritage, Cookie. Besides, like I said. The pack, my poker buddies, all have shifter blood in them, too. And some of them can still shift. I've seen them."

Could her grandfather and all his friends be delusional? Was this a form of old age dementia? Tala studied her grandfather's earnest expression and knew he had all his mental capacities intact. Unless. "Gramps, doesn't Luther use medicinal marijuana for his glaucoma?"

His laughter echoed around the small room. "So you think we're just a bunch of old farts getting high and imagining we're werewolves?"

"Well..." Leave it to Gramps to put her in her place. "At least that would make more sense."

His laughter died down as he took her by the arms, hugged her to him, and then put her at arms' length. "You know what? If I could get old Luther to share his stash with me I would. But he's tighter than a virgin with her cherry with his stuff. Damned if I wouldn't enjoy a little toke once in awhile."

She grinned, grateful he hadn't taken her question the wrong way. But then, when did he ever take anything she said the wrong way?

"But Cookie, you're barking up the wrong pot plant. Pun intended." He chuckled, pleased with his own humor. "You've got shifter blood in you. Don't just trust me on this. Look inside yourself for confirmation."

When she sighed, he narrowed his eyes, zeroing in on her. "Now I've got a question. What brought all this up? You start howling at the moon lately?"

*****

Devlin wasn't at the apartment when Tala got home. *Where could he be? Getting tossed into jail again?* The thought of having to bail him out a second time left a bad taste in her mouth. Would she come to his rescue again? Yet there was no question she would. She hadn't told him to get lost or anything. Not permanently, anyway.

She flopped onto the couch and rested her head against the sweet softness. Could she be mentally unstable and not even realize it? Maybe she'd conked her head too hard when she'd fallen down during the moonlight dance summoning an immortal. After all, hadn't everything started after that night?

But I didn't fall down. I crouched down. Like a four-legged animal. Like a wolf. And I howled. Damn it all to hell and back, I howled.

The only other explanation was even harder to believe. Had she really summoned her immortal man? How ridiculous! The urge to scream again crawled up her throat, but she fought it back down. She could handle this. Even if she wasn't about to look at the wolf family poster.

To keep her eyes away from the poster, she deliberately punched a couple of buttons on the remote and turned on the television. "Maybe an old movie will get my thoughts off this lunacy for awhile. Then I can think later, once my head's clear." Skimming through the channels, she landed on the *Discovery Channel* and one of her favorite programs. "Yay. This'll get my mind off my problems."

She sighed and waited for the commercials to end. After a middle-aged man finished extolling the virtues of a pill for penis enlargement...*damn, are those ads everywhere now?*...a lush, green forest in the mountains covered the screen. Out of the forest loped a canine, gray and white, a gorgeous creature by anyone's standards. Tala squinted, trying to place the familiar image.

The wolf dashed over to the edge of a clearing as the camera zoomed in for a close-up. Italicized words scrolled across the bottom of the picture. *The male wolf searches for his mate.*

"Oh, crap. Uh, uh." She talked to the canine in the screen. "You know how I love wolves and wolf shows, but now is not the day for this." Clutching the remote, she switched to another channel.

A town, dark and hidden by the night's shadows, focused on the screen. As a backdrop to the town, the light from a full moon blanketed a meadow, highlighting a sole inhabitant as it moved swiftly across the glade. Suddenly, the focus zoomed closer to the man, who bent down next to a building at the edge of town. Inching nearer, his face grew clearer. His jaw changed, hair sprouting over his skin, as his features twisted into grotesque display of human to wolf metamorphosis. Claws sprang out from his changing hands as he gripped the wall and lifted his head to howl.

"Oh, come on. *The Wolf Man*? What next?" Tala thumbed her way to a tried-and-true favorite program, *Classic Movies*. "Now we're talking. Abbott and Costello. Some funny stuff is just what I need. Frankenstein, yes. Werewolves, no."

Abbott and Costello ran through the house of horrors while Frankenstein chased after them. Tala laughed at their hilarious antics, letting the tension slip away. "Finally. The perfect show." She snuggled down into the couch and rested her feet on the coffee table to enjoy the movie, and was soon immersed in the show.

"What the hell?" Tala lurched upward as the Wolf Man jumped in front of Costello. "No! This isn't right. Frankenstein's the bad guy in this movie. It's called *Abbot and Costello Meet Frankenstein*. Not the Wolf Man." She tossed a pillow at the TV, grabbed the remote, and clicked the "Off" button.

She was doomed to think about her situation. Forced to ponder her grandfather's words. Thrown into contemplating Devlin and his fantasy.

What if his fantasy is true? She frowned and recalled her grandfather's words. Gramps had always been the rock in her life, so steadfast, so secure. So *normal*. Until now. Until he'd professed to having werewolf blood running through their family's veins.

"Oh, excuse me," she said to an invisible Gramps. "Shifter blood." She tracked her fingers through her hair and paced over to the desk where her computer rested. "Do I dare try again? Do I really want to know?" She eyed the screensaver depicting a pack of gray wolves. "I'd be better off knowing the truth, right? Or would I?"

Slipping into place before the computer, she tapped on the mouse and brought up a search engine. "Between my one-track mind and the rest of the world," she glanced at the television, its blank screen mocking her. "...I guess I'm destined to know everything I ever wanted to know about werewolves, but was afraid to ask."

Taking a deep breath, she steeled her nerves, and typed key words into the search criteria. "Here goes nothing." A quick bark of a laugh escaped her. "Or everything."

A list of sites popped up on the screen. Why hadn't she seen these before? "Popular subject." Leaning toward the screen, Tala brought up the first site and read aloud. "'The term werewolf means 'manwolf.' Well, duh." She skipped past some general information she'd read earlier. "Now here's some new info. 'Lycanthrope, another term used for werewolves, also refers to a mental disease where the individual fantasizes about being a wolf.'"

Could Devlin be mentally ill for real? Tala thought about him spying on her and sleeping on her patio. "Not exactly your average everyday things to do." Still, her heart wouldn't let her mind accept the insanity explanation.

Moving on to another site, she scanned the material, cringing when she read information that made her uneasy. Although the history and origin of werewolves was interesting to read, her pulse skipped a beat when she landed on a section called *Modern Cases*. Reading the information didn't help her agitated stomach, though. "God, these poor people. They truly believe they're werewolves." Like Devlin did. Like Gramps did.

Like I do.

Unable to stand the images and facts any longer, she clicked on the mouse and shut down all the websites. Pushing back her chair, she slumped down, and crossed her arms in front of her. "No. I won't. I won't let myself believe Devlin or my grandfather is crazy. Or myself, either."

Then how do I explain what I saw? Her thought caught her unaware, lurching her upset stomach into her throat. Did I really see Devlin change? See him shift? She closed her eyes, picturing an image of Devlin as he reacted to the smell of George's aftershave. She'd seen fangs. Not teeth. Honest-to-God, sharp-as-a-knife fangs. Hadn't she?

Another image came of Devlin, his head shaped differently, grabbing George and coming to the she-wolf's rescue. He'd shifted then, too. She'd dismissed what she'd seen at the time, but could she now?

Shaking her head, she rose and crossed over to stand in front of the mirror on the wall. What if Devlin's explanation was true? And what if everything Gramps had told her was true? She stared at her image and smiled, stretching her lips to expose her teeth. "Looks like normal teeth to me."

Bending to the mirror, she hooked her thumbs on either side of her mouth and pulled up her upper lip. Studying her eyeteeth, she voiced what she saw as if relaying the facts in a scientific examination. "Shape, normal. Color, normal. Length normal. Hardly anything canine-like."

She laughed, relieved as much as embarrassed by her self-examination. "You're acting stupid, Tala. Pure and simple." Rubbing a hand over her neck, she shook her head, dropping her gaze.

A simple silver bracelet rested in a crystal bowl on the side table beneath the mirror. Tala bit her lip and fingered the bracelet, moving it around the bowl. "Too bad Carly didn't know how silver affects me before she gave me this." Cocking her head to the side, she asked her mirror image. "But I wonder if this is why I can't wear silver." Silver of any kind had always made her vaguely ill. The more silver the object contained, the more ill she became. So if a silver bullet could kill a werewolf, then maybe a little silver could make one sick?

The absurdity of her question hit her and she picked up the bracelet to inspect it. Turning it over in her hand, she shook her head again. "Lots of people are allergic to different metals. I just happen to be allergic to silver, that's all." Satisfied with her logic, she let the bracelet *clang* into the bowl.

It's better to know. At the whisper in her head, she turned and walked through the glass doors and onto the patio. Above her, the moon glowed a brilliant white against the dark sky. "This is so ridiculous." Glancing around, she checked to make certain no one else was around. "At least this time, I won't have an audience with camera phones." A shiver of anticipation zipped through her. "Here's hoping nothing happens." She cleared her throat, raised her chin toward the sky, and howled.

Tala's first attempt was weak and breathy. *Hell, I sounded more like a sick hyena than a wolf baying at the moon. Pitiful, Tala. Really pitiful.* Setting her feet apart, she fisted her hands on her hips, circled her neck to loosen the muscles, and let out a longer, stronger call. A third, more forceful cry followed, this one surprising her. The sound of her last howl carried on the wind, echoing through the air.

"Wow. Not bad."

"Mommy, there's a doggy upstairs."

Tala jolted, clamped a hand over her mouth, and slinked over to the glass doors. *Crap, Tracy heard me.* Deciding Tracy would hear her if she opened the doors to sneak inside, Tala held her breath and waited.

"No playing with imaginary pets right now, sweetie."

Please don't let Caroline come outside. Tala pressed against the glass, trying to get as close as possible to the building. *And definitely not Bobby Lee with his shotgun.*

"But Mommy. The doggy's crying."

So much for sounding like a vicious werewolf. Tala's hand tightened over her mouth as she stifled a giggle.

"Good grief, Tracy. First a monkey and now a doggie. You know people can't have pets in our building. Enough is enough. Close the patio door and come eat your apple."

Tracy whined, protesting a little more, but slid the door closed with a *bang*. Tala could hear mother and daughter continuing to fuss.

Trying to move as quietly as possible...*like a wolf?*...Tala slipped inside her apartment. Once safely on the couch, she clutched her tummy and burst into a fit of giggles. "Okay, so baying at the moon isn't my thing. Thank God for small mercies."

Without thinking, she flicked on the television again, returning to the comedy-slash-horror flick. Once more, the Wolf Man filled the screen, morphing from man to animal. Staring at the transformation, Tala leaned forward and scrutinized the way his body changed in bone structure and appearance. Granted, it was a movie, but maybe...

"So werewolves, uh, shifters have to change their whole skeleton." Intrigued, she watched as the Wolf Man's face twisted and contorted. He jutted out his chin as the length of his jaw expanded. Thrusting her own chin forward, she tried to imagine the pain of such a transformation. "No wonder they always make a lot of noise."

The Wolf Man continued to change, hunching over as his clothes shredded across his back and shortened on his arms. She slipped off the couch and crawled to the television, wanting to get closer to the images.

Tala copied his conversion step by step. When he wrenched a body part one way, she tried to do the same. When he rumbled one of his growls, she mimicked it with one of her own. Concentrating, she envisioned coarse hair sprouting all over her body, claws striking out from the tips of her fingernails, ears growing to fur-tipped triangles on her head.

"Grrrr." She let the sound roll from the back of her throat and over her tongue. She shook her head when he shook his, ready to feel his anguish as he cried into the night sky. Tala bared her teeth and could almost, just almost, feel the tips of fangs on her lower lip. Could she be changing?

"Having fun?"

Tala shrieked, pushed up from the floor, stumbled, and landed on her butt. "Damn it all to hell and back!" She glared at Devlin, too embarrassed to think what to do next.

Devlin's gaze skimmed from her to the television and around to her again. "Are you trying to do what I think you're trying to do?" A wide smirk covered his face as a twinkle came to his eye.

Recovering, Tala scrambled to her feet. Who did he think he was, making fun of her? "I'm just watching a movie." When she saw his raised eyebrows and his pointed look at the spot on the floor where she'd tried to shift, she hurried on. "And exercising."

One eyebrow cocked a bit higher, relaying his disbelief. "Right." The bemused expression matched his growing smirk.

Tala tugged at her disheveled shirt and thrust her chin higher. "It's a new fitness trend sweeping the nation."

"Really?"

She glared at him, tired of his superior attitude and smugness. "Yeah. Really."

"And what do you call this new workout? Abs of Steel for the Alpha Wolf? Pilates for Predators? Jazzercise for Canines? Tae Bo for Timber Wolves?"

Okay, yes, the guy was funny. She stammered, searching her brain for any title halfway plausible. "Um, it's called *Maniacal Yoga.*"

Devlin laughed and crossed his arms over his wide chest. "Hum. Kind of a weird name. Even weirder than mine."

Unable to stand his man-are-you-full-of-shit stare, Tala tossed her hair over her shoulders and strode to the kitchen. Placing her back to him, she reached for the refrigerator handle and pulled open the door. Scanning the interior, she tried to choose something to eat. Not that she actually wanted food. But she needed to do something, anything rather than look at him. "I didn't pick the name, you know."

"Course not. But, you know, from the way you were moving your body and all, I'd swear you were trying to shift."

The cold can of soda she'd picked up slipped through her fingers, but she caught the can halfway to the floor. Since when had her reflexes gotten so fast? Keeping her face turned from him, she gulped in some air and worked to keep her voice even. "Don't be ridiculous."

"So you weren't trying to shift?"

She popped the top on the can and took a drink, forcing the liquid down to the twisted pit in her stomach. "Of course not."

"Good. Because if you ever wanted to shift, it would look like this."

*****

Sweet release erupted within Devlin as he allowed the other part of him to rise to the surface. Keeping his eyes on Tala's ramrod straight form, he willed her to turn around and watch him. The smell of her apprehension drifted to him, saddening him. Above all else, he didn't want her to fear him.

Stripping his clothes from him, he let the transformation continue. Still, she kept her back to him. "Tala, you have to watch to understand. Watch.

Now." Although spoken in a whisper, his command took hold and she pivoted, slowly moving to face him.

As expected, the shock on her face made his heart ache for her. Her eyes, wide and staring like a deer caught in a hunter's scope, scanned him up and down. But he kept on shifting.

"It's okay, Tala." Years of practice had taught him how to speak even while his fangs sharpened and his skull shape morphed. "I'm Devlin. No matter what form my body is in." Claws grew on both feet and hands, and he held up one hand for her inspection.

She struggled to speak, but nothing came out. Falling against the refrigerator door, she shook her head and gawked.

He stretched, getting used to his other body structure, and she jumped. "I would never hurt you, Tala. Never."

Within seconds, Devlin stood before Tala as a large, black wolf. A rumble echoed from his chest, the need to howl rushing through him, but he kept his urge under control. Instead, he did something he'd never expected he would do. Dipping his head in a low bow, he offered himself to her.

To pet.

Damn, I must really love this woman to submit to her like this. His love for her lanced through his heart as he realized the extent of his emotion. Was this what love did to a person? Here he was, Devlin, leader of Morgan Pack, bowing to a female. Yet he knew he'd do anything for her to understand and not fear him. Even bow.

With his head lowered, he couldn't see Tala's reaction. He took shallow breaths, trying to make little to no sound, afraid he might frighten her. And waited.

When her hand touched the top of his head, he let out a long sigh, releasing his apprehension. Devlin remained motionless, not wanting to scare her from making another move, and was rewarded when her fingers bent, catching a bit of his fur in between them. She moaned, running her hand down the length of his neck, holding his neck and his hope in her palm. Still stroking him, she petted him as she would a beloved dog.

Devlin raised his head and smiled a wolfish smile. "See? I won't bite you again." His smile widened, a mischievous idea zipping through his mind. "At least, not unless you want me to."

Tala gazed at him, her eyes locking with his. At long last, she blew out a puff of air, loosening up her whole body. "I...I don't believe this."

"Why not? You saw me shift. You see me now. What more can I do to convince you?" He reached out to her, claws retracted, to take her in his embrace. She, however, wasn't ready for closeness as she yelped and slipped away from him. Trying not to let his disappointment show, he followed her to the living room.

"Everything you told me is the truth."

Although her words seemed more like a statement of fact than a question, Devlin answered. "I wouldn't lie to you. I'm Devlin Morgan of the Morgan Pack. I *am* a shifter." He studied her, sizing her up. Was she ready for all the truth?

Tala slanted her head as she continued to scrutinize him. At least she appeared calmer than before even though those icy blue eyes never blinked.

"Tala, I haven't lied to you, but I haven't told you everything either."

Anger flashed in her eyes, and he smiled. *Ah, there's the feisty female I know and love.* "Hold on. I couldn't tell you before. You'd have freaked out worse than you did."

She considered his explanation, and accepted it with a curt nod. "Go on then. Tell me everything." Her sarcastic laugh bit at him. "But damn it all to hell and back. What more can there be?"

"I tried to tell you before. I came to the city to find a mate. You're my mate."

At last she blinked, as if he'd surprised her with a snake held to her nose. "But why me? I don't believe you." Tala ran her gaze up and down his body, her forehead creasing in dismay.

How could she not believe him? After everything she'd seen, how could being his mate prove to be the most unbelievable part? "I haven't misled you, have I?"

She shook her head, but looked unconvinced. "But how can I be your mate? I'm not a shifter."

He'd opened his mouth to explain how he could change her when she gasped and clamped a hand over her mouth. "What, Tala? What's wrong?"

Chapter Twelve

Amazement sparkled in her eyes as she lowered her hand from her mouth. "My grandfather."

"What about him?"

She laced the fingers of both hands behind her head and crossed to sit down on the couch while he followed behind. "My grandfather is a retired zoologist. When you made those wild claims, I did some research on the Web and went to talk to him."

Tired of trying to maintain an upright position...being on all fours was so much more comfortable in this form...Devlin lowered to the floor and rubbed up beside her. "Yeah? Go on."

She swiveled on the couch to face him. "He said I have shifter blood in me. Diluted through generations of marriages to humans, but shifter blood, nonetheless."

Rising to place his forepaws beside her on the couch, he issued a low, satisfied growl. "I thought you might. Otherwise, I don't think I'd have heard your call."

Tears sprang to her eyes. "Oh, shit, Devlin. Oh, shit."

He needed to take her in his arms to comfort her. To comfort him. Wanting her body next to his, he began the shift back to human.

This time, she studied him. Mesmerized, she stood, unmoving, her eyes taking in every change, every detail of the process. Until he stood before her, naked, and ready.

"Uh, Devlin?"

"Yeah?"

"Do you always get an erection when you shift?"

Of all of the questions she could have asked, he hadn't expected *that* one. Glancing down, he laughed and shook his head. "No, and thank goodness. Having a hard-on every time I shifted would cause major complications. And quite a few stares, if I say so myself." He chuckled, hoping for one in return. But she acted as if she hadn't even noticed his joke about the substantial size of his shaft.

"So the big, bad, black wolf is what you always look like?"

Was she kidding? He frowned at her, unsure of what answer he should give. He opted for humor again. "Only when I'm around beautiful blondes like you and Goldilocks."

This time his joke hit home and she chuckled. Relief flooded through him and he grinned at her, happy to smell her fear leaving her. He was even more thrilled when she accepted his outstretched hand and stood alongside him. "Does this mean you'll come home with me to the mountains?"

Her hand squeezed his. "What? No. I mean, how can I? I don't shift. Just because I have a little shifter blood in me doesn't mean I could live with your people. Or that I'd want to."

The joy he'd allowed himself evaporated. "No, Tala, you don't understand." He took both her hands in his. "I can change you. You have shifter blood in you. All we have to do is bring it out."

"You mean like my sad attempt when you came in?"

"Good. So you admit it. You were trying to shift, huh? But, no. You'll change. Don't worry. When I bit you, I started the conversion."

She broke from his hold and moved away, putting both physical and emotional distance between them. He ached to follow her, but knew he'd better not.

"You mean the other day? That wasn't a hickey gone wrong? You meant to sink your teeth into me? Without asking me?"

Had he told her too much too soon? Yet, the truth was out and he had to make her understand. "I'm sorry you're upset. But it was a natural thing for me to do. I couldn't control myself."

Her words came out fast and furious. "I don't give a fuck what you think is natural. You had no right, Devlin. No right at all. And then you lied to me about what you'd done."

He cringed at the sight of moisture coming to her eyes and prayed the tears wouldn't fall. He hated to see her cry. Ever. But especially because of him. "I'm sorry, but you were so upset, I couldn't tell you the truth. Not then. Tala, you're my mate. My lifelong partner. It's destiny for us to be together."

"Destiny? What the hell are you talking about?"

He nodded, hoping she would come to see the reality, the history of it all. "We're meant to mate, Tala. Think about it for a minute. Your ancestors are shifters. Your family is shifter." A memory of his mother, her eyes glowing as she talked about finding his one, true mate, filled his mind. "Shifters are like wolves. We mate for life with the one who was meant for us. Tala, just imagine the future. You, me, and a pack of kids."

She stared at him, glanced at the wolf family poster, and blanched. His words about a family had sunk in. "A family?"

"Sure, why not?"

"Kids?"

"Uh, yeah."

"Shifter kids?"

He cocked his head at her, trying to understand her thoughts. "Well, kids, really. But yeah, they'll shift like we can."

"Oh. My. God."

"Tala, it's all right. We can talk about it all later."

She took another look at the poster and shook her head. "I have my friends, my grandfather, my work here. I can't go running off with you to live in the woods."

"You'd love the freedom, Tala. I know you would. I could see the freedom in you wanting to break out the night I watched you dance."

A wild race of emotions cascaded over her features. Anger, lust, desire, and need came and went until only apprehension remained. "No. I can't."

Frustration held in check far too long roared out of Devlin. "Damn it, we belong together. I know it and you know it, too. You called to me, Tala, and I came for you." Striding over to her, he took her by the shoulders and forced her to look him in the eye. "I need you and I want you. And I'm going to have you."

Her mouth opened to speak and he took it as an invitation. Crushing his mouth to hers, he slid a hand behind her neck and held her to him. Her smell, so hot, so spicy, so *her*, filled his nostrils. Drinking in the warm nectar of her, he fought to control the aggressiveness raging through him. Although she responded, clinging to him as her arms slid beneath his, he felt her body tense at the unexpected embrace.

Devlin jerked away from her, abrupt and wrenching, leaving Tala gasping for air. He wouldn't force her even though the primal urges screaming within him demanded he push her down and take her as his female. Instead, he picked her up, carrying her like a piece of fragile crystal, and strode into the bedroom.

She tucked her head against his chest and murmured soft, indecipherable sounds, shooting his pulse rate higher. With all the tenderness he could manage, he lowered her to her feet.

"Trust me, Tala. You're mine and I'm yours. Forever."

Keeping his gaze fixed on hers, he slipped his hands under her shirt, letting the fabric glide over the curves of her breasts. Free of her bra next, he took her face in his hands and pressed butterfly kisses to her lips. She whimpered, but made no move to stop him.

Unsnapping her jeans, he thumbed them over her lush hips and let them drop to her ankles. Daring to break free of her blue magnetic pools, he let his sight skim down her flat stomach, drawn to the lacy white of her panties.

Bending to his knees, he nipped at the pink rosebud on the front and tugged. His fingers joined his mouth to slip the silky material over her pelvis. With all her clothes gathered at her feet, he tapped one ankle, coaxing her away from the pile. She stepped to the bed and sat on the edge.

Altering his position on his knees to turn toward her, he ran both hands over the smooth skin of her legs, giving her gentle encouragement to spread them wider. When she did, he shot her a playful look and lifted her legs over his shoulders.

Tala sighed a low, contented sigh, and lay back on the bedspread, spreading her arms over her head. "Devlin?"

"Shh. You can trust me, Tala." This time she'd know they weren't having sex. This time she'd know they were making love.

A quiver ran down her leg as he lowered his head to her bush and nuzzled his face in her furry softness. Teasing her, he licked the inside of her thigh with a slow, leisurely lap. Startled, she jerked, but he held her firmly in place. While his thumbs played with the edge of her folds, his tongue slipped inside to fondle and suck her already wet nub.

Tala was his. Not as a possession or submissive female, but as his mate, his other half, his partner in life. As she bucked under the lashings of his tongue, he stayed focused on the main objective. To make Tala understand they would stay together forever.

He rose and she growled her displeasure at him for stopping. A smirk crooked the corner of his mouth as he climbed on top of her, shoving her farther onto the bed. "Don't get frustrated. I'm nowhere near finished." Falling on top of her to pin her to the bed, he saw the heat flicker in her eyes.

"Relax and enjoy." Gathering up all his love, he kissed her again, nipping her lip with gentle tugs. He grasped her breast, rubbed her hard nipple with his thumb, and rumbled his satisfaction into her throat.

The shift broke over him and he stopped, stunned at its intensity. He squeezed his eyes shut in the struggle to maintain control. He wouldn't shift. Not yet.

When he opened them again, the brilliance of her sapphire eyes shone against her tan face. Her blonde hair, spread out around her head, sent a pleasurable ache through him. An ache to bury his hands in her hair and run its silkiness over his body. An ache to grab onto her and never let her go.

Damn, she's beautiful. He remained quiet for a moment, soaking in the sight of her. "Damn, you're beautiful."

Her startled expression, as if she'd expected him to say anything else, confused him. "Tala, don't you know how beautiful you are? Hasn't anyone told you?"

Tears gathered at the corners of her eyes. "Not for a long time." The rest of her words strangled in her throat. She averted her eyes from his, but not before he saw the pain lingering there.

The shift started again without the usual warning buildup, a result of the anguish searing through Devlin. How could such a glorious woman not have experienced her own beauty? Were the men she'd had before him been blind? His breathing grew shorter, panting in his ache for her pain. Razor-like claws ripped into the covers underneath them, while his facial structure began to distort along with the rest of his body. As his strength increased, he raised his massive head to roar his frustration. Yet just as he was about to cry out, her palm cupped his cheek, bringing his hot glare down to her.

The tenderness on her face knocked all the emotion, save love, from him. He gasped, stunned, amazed, and thrilled to see her expression. No one had ever looked at him like that. She was open to him, all her emotions, all her fear and hopes, all her love on display for him. Only for him.

"Stay with me, Devlin. As a man. I need you."

His body relaxed in an instant, losing the wolf-like characteristics. As the power within him lessened, he regained control, and met her longing gaze with one of his own. She wrapped herself around him, urging him to fulfillment and he answered her.

Driving into her, they kept their hold with their eyes, each thrusting against the other with unbridled need. Perspiration poured from him to drip on her own sweat-soaked body as they moaned and growled in turns.

Devlin held on, wanting to let her come first, wanting her pleasure before his. Yet he was unprepared for her command.

"Devlin, mark me again."

Lifting his upper torso away from her, he stared at her, wondering if he'd heard her correctly. "What?"

The determination in her expression left no doubt behind her words. "Mark me again. Do it." With one last silent signal to obey her, she turned her head to the right, exposing more of her left shoulder.

His release tore through him, stiffening his body even as the surges continued. Crying out in ecstasy, he shifted, bringing forth his fangs. Spreading his lips wide, he plunged his teeth into her.

*****

"This is freakin' sinful."

Tala stretched her long body next to Devlin's naked skin; delighting in the sensation of his strong, lean form next to her nude one. *Could her life get any better?*

Devlin murmured his agreement and ran his hand along the curves from the top of her shoulder to the bottom of her thigh. His eyes burned with lustful fever even though they'd just finished making love a few minutes earlier.

With his hair spread across his pillow, his other arm supported her head, and she nuzzled her nose into his chest. His rich, dark scent filled her nostrils, making her feel safe and loved. "I'm glad I took the time off from work. Even if we never got out of the house during the whole three days." She sighed, happy and contented for the first time in years.

"*Because* we never got out of the house." Devlin sported his mischievous twinkle and pulled her closer. "I may never let you out of bed again."

"Promise?" Tala batted her eyes at him. "If I had my way, we'd stay in bed forever."

"We can make your wish come true, you know. Come home with me and we'll spend all day, every day, together. Playing in the sun, making love whenever we want, hunting. Doing anything we want." He kissed her, holding the kiss until she almost forgot what she meant to say.

"I'm not too sure about the hunting thing. All the blood and guts. Yuck." She wrinkled her nose at him. "Besides, I couldn't hurt Bambi."

"Trust me. Bambi could hurt you if he wanted to. But you'll get used to hunting. In fact, as soon as you shift the first time, you'll find you'll have a real appetite for hunting." He rose up, bending over her to nip her on the shoulder.

Tala laughed and pushed him back. "If you say so. But I'd still prefer a four-star hotel with room service." But would she ever shift? Hadn't she tried to morph many times during their self-imposed seclusion? And failed every time?

Devlin noted her turned-down mouth and lifted his chin so she'd pay closer attention to him. "I know what you're thinking."

"Oh, you do, do you?" She wrinkled her nose at him. "Think you know me so well, huh?"

"Sure I do." His palm slid over her cheek, a loving, cherishing gesture. "Don't worry. You'll change when you're ready. Quit worrying about it."

She blew out a frustrated sigh and concentrated on the sexy body next hers. "Okay. I'll try." Her fingers traced a path over his hard pecs and she reveled how her life had changed since Devlin's appearance. "You know I've got to go into work tomorrow."

Devlin growled and flipped on his side to face her. "No. Stay with me." His eyes grew darker with worry. "Besides, the hunters I told you about might still be around. They might follow you again like they did the other day when Mickale showed up. I want you safe in my arms."

"I can't believe there's this whole other world filled with shifters and men who hunt them." She shook her head, more concerned for him than for herself. "Besides, why would they care about me? I'm not a shifter. At least, not yet."

He tightened his hold on her as if he'd never let her go. Which, she thought, was not a bad way to live.

"They might use you to get to me."

A chill passed over her as she envisioned Devlin's bloodied body, cold and lifeless, because of her. "I'd never let them use me to hurt you. Or your family."

"You might not have a choice." His eyes locked onto hers, pulling her down into their dark depths.

Running her fingertip over his full lips, she gasped as he sucked the whole finger into his mouth. A flash of pleasure erupted in her belly as she watched him run his tongue around and around her finger. "You're so bad for me, Devlin."

"Yeah, but I'm a good kind of bad." He wiggled his eyebrows at her, mimicking Groucho Marx. "And you love being bad with me."

"True. But someone's got to pay the rent. And I like the idea of having a kept man."

He nuzzled into her neck, nipping at the hollow between her collarbone. "You can keep me any way you want."

"And you'd be worth every penny."

He growled, lifting up on his elbow to stare at her, a seriousness replacing his lighthearted manner. "I'll pay it."

Pulling her finger out of his mouth, she gazed into his eyes. "Just how do you get money? I mean, you said you're in the import/export industry, but you never go to work or get business calls or anything." Like him, she raised up on her elbow to study him, poking him playfully in the chest. "What are you, connected to the Mafia? Don't tell me there's a shifter Mafioso."

He puffed out his cheeks, Marlon Brando style, mimicking the actor in his Godfather portrayal.

"People do favors for me. I ask and they do whatever I say. Capish?"

She squealed when he hoisted her body on top of his. His hands glided down her torso and clamped onto her butt. "See, woman? You'd better behave or you could end up with a horse's head in your bed."

"Better a head of a horse than an asshole of a wolf."

"Why, you little—"

Tala pinched his nipples, urging him to stop his tickling. "No, seriously. Truth."

"Okay, okay. No need to get rough." He tilted his head, moving one hand through the hair falling forward over her face. "Truth is, I have many lucrative investments making very substantial profits. And, due to my incredible business savvy, I've got good people who oversee the daily operations, so I don't have to. Working to earn money isn't a necessity. It's not for me and it won't be for you."

Her mouth fell open. "Are you saying you're independently wealthy?"

Clutching a bunch of her hair in his hand, he ran a thumb along the top of her ear. "Let's just say, money will never be a problem."

"Holy shit, Devlin. Why didn't you tell me?"

"Should I have?" His dark eyes grew grave as he explored her face. "Why?"

"Because I'd have made you pay some freakin' rent, that's why."

For a second she was afraid he'd not understood her joke. Until he laughed a deep, rolling laugh. Grasping her hair at the nape of her neck, he pulled her mouth to his.

*****

"Yeah, I'll be back at work in an hour. I took an early lunch because of the meeting later today." Tala changed hands, hoping to get better reception from her cell phone. "I'm glad they were okay about postponing last week's meeting until today. I needed the vacation." Remembering her time alone with Devlin sent a tingling sensation through her.

She answered a few quick questions from her assistant while she signaled to the clerk behind the lunch counter. Since she was a regular customer at Jake's, the deli type luncheonette located across from the zoo, the clerk interpreted her gestures and gathered together her order.

The impromptu vacation she'd taken for a few days...all spent in bed with Devlin...had left the work piled high on her desk at the zoo. But she wouldn't have traded their time together for anything. She grinned, gave her assistant a few assignments, and ended the conversation.

"Hi."

Tala swiveled toward the voice behind her to find a handsome, formidable man standing behind her. Black hair fell to his shoulders, while a snow-white streak blazoned a trail along the side. His form-fitting shirt highlighted a strong muscular body while forceful dark eyes seemed to laugh at a private joke.

"Uh, hi." She squinted at him, unsure if he'd spoken to her or someone else. "Do I know you?" His build, his confidence, his attitude were familiar to her and her heart doubled its pace once she realized where the familiarity lay. This man reminded her of Devlin.

A slightly older, harder-looking Devlin. He smiled and she returned his smile.

"I'm Mickale."

Devlin's brother. In human form. And one hellova good-looking human form, too. "You're Devlin's brother." She took his outstretched hand more out of courtesy than a true wish to touch him. Something about him unnerved her. "Tala Wilde."

"Yes, I know."

Tala withdrew her hand from his lingering handshake. "From following Devlin and me around?" Hearing the clerk behind her, she pivoted and paid for her coffee and sandwich before confronting the man again. "Is that how you know me?"

"Devlin's told me about you."

Caught off-guard, she studied him, buying a little time. As far as she knew Devlin hadn't left her apartment in days. Had he told his brother about her before their secluded time? Not that it mattered, but she was curious.

"Devlin's mentioned you, but I didn't realize he'd told you about me." *At least, not about me and recent developments, I bet.* "Are you looking for Devlin? If you are, he's back at my place, watching tapes of my public service programs, sleeping, and eating huge quantities of pizza." Did Mickale know about *them*?

She inclined her head toward a small table nearby. Settling into the metal chair, she waited for him to sit down before asking the obvious question. "So when did Devlin tell you about me?"

He laced his hands and placed them on his lap. One corner of his mouth twitched upward, making her notice the scar running along the side of his jaw.

She took a quick sip of scalding coffee. Devlin had mentioned his brother and the incident at the zoo parking lot as well as their run-in with the hunters at the bar. But nothing about telling his brother about her. They'd assumed his brother had returned to the mountains and the rest of Devlin's immediate family. She blew on her coffee, giving her time to reflect. Talk about a *Guess Who's Coming to Dinner?* moment. Although this was lunch, not dinner, and she hadn't known he was still around.

Disturbed by his lack of response to her question, she tried again. "So you're Devlin's brother?" *Great, Tala, let the first relative you meet think you're slow-witted.* Hadn't they already gone over this tidbit of information? She frowned and continued, "Sorry. I'm a bit ditsy today. We already covered that info, huh?"

A flicker of surprise drifted across his face. "Devlin's told you about me?"

Okay, now he's doing the same ditsy thing. What's going on here?

His look penetrated into her, searching her for answers to questions he hadn't asked. "What has he told you about me?"

Tala's inner warning system shrilled and she decided to play it safe. "Not much. Just that he has a brother and a father. And that your mother's passed on." She saw the sadness flicker across his features. *Good. His mother's death bothers him. Which means he can't be a bad guy, right?*

"She is. And my father's getting on in years. Which is why he's left me in charge."

"You?" She paused, giving him a chance to react. When he didn't, she kept on pressing the issue.

"Devlin told me his father wanted him to take over the, uh, family business."

Mickale's mouth tweaked upward for a second before transfixing into a bemused smile. "Devlin's mistaken. I'm the one who'll take over." His determination showed in the way his body tensed at the mention of Devlin leading in his father's place.

He and Devlin are competitors. For a company? Or for a wolf pack? Tala dropped her eyes, not wanting her thoughts to show in her eyes. "I see."

"Did he mention anything else?"

"Like what?" No way would she say anything about shifters.

"Such as his problem."

Tala put the coffee cup on the table, ready for whatever came up. "What problem? Is something wrong with his father? Or are you saying something's wrong with Devlin?"

Mickale leaned over the small table, piercing her with a hard look. "Devlin has, shall we say, delusions."

A shiver ran through her as she threw up a barrier to his words. Why would his brother say such a horrible thing? Devlin didn't have any delusions. "I don't understand. What do you mean?"

"Devlin suffers from lycanthropy."

"I'm sorry?" She knew what the word meant from her Internet explorations, but she wanted to hear what he'd say.

"Lycanthropy. It's a mental disease where a person thinks he's a nonhuman, an animal. Sorry for the bluntness, but Devlin thinks he's a werewolf."

Tala leaned forward, wanting to see deeper into his eyes. Why would his brother try to convince her that Devlin had a mental problem? Especially since Mickale was a werewolf, too? "A werewolf?"

A squeal broke her concentration on Mickale as they both swiveled toward the sound. Coffee flowed over a table in the corner of the deli, but, surprisingly, the man who'd knocked his cup over didn't put down his newspaper. Instead, he continued to hold it up, hiding his face from view, as the deli clerk hastened over to wipe up the spill. Yet even when the clerk tried to help, the man refused to lower his paper.

"Sir, if you'd like, I'll take your wet newspaper and get you a new one." The young girl grasped the end of the paper, only to have the man-behind-the-page yank it away.

"No! I'm fine. Just leave me alone."

Something about the odd, high-pitched voice sounded fake to Tala. She glanced at Mickale who shrugged and turned back to the scene playing out before them.

"But, sir, don't you want a fresh cup and a dry—"

"No, I said. I—I like my news wet."

"But it's dripping on your pants. Are you burned?"

"Uh, yes, no. I don't care. I'm okay. I like hot pants."

"Huh?" Rolling her lips under, the clerk tried to keep from laughing, then stood for a moment, unsure of what to do. At last, she shook her head and left the man to return to the counter.

"I'm afraid so."

"What?" Tala darted her gaze between the strange man and Mickale. "What'd you say?"

"I said, I'm afraid Devlin does think he's a werewolf."

She scooted her chair so she was square with Mickale. *He's lying.* But again she wondered about the question of motive. Would he lie for leadership of the pack? She adopted as sincere an expression of concern as she could. "He's never said anything about werewolves to me. Much less about being one."

He leaned against his seat and heaved a big sigh. The perfect image of a devoted brother worried for his mentally ill sibling. "No doubt he will. He always does. After he lures a woman into trusting him, he lets his neurosis out. But by then, it's too late."

Oh, this guy's good. So genuine. So believable. If she hadn't grown close to Devlin in the past few days, if she hadn't seen Devlin shift, she'd have hooked onto his story and swallowed it whole. "Too late? Too late for what?"

Mickale glanced around him as if making sure no one else could hear. "Has anything unusual happened with Devlin since you two met? Anything involving small animals?"

Her mask slipped before she could conceal her astonishment. Did he know about the poodle in the park? Tala frowned, trying to sort through the possibilities. Could Mickale have found out about the animal abuse charge against Devlin? Would his arrest be a matter of record? Mickale's hard stare bored into her, forcing her to answer. "Uh, no. Nothing."

He blinked and arched one eyebrow. *Crap, he knows I'm lying.* But she wasn't about to confirm his suspicion. "In fact, Devlin has a real way with animals. Even wild ones." *Wilde, like me.* She blushed at the image her thought provoked. Putting on her game face, she smiled at Mickale, daring him to challenge her, and held her breath.

He studied her through narrowed eyes for a moment. "Good. I'm glad."

Tala's neck stiffened as he continued to examine her. Lifting her cup to her mouth, she blew on her coffee to release the confusion, the irritation building inside her. But the ordeal wasn't over yet.

"The family's main concern is keeping him from doing harm to anything else. Or anyone else."

Stunned fury hit her with a cold blast and she started to rise. She had to get away from this man. This liar. As she rose, he caught her arm, forcing her to listen.

"I'm sorry if I shocked you. But you needed to know."

"I've heard all I want to hear." She glanced at his hand on her arm and scowled at him. Taking the anger rising in her and directing it at him, she sent him a hard, icy stare and stretched her lips wide. A mean, rumbling sound drifted out of her. "Get your paw off me."

*****

Hiding in a corner of the deli behind a wall of newspaper, George attempted to keep his soppy slacks away from his groin area. The hot coffee scalded him, but he was determined not to show his face. What was a little burn when you'd lost your job and your dignity? Revenge would heal all his wounds.

Yet when Tala growled at the man sitting across from her, he'd thought he'd choke on what little coffee was left in his cup. If she'd snarled at him that way, he'd have come damn close to wetting his pants. At least if he had, maybe he would have cooled off the area.

"Crap. She sounds like her new boyfriend." He brought the coffee cup to his lips and was shocked to see his hand shake. "Shit." Placing the cup down before he let it slip...again...through his trembling grasp, he watched Tala as she jumped up from the table and strode from the deli. Her companion's stunned expression faded soon enough, replaced by the poker face he'd used through most of their conversation. But he remained seated.

Something was familiar about the man. George couldn't shake the uneasy impression. Something bothered him about the stranger. As he took another sip, realization struck him and he wondered why he hadn't recognized the resemblance before. This man had to be related to Tala's animal-man. His heart thudded in his chest as an image of the man who'd attacked him passed through his mind.

Devlin. She'd called her boyfriend Devlin. Remembering Devlin's hands on him wasn't half as scary as remembering the way the man's, the freak's, features had morphed into with long, vicious-looking teeth protruding from his mouth.

George swallowed the bile rising up his throat as alarm swept through him. Damn, were there two of these mutants? Yet Tala's fierce reaction to the man left little doubt in his mind that she hadn't liked this man. Even if he and her new lover boy were related.

He waited until the man's attention was hooked on the cute counter girl before throwing a couple of dollars on the tabletop and lurching out of his chair, through the door. Tala was several yards away, moving at a rapid speed. He frowned as he stretched his stocky legs to keep up with her incredible pace. Since when had she gotten so fast? The way she moved her body had changed, too. Instead of short movements, she flowed along with more fluid, more powerful strides.

"Doesn't matter. She'll soon find out she can't fire someone like me and not get punished." He licked his lips, the thrill of imagining her cowering before him gave him an added burst of adrenalin. "You're gonna come crawlin' on your knees. It's payback time, babe."

George followed her across the street and through the entrance of the zoo. As he was about to approach Tala, however, a box-shaped man slid out from behind a vendor's stall, placing himself behind Tala. Two other men joined him, keeping their distance from each other and Tala. But George could see they were together by the unspoken signals they sent each other.

"Hmm, seems sweet Tala has more admirers." George slacked off his pace so they wouldn't notice him. "What's going on with you, babe?"

He continued to trail the men at a greater distance as they followed Tala. When she entered the building housing her office, they stopped and took up different positions outside. Sliding onto a bench, George picked up a discarded zoo map and pretended to study it.

"Mommy, that man made a boo-boo in his pants."

The map slipped from his fingers as George jumped at the little girl's words. Her mother, pushing another child in a carriage, scrunched up her features in disgust as her gaze landed on the large wet spot on his slacks.

"Did you do a bad tinkle?" The curly-headed blonde toddler pointed at him before covering her giggles with her hand.

George felt the heat zip into his face as he desperately snatched up the small map to try and cover the wet area. "Go away, you little brat."

"Kristi, don't stare at strangers. Just keep walking." The young mother cupped her daughter's hand in hers, picking up speed as she pushed the stroller ahead of them.

"God, how I hate kids." He scowled as the mother shot him a glare. "I always wanted to give a zoo visitor a little birdie. So here's yours." Keeping one hand over his crotch, he flipped her a middle finger salute, sending her charging off as fast as she could.

Remembering his goal, he resumed his hiding position behind the flimsy piece of paper. Thankfully, the men tailing Tala hadn't noticed the brief disturbance.

Why were these men following Tala? He checked them out and noted their similar, beige, non-descript clothing. All were trying to appear nonchalant, typical zoo visitors, but he saw the way they kept glancing at the door. They'd tracked her for some reason. But why? He got comfortable on the bench and waited.

George checked his watch and realized thirty minutes had passed since they'd taken up their various positions. "Come on, guys. Make a move. She's not coming out any time soon."

As if on command, the chunky man signaled to the others and walked away, scooting around the corner of the restroom building. His companions, however, remained in their posts.

"Oh, sure. Go take a leak. Don't worry about keeping your watch." George scowled and squirmed in place. He wasn't the only one needing a break. But he'd be damned if he'd leave and miss anything.

When one of the men glanced in his direction, George whipped the map back in front of him and ducked his head. *Don't get stupid. Stay alert.* He mentally kicked himself for almost getting caught.

"What do you have that they want, Tala?" He peeked over the edge of the map. "Five bucks say these guys have something to do with your freaky boyfriend."

"Now there's a bet you'd win."

George started to turn around just as a large hand clamped over his mouth. He let out a squeal seconds before the terrifying darkness swept over him.

Chapter Thirteen

George struggled against the giant pinning his arms behind him. "Who the fuck are you guys?"

The squat man stood in front of him, arms crossed, and not in a pleasant mood. "I'm gonna ask you the same thing." A long scar ran down the side of the man's neck. The type of scar a person got after a battle for his life.

"None of your damn business." George scanned the inside of the work shed. Dim light filtered through the cracks in the small wooded building, and he contemplated shouting for help. Until a strong hand throttled his neck, cutting off his air supply.

"Watch how you talk, little man." His tormentor pressed his nose close to his. "I don't take shit from a nobody like you."

The man let go of his throat, giving much needed oxygen to George's brain. Once the fuzziness left him, he tried another approach. Maybe he wasn't a brave man, but he wasn't an idiot, either. He coughed and sputtered out the words. "S-sorry. Didn't know you were so touchy."

The satisfied smirk his attacker sported held no warmth or mercy. "Like I said. Who are you?"

He rolled his head around, trying to ease some of the pain throbbing at the base of his skull. "Name's George. And you?"

"His name's Skanland and I'm Carl."

George cringed as Skanland struck out in his direction, barely missing him to whack the brute holding his arms. At least the hit hadn't been meant for him.

"Shut up. I'll do the talking, dumb ass."

The big man didn't budge and tightened the grip on his arms. "Hey, not so rough."

"Why were you watching us?" Skanland fingered a toothpick out of his pocket and stuck it in the side of his mouth.

Should he tell the truth? He studied the man before him. Granted, he didn't appear to be the brightest chunk of brick, but just how stupid was he? Still, he had nothing to gain by telling a lie. Especially when the truth might serve his purpose better. "Doing like you. Following the bitch."

Interest popped into Skanland's eyes. "Is that so? You know the pretty lady?"

George, never one to let a lie stand in his way, nodded. "Sure do. Intimately."

"Intimately?" Carl's sour breath slid over George's shoulder. He swallowed the bad taste and hoped he wouldn't hurl.

"He means he's fucked her, asshole." Skanland chuckled and grabbed his crotch for emphasis. "And I bet she's hot in bed, huh?"

Happy that Skanland bought his story, he winked, enjoying the opportunity to embellish his fib. "You don't know the half of it. She can suck the lid off a beer can. Especially when you slap her around first. As an incentive, you know."

Skanland's interest jumped ten degrees. "She likes getting roughed up, huh?"

"Doesn't matter what she likes." He recognized a man who liked to beat up women. Took one to know one.

The three men shared a laugh. Skanland ran his gaze up and down George and waved his hand at Carl. "Let him go."

"Aw, do I have to? He's so...soft."

Huh? Carl's fingers slid down George's arms, sweeping to squeeze his elbows. With a groan of displeasure, Carl released George.

"Ugh." He stumbled forward a few inches before gaining his stability. Rolling his shoulders around and shaking his arms to loosen up the soreness, he glanced furtively around the enclosure for any possible route of escape. "I told you my little secret." Fixing his eyes on Skanland's, he added, "Now tell me yours."

But Skanland wasn't ready yet. He walked over to the side of the building and peered through a slot in the wall. "I'm betting you aren't too cozy with the female any more." Turning back to him, he took out the toothpick and pointed it at him. "Are you?"

Female? George chomped down the words he wanted to spit at him. Instead, he played along with the man's assumptions. Since they happened to be true. "Naw. The uh, female, has a little ego problem right now. She fired me and thinks she won't get punished for it. Nobody fires a man like me."

Skanland snorted. "Everybody fires a dick like you."

Rankled, he started to object, but Carl's wink caught him by surprise. *Did the big man just flirt with him? Argh.*

"And what about her new friend?" Skanland grinned, letting George know he knew about Devlin. "She throw you over for him?"

He scowled, unhappy to be put in a position of ridicule. "The freak? He won't last long."

Skanland threw away the toothpick, shot a wad of spit onto the floor, and stepped closer to him. The body odor from the man almost brought George to his knees. *Shit. Metro-sexual he's not.*

"I think we have a mutual interest in those two. You want to pay her back? And get rid of him? What'd ya say?"

Forgetting about the foul smell, George cocked his head to the side, ready to hear what the burly man had to say. "I'd say, tell me what you've got in mind."

"We don't give a shit about your bitch. What we want is her new boyfriend. But I'm thinking once he's out of the way, you can move in on her."

"And what about the other one?"

Surprise flickered across Skanland's face. "The other one? You mean the one in the parking lot? He's still around?"

George sneered at the two men. "I don't know anything about a parking lot, but I do know there's another like him. In fact, Tala was talking to the other one in the deli across the way." He snorted, adding to his derisive tone. "You guys aren't very good at tracking someone, are you?"

Skanland whirled around to smack Carl in the head. "You prick. You were supposed to keep your eyes on her." Without waiting for an answer, Skanland jerked around to George and raised his hand, threatening to lock onto his neck again. "And you. Don't push me."

Holding up his palms, George scooted out of reach. "Calm down. Just kidding." Once the other man had lowered his hand, he continued with his proposition. "But if you want to get both of them, then listen up."

Skanland and Carl shut up, their eyes leveled on him. Control, unlike he'd ever experienced rushed through him, and he grinned in delight. Neither one moved as they waited for him to lay out his plan.

George took a moment to bask in their attention, crossed his arms, and adopted the stance Skanland had used earlier. "Okay, so here's what we're going to do."

*****

The hairs on the back of Tala's neck stood on end all the way home from the zoo. Glancing into her rearview mirror, she couldn't shake the uneasy sensation crawling through her. In fact, she'd had the same feeling all day long.

Was that car following her? As she'd done many times during the drive, she whipped her head around to stare at the headlights glaring behind her. She shook her head, and grumbled under her breath. "Great, Tala. You're getting paranoid. Shake it off."

When the car made a signal and exited onto a side street, she relaxed a little and blew out a puff of air. Taking one hand off at a time, she wiped her palms on her jeans, consciously realizing for the first time just how nervous she was. She needed to calm herself down. "See? The car turned off. You're jumping to stupid conclusions, girl." But she couldn't get rid of the warning alarms blaring in her mind.

Tala drove on and tried to ignore the cars behind her. After what seemed like the longest drive home in history, she swerved into her apartment complex and pulled into her reserved spot. Gathering up her purse, she left the car and took quick strides to reach the stairs up to her apartment. Her breathing slowed as she neared her front door, and she fought the urge to call for Devlin, praying he hadn't gone anywhere.

"If you do, he'll think you're some kind of clinger. Or worse, a dick-whipped female." Chuckling a tight, high-pitched titter, she pushed her key into the lock and twisted the doorknob.

A brilliant light fixed on her and she spun away from the door, toward the glare, only to be blinded by its brilliance. "What the hell?" Holding up her hands as shields, she peered ahead and saw the dark outline of a man.

"You okay, miss?"

Her heart started beating an even rhythm again. "Oh, Mr. Conroy. It's you."

Mr. Conroy, one of the complex's senior security men, lowered his flashlight. "Sorry. I always forget about the light. I heard about your prowler of the other week. Wish I'd been on duty, 'cause I'd have taught him not to hang around outside a young lady's home. But me and the missus took our first vacation in ten years. We headed down to Miami."

Like his seventy-year-old body would have been any match for Devlin. Tala sent him a shaky smile. *My prowler. Man, if only he knew.* "Good for you. You deserved some time off."

"That's what the missus thought, too." He shone the light on her face, blinding her once again. "I heard you've got someone staying with you. A man?"

Tala could hear the judgment in his voice, but she knew his concern came from caring for the tenants rather than any moral stance. "Uh, yeah. I do. Uh, my cousin came in from Utah."

"Your cousin, huh?" Skepticism laced his tone.

Lying to kindly, old Mr. Conroy was harder than lying to anyone else. "Yep. My cousin, Devlin."

"Devil?"

She giggled at the thought of Devlin with horns and a long tail. *Okay, so maybe he did have a tail sometimes.* "No. Not 'devil.' Dev*lin*. Please, Mr. Conroy. The light?"

He lowered the flashlight to his side. "Right. Deville. Got it."

Tala gave up trying to get him say the name correctly. Maybe he'd get a hearing aid soon, because God knows he needed one. "Right. Well, if you'll excuse me." She gave him a quick wave of her hand and opened her door. "'Night, Mr. Conroy."

"'Night, miss. You be careful. You and Devo."

Thankful to get away, Tala burst into the apartment. Stumbling over an object on the floor, she fell forward, reaching out for the nearby side table to keep herself from falling. "Shit!"

Devlin sprang off the couch, ready to catch her, sticking a slice of pepperoni pizza on the front of her shirt. Thick sauce smeared on her chest and pepperoni dropped down the v-neck front, lodging between her heaving breasts.

"Oh, yuck." Tala peeled the pizza off her shirt and handed it to Devlin. Surveying the area around her couch, she counted six pizza boxes scattered on top of the table, couch, and carpet. "I guess I don't have to ask what you've done all day."

The skin around Devlin's big velvet eyes crinkled with his smile. "What can I say? Except maybe 'Hi. My name's Devlin and I'm a pizza addict.'"

She retrieved another chunk of pepperoni from inside her shirt and popped it into her mouth. "No shit. But couldn't you have put down the pizza long enough to say hello?" She giggled when he threw the pieces he held in each hand on the floor and hauled her to him. "Devlin!"

Devlin's tongue licked across the swell of her breasts. Glancing up at her with sauce all over his face, he quipped, "Yum. You're the best piece in town." Another lick across her boobs had her squirming and giggling from the raspy texture of his tongue.

"Should I come back later after you've finished eating your female?"

Devlin and Tala jumped at the sound of the amused voice, and spun to face the sound.

*****

"Mickale? What're you doing here?" Devlin swung Tala away from the door and away from Mickale.

"Checking up on you, little brother. I wanted to make sure you're having a good time in the big city." Mickale's eyes glittered as he walked into the apartment, his gaze latching onto Tala's saucy breasts. "Although it looks like you're having a damn good time without me."

"I repeat. What're you doing here?" Devlin kept his voice level although his thoughts were anything but calm. Since he hadn't heard anything from Mickale for the past few days, he'd assumed his brother had hightailed it home to the mountains.

"Relax, bro. Tala and I've met. Haven't we, babe?"

The smirk on his brother's face pushed at Devlin's last nerve. Did he mean other than when Mickale had appeared in wolf form during the chase at the parking lot? Or somewhere else? Devlin tossed a questioning look at Tala who blinked at him and switched her frosty glare to Mickale.

"Don't call me 'babe.'" Tala's expression left little doubt in Devlin's mind that their meeting hadn't been a pleasant one. Which meant Mickale wasn't welcome in her apartment. "Did you follow me? Was it you?" Tala fisted her hands on her hips and scowled at Mickale.

"He followed you?" Devlin put himself between Mickale and Tala, ready to protect her. Even from his brother. "Why would you track her?"

Mickale stopped his perusal of her apartment and shot them an I-don't-know-what-the-fuck-you're-talking-about frown. "Why would I do that? I knew where she lived. Besides, I thought our conversation at the deli got cut short and we could continue our discussion here. But follow you? Nope."

"You mean the discussion where you called Devlin a mental case?"

Devlin tipped his head to eye his brother. "A mental case? Gee, Mick. You've called me a lot of things in the past, but never a 'mental case.'"

Mickale shook his head and walked around the room, picking up knickknacks and pictures to examine. He stared at the photo of Tala's grandfather for a moment before gesturing at the walls. "Love the wolf posters, by the way. Which explains your willingness to get involved with someone suffering from lycanthropy."

Devlin searched his brain for a definition. Lycans were werewolves, but was there a disease for wolves? "Suffering from what?"

Tala jumped to answer before Mickale could. "It's a mental disease where a human thinks he's a nonhuman thing. Like a wolf. Which, of course, doesn't apply here."

Devlin crossed over to where Mickale stood studying her computer screen. He seized Mickale's collar, yanking him around to face him. "So you told her I'm some sort of weirdo?"

As he'd expected, Mickale let out a snarl and jerked out of Devlin's hold. "The first step to getting well is admitting you have a problem, bro. I just want to make sure no one gets hurt. So, if you'll come with me…"

Devlin didn't know whether to laugh at him or punch him out. "Hurt? What the hell are you talking about? Nobody's in any danger from me. Except maybe you."

"Oh yeah? Tell that to the poodle."

Devlin slammed Mickale against the wall nearly four feet behind him, lifting him off the floor and nailing him there. "Shut up. You know I didn't do anything to the poodle."

His teeth extended before he knew the transformation had started. Strength leapt through Devlin's body as the shift progressed, and he did nothing to stop the flow. His denim shirt ripped against the expansion of his torso and he growled as his power grew.

Mickale's features contorted into a gruesome, terrified mask of fear. "Oh, my God. What's wrong with him? He's foaming at the mouth!" Twisting his head toward Tala, he reached out his hand and implored her. "Call nine-one-one! He's having some kind of fit. He needs his medication."

Devlin roared, laughter threatening to alter the anger in the howl, and pushed his brother up another few inches. His hand closed around his brother's neck as a small part, the jokester part of him egged him on. If Mickale wanted to act like a victim, he'd play his part of the attacker.

"Devlin. Stop." Tala's hand on his arm broke his fixation on his brother and he glanced sideways at her. Her azure eyes, so beautiful and calm, fixed on him. "Let him go. I know you're not really angry."

At her request, he dropped Mickale, pivoting on his heel to stalk to the other side of the room. He swiveled to face Tala and Mickale, his fists clenching and unclenching as the return to human swept over him, relieving the stress on his body and clothes.

Coughing and gasping for air, Mickale pointed at him. "Do you see, Tala? He's dangerous. Get him out of here while you can." He pushed away from the wall and reached for her, imploring her with his eyes. "He'll hurt you."

"Cut the bad act, Mickale." Devlin growled his displeasure and started forward, but Tala raised her hand, stopping him. He could sense she wanted to handle the situation, so he took a wide stance and watched.

"Dangerous? Yeah, probably so. To liars like you." She spit out the words, accenting each one in her annoyance. "Do you think I'm blind, Mickale?"

Mickale, seeing his argument lose any hope of succeeding, shook his head. "No, of course not. You saw his anger problem, didn't you? He's dangerous. And not just to poor, defenseless animals, either."

"Oh, so that's your plan. You're trying to scare me into leaving Devlin." She blew out a *puh* sound and sneered at Mickale.

Was Mickale so desperate to rule Morgan Pack that he'd try to keep him from taking his mate? Devlin growled again, hurt causing his gut to twist. He'd known Mickale had wanted the leadership role. He just hadn't realized how much. "Shit. I never would have guessed you'd go this far."

"Forget it, Mickale. I'm not some dumb blonde who can't see what happened right before my own eyes. I saw him shift. In fact, Devlin's shifted many times in my presence, so give up the lame story."

Mickale straightened up, glanced at Devlin and Tala, and slumped against the wall as the fight left his body. "I see." He shrugged and shot her a pointed look. "So you know?"

Maybe once Mickale knew the extent of their relationship, he'd stop trying to sabotage them. "She not only knows about me, she knows about you. As well as Father and the rest of the pack." He caught and held his brother's gaze. "I've marked her twice, once with her permission."

Tala moved over to Devlin to snake her arms around his waist. "Yep. I'm Devlin's mate. And nothing and no one is ever going to change that fact. So get used to it. *Bro.*"

Mickale's face flinched with conflicting emotions. Knowing his brother well, Devlin knew he wrestled with anger and disappointment. But not resignation. Because his brother never gave up.

"So? What'd ya say?" Tala broke free of Delvin's squeeze and moved toward Mickale. As she opened her arms for Mickale, jealousy, pure and simple, crashed into Devlin's heart. Still, he remained motionless, letting Tala do what she wanted to do. "Want to give your brother's mate a welcome-to-the-family hug?"

A devilish grin spread over Mickale's face, tempting Devlin to jump between them. Instead, he gritted his teeth and controlled his first reaction. Tala was right in trying to form a union between them, and he'd have to keep his emotions, his jealousy, restrained.

Mickale tugged Tala's arms to hug her to him. Resting his head on her shoulder, he wiggled his eyebrows at Devlin, daring him to break them apart. Again, Devlin resisted his initial thought of wrestling his brother aside. That is, until Mickale's hand slid down and grabbed Tala's butt. "Actually, we give a welcome-to-the-family rump rub, instead."

Devlin, lunging forward, wasn't as quick as Tala. Her hand whipped around to grasp Mickale's and twisted, wrenching his fingers backward toward the top of his hand. Mickale hollered, pulling his hand away, as he backpedaled away from her. Tsking at Mickale, she slid into Devlin's arms, and he couldn't resist wiggling his eyebrows at his brother. "She's something, huh?"

"I'd say so." Mickale massaged his sore fingers. "But does that mean the rump rubbing is off?"

Yet before Devlin could answer, the phone rang, startling all of them. Devlin shook his head at

Tala and beat her to the punch. "No, I'll get it. And if it's your work, I'll tell them you're busy meeting your new wolf family."

"They'll never believe the crew I've gotten hooked up with." Tala darted her gaze to Mickale. "Oh, and tell them I'll give them a call back." Lifting her chin, she howled. "Wolf style."

Damn, she really is something. Warmed by her acceptance of his family, Devlin laughed and picked up the phone. "Wilde residence."

"Hey, Freak. Bitten anyone lately?"

Recognizing the voice, Devlin scowled and put his back to Tala. *The little man who'd beaten the she-wolf. George.* "Fuck off." In one quick motion, he disconnected the call and took a deep breath. No need for Tala to know who was on the other line.

"Who was it?"

Crap, she had to ask. He let Tala's question wait a sec before deciding to lie. "Wrong number."

"A little harsh weren't you? I mean, a wrong number is a simple mistake."

"Meanwhile," Mickale, as usual, wanted all the attention on him, "what'd ya say we sit—"

The jangle of the phone came again, interrupting Mickale's suggestion. "Damn." Devlin scooped up the phone before Tala could get past his body blocking the way. Holding the earpiece close, he cupped his hand over the receiver, and hoped his posture wouldn't relay his fury to Tala. "Talk."

"Don't hang up on me again, Freakazoid. I know all about you and your relative. Just how many of you freaks are there?"

His hatred of George sent his blood boiling, but he managed to keep his tone level. "Don't call again."

Devlin started to hang up when he heard George shouting.

"You'll be sorry!"

Tala's eyebrows darted downward as she yanked on his arm to get him to answer her questioning gestures. "Is something wrong?"

"Naw. Probably just the pack wanting him to bring home some dog biscuits." Mickale hopped away as Tala tried to swat him.

"You don't give up, do you?"

"Never."

Devlin concentrated on keeping the phone turned away from her, and stuck to the conversation. "I don't think so." What he wouldn't give to be able to reach through the line and throttle the guy.

"Oh, but you're gonna want to hear what I have to say."

Devlin spoke softer as Tala inched nearer. "Again. I don't think I do."

"Yeah, you do. Unless you want something to happen to pretty Tala. Something real bad."

He squeezed the phone tighter, his knuckles turning white from the strength of his grip. Tala moved a little closer, forcing Devlin to put on an act. "Hey, buddy." Looking at Tala, he feigned a big smile and covered the phone as he told yet another lie. "It's a friend of mine. And no to the dog biscuits."

Tala seemed unconvinced, but took his not-so-subtle hint, and headed for the kitchen. "You two have a weird way of relating to each other, whoever this guy is."

She trusts me and I'm lying to her. He thought about telling her the truth and opted against the idea.

No, I have to keep Tala safe. Even if it means keeping secrets from her.

Mickale, however, hadn't fallen for the fib. Instead, he drew next to Devlin and narrowed his eyes to let him know he hadn't bought his lie. With Mickale's sensitive hearing, Devlin didn't doubt his brother could hear everything.

Devlin jerked his head at Tala in a silent don't-let-on message. Again putting his back to Tala, he spat out his whispered warning. "If you hurt Tala in any way, I promise you I'll snap your neck. After I tear the skin off your body in tiny, agonizing strips."

"And what? Eat me alive?"

This smile was genuine. "Yeah, but with lots of ketchup to take away the nasty taste."

The silence on the other side told Devlin he'd hit home. Unfortunately, the silence didn't last long enough.

"Listen up, Wolf Man."

So he does know. He guessed George was brighter than he'd looked.

"If you want to keep Tala safe and sound, you'll meet me tomorrow at the downtown park around four o'clock. You and your freaklative. And don't bring anyone else, especially Tala."

"And why should we?"

Tala waved at him from the kitchen and held up a sandwich. Devlin nodded telling her he wanted her to fix him one.

"Because if you don't, I'll visit Tala when you're not around, and she'll get a taste of my tender loving care. You know, like I showed the female wolf? Or maybe I'll give Tala a treat with a little booty action. That's how you doggies like it, isn't it?"

Devlin tipped his chin at Mickale and waited for his agreement. Mickale licked his lips and smiled, always ready for action. "Consider us there."

"Good doggy."

Chapter Fourteen

"I don't get it. Why are you acting so mysterious?" Tala flopped on the bed to watch Devlin get dressed. The man had a body other men would kill for and women would die for. She ran her tongue over her lips to draw his attention.

Devlin stopped buttoning his shirt to stare at her. "Damn it, Tala. Don't tempt me." The low rumble in his throat sent pleasurable chills through her. "I've got something I have to do."

"With Mickale." She slid her hands over her breasts and tweaked her hardened nipples to elicit another growl from him. "What's so important you can't take a little time...for me?" She pouted, putting on her best Marilyn Monroe sweet and innocent, yet don't-you-think-I'm-sexy expression. "Wouldn't you rather get busy with me?"

He laughed and turned away from her. "You are a devil in disguise, woman. Get busy? So we've gone from making love to plain old getting busy?"

"Oh, Dev-lin." Her singsong tone brought him around to face her. Grinning, she whipped her nightgown over her head and tossed the red silk at him. Jiggling her breasts at him, she raised one breast upward and swiped her tongue over the brown tip.

Devlin's mouth dropped open and his eyes gleamed with unmistakable lust. "You're killing me. You know that, right?" At her come-take-me look and wink, he moved closer to her, reaching out his hands. Abruptly, he jerked away at the last moment, sending Tala's hopes dashing to the floor. "No! I can't. Mickale's waiting."

Deflated, she fell back on the bed, her arms flailing out to the side in a dramatic gesture. "Wow. We're not even married yet and you're leaving me to go hang with your brother."

He tilted his head to quiz her. "Married? The pack has a mating ceremony, but not a wedding like you're thinking of. As far as I'm concerned, we're already mated. The pack thing is just a formality."

She frowned for a moment and decided not to push the marriage idea. Skimming her hands along her body, she once more tempted him to stay. Her fingertips slid under her thong to play with herself. "Stay, Devlin. I need you."

He bit his lips in response, moved a step nearer to her, and then strode away from her. Damn, she'd almost gotten to him. What was so urgent to make him leave her like this? "Besides, I thought you two didn't get along well."

"Mickale's my brother and we may fight, but we stick together, too."

Rising up on her elbows, she peered at him, searching for his hidden agenda. "So why now? What's going on, Devlin? You're not telling me something. I know it."

He tucked his head, averting her scrutiny. "You're paranoid. Nothing is going on."

Tala rose from the bed to skulk into her walk-in closet. "Maybe not, but the results are the same. You're not staying with me. What am I supposed to do while you're off doing wolf men stuff?" She chose a dark green t-shirt and black jeans and exited the closet to toss them on the bed, once again narrowing her eyes at him. "Come on. Spill. What exactly are you guys up to?

For the umpteenth time, Devlin avoided meeting her gaze and gave her another lame excuse. "Oh, you know. Guy stuff."

"Okay. So how about I come along? I like guy stuff. Especially when the guy is you."

Devlin wheeled around to confront her, unnerving her with the fierceness of his expression. "No!"

When he saw her jump, his face relaxed and he took a deep breath as if trying to steady himself. "Sorry, I didn't mean to startle you. But why all the questions? Don't you trust me?"

Tala paused as she pulled the t-shirt over her head. "I do trust you. I'm wondering if you trust me."

If he hadn't taken her in his arms right then she'd have worried about their relationship. But his strong arms holding her body next to his left her with no doubt. Pack ceremony and wedding aside, they were already a pair.

"We're already mated, Tala. But maybe you'd like a traditional wedding? With all your family and friends?"

She dove into his eyes, searching for any hint of a joke. He was serious. "Devlin Morgan, are you officially asking me to marry you? Human to semi-human?" She wiggled her nose at him, hoping to prod him into challenging her jab.

"Real cute." Cocking his head to the side, he arched one eyebrow and nodded. "I am, Tala Wilde. So what do you say? Wanna marry the Wolf Man?"

"Will you follow me around for the rest of my life?"

Devlin slipped his hands under her shirt to fondle her breasts. "I'll nip at your heels every day of the week, begging for a treat."

She pretended to play coy and consider his proposal. "Well, okay. I guess I'll have to say yes. Besides, you've already marked me and we're mated, so what else can I do?"

Devlin boosted her into the air and twirled her around in a circle. Giddy with happiness, Tala pulled him to her and kissed him long and hard.

"The ladies are not going to believe this."

Devlin held her against him, her feet dangling in the air. "You mean your group of single ladies? Will they let you stay in the group once you're married? Do you think they'll approve of me?"

She tracked her fingers through his long, silky hair. "They'll always be my friends, no matter what. And they'd better like you. Or I'll let you shift and scare the panties off them."

A wicked glint appeared in his eyes as the mischievous grin she'd come to love spread across his face. "Hmm. Scare the panties off them, huh? Sounds like a job I'd love to do."

She good-humoredly slapped him on the chest. "Watch it, Wolfie. You're all mine."

"And glad of it."

He kissed her again and she smiled into the kiss. *How lucky could she get?* Her feet hit the floor as he dropped her, jarring her out of her blissfulness. "Hey! Watch how you treat your future bride."

"Sorry." He delicately pecked her on the cheek this time, leaving her wanting more. "Gotta go."

She clasped her hands around his neck and tugged. Knowing something was up. Knowing she should keep him close. "No. Come on, Devlin. Blow your brother off."

"Blech, what a thought." He shook himself at the revolting thought.

"Quit trying to change the subject. You know what I meant." Batting her eyelids at him, she tried one last proposition. "I promise I'll show you a good time." She laughed, hoping he'd take the bait. "A real good time."

But his serious expression squelched her humor as he took her hands away. *He's way too serious. Something's definitely up.* A shot of dread coursed through her, reinforcing the urge to keep him by her side. "You're hiding something from me. Aren't you?" She fixed her eyes on him, not letting him turn away from her.

Still he denied her suspicions. Breaking free, he pivoted and headed out of the room, calling to her as he strode through the apartment and out the door. "Wrong, Wilde. I'll get back as soon as I can and *then* we'll get busy."

Her mouth stayed open, gaping at the emptiness surrounding her, until she heard the door slam shut. "What the hell just happened?"

The silence Devlin's departure left behind pounded against Tala's nerves as she loped through the apartment toward the door. "No way, Dev. I'm going to find out what you've got going on."

She swung open the door and peeked down the deserted hallway. Grumbling under her breath, she grabbed her keys to shove them in her jeans' pocket as she pulled the door shut behind her. "Gotta catch up with him." Since Devlin wasn't driving...no way would he ever drive again if she could help it...she was determined to stay on his heels. At a discreet distance, of course.

Taking the stairs two at a time, she scanned the area around the apartment building. Off in the distance, she picked out Devlin as he jogged down the sidewalk across the two-lane road running adjacent to the apartment complex. Pulling in a breath, she started after him.

A shout tore from her throat as rough hands latched onto her, dragging her to the side of the building. Strong arms pinned hers behind her back while another man hooked her legs under his arms. Tala cried out again, but the sound was suffocated against the cloth pressed over her mouth.

*****

The blackness dissolved in a slow, gradual mist, changing from pitch black to gray then, at long last, to a dingy haze. Tala groaned, her head a heavy ball of stabbing pain balancing on top of her neck. "Aw, crap. I feel like shit."

"The effects of the drug will wear off soon enough."

Painful pinpricks seared up her arms as she attempted to move them, perplexed at why they wouldn't obey her commands. Coarse ropes bound her by her arms and legs to the chair, and trussed her hands behind her. She flexed her fingers, hoping to regain some sensation in them.

Widening her eyes in an effort to clear her vision, Tala gaped at the squat man sitting across from her. Yet the clearer his image grew, the more she wished she couldn't see. The man was a poster child for *Dirty People Against Baths,* and his greasy strands of hair were a testament of his aversion to shampoo. His shirt, almost stiff with the grime clinging to the material, billowed over kaki slacks that hadn't seen the inside of a washing machine since they'd left the factory.

Tala glanced around the small, dimly lit room, furnished only with the chair she sat in and the cot he used. The overhead light hung from a wire in the ceiling while a dark blind blanketed one small, rectangular-shaped window. An image of an old war movie flashed through Tala's mind. "Where am I? Your interrogation room?" She shot him a piercing look and wished looks could kill. Or at least dismember. "I ain't tellin' you nothing, you Commie, you."

"Commie?" His broad forehead crinkled as he frowned at her. "I'm no Commie. Hell, I don't even vote."

"Figures." She rolled her eyes at him before checking out the door. "And I don't suppose you're the sole survivor of some anti-social cult, are you?"

As if answering her question, a tall man with an I'm-so-stupid-I-don't-even-know-I'm-so-stupid expression barged into the room. "Skanland. You told me to tell you when it was time." He stared at Tala, running his gaze up and down her while his tongue snaked out to caress his upper lip. "Uh, it's time."

Tala sneered at him, letting him know he had as much chance with her as a slug would with a bunny. "Who are you jerks?" She sent a silent prayer of gratitude for the anger sweeping through her. Better anger than fear.

Skanland rose from the dirty cot in front of her, moving close enough for her to smell his foul odor. He pinched her chin and forced her to raise her gaze to his. Bloodshot, tired eyes dove into hers and she saw the hatred they contained. "Quite an ugly mouth on such a pretty lady. Or should I say, pretty bitch?"

"Yeah. Pretty bee-atch."

Both Skanland and Tala shot Carl questioning looks, but Skanland added a jab to the shoulder.

These guys are a joke. "You shouldn't say anything. Not until you've poured a gallon of mouthwash down your mouth. You reek, man."

"Shut up."

The sting of his hand across her cheek was unexpected. *He hit me?* Tala glowered at Skanland and growled, "You do *not* want to do that again."

She prepared for the next slap, ducking her head right before contact. *Ha, ha! Missed me!*

"Ow! You hit me." Carl rubbed his arm, a hurt expression overtaking the blank one of before.

Skanland fumed, embarrassment evident in his scowl. "Then get out of the way, moron."

"I wasn't in the way."

Tala bit the inside of her lip to keep from laughing. "Are you two for real?" *Ladies and gentlemen, may I present for your amusement, Squatty and Stupid.*

Carl's tough expression dropped as he buckled under the other man's glare. "You shouldn't hit her again. We're supposed to swap her for the shifters. Besides, my momma taught me to never hit a woman."

Skanland paused and stared at Carl in disbelief. His deep belly laugh vibrated against the walls of the room and he clutched his stomach as he stumbled a few feet away. "A woman?" Pointing at Tala, he tried to catch his breath between laughs. "She's no woman, moron. She's a shifter."

Tala's mouth dropped open. He thinks I'm a shifter? At first incredulous at his statement, she smiled to herself as an idea dawned on her. Could they tell? Even though she hadn't shifted yet, could she be considered one? Either from her ancestral blood or from Devlin's marking her?

"She don't act like one." Carl bent closer to examine her. "Besides, hitting any female ain't nice."

Again Skanland belly-laughed at his big friend. "Crap, but you are such a girl. Your mamma truss you up in dresses when you was little?"

Carl's pink complexion told the story. "Well, we did used to have a good time trying on each other's clothes."

Tala met Skanland's eyes with a wicked grin. "Some bosom buddy you have there, Skanland."

"But, Skanland, wouldn't she have shifted by now if she was one?"

The moron did have a point, she thought. Dismay pushed out all the pride she'd felt a moment earlier.

"How's she gonna shift while she's knocked out? But it don't matter." Skanland's filthy hand pulled her shirt's collar aside to expose the large mark of Devlin's bite. "One of them's marked her. She's his female now."

Carl grimaced at the mark on her shoulder. "Damn. Why would such a pretty woman want such a thing?"

Skanland let her shirt go and shrugged. "Damned if I know. But once a woman lies down with dogs, she's no longer a woman. She's just another bitch in heat." He let his hand slide over her hair to finger the end of a strand. "Doesn't mean we can't have a little fun before she starts shifting like the rest of the beasts."

Tala jerked away from him as much as her restraints would allow. "I wouldn't let you touch me with your skuzzy dick if you boiled your cock in hot water first." She grinned, a challenge to her smirk. "But you go ahead and try it, and I'll see."

Rage stiffened Skanland's body as he raised his arm to hit her again. She readied herself, prepared to dodge another blow, yet as he put his arm over his head, the door swung open and two more men fell into the room.

"Skanland. George called. They're at the park now. I told him we'd meet him at *The Lucky Lady* when we're finished."

For the first time since coming to, fear pierced Tala's heart and she swiveled her head to the other men. "Who's at the park?"

Skanland cackled, enjoying her alarmed tone. "Your animal boyfriend and his litter mate. They're getting the word right now. And soon, they'll join us for a party. A shifter-skinning party."

All four men chuckled then, hurling panicked signals through Tala's brain. "What are you going to do?"

Skanland leaned over to rest his hands on the arms of her chair. "First, we're gonna to trap 'em and give them a good neutering. Then, we're gonna skin 'em alive. I need a couple of new hides for my walls."

Tala tried to keep her terror from showing, but judging by his face, she failed. "Why? What do you have against Devlin and Mickale? What'd they ever do to you?"

Skanland's lips twisted into a half-sneer, half-smile. "They're shifter scum. Freaks of nature who don't deserve to live." He rose and took a gun from one of the other men. Holding the gun in front of him, he shook it at her. "And we're the ones who're going to wipe their kind...your kind...off the face of the planet."

What could she do? Nothing, no words, no action came to her. Would she be an unwilling witness to Devlin's death? Tears of anger welled up inside her even as one comforting thought came to her. *At least, they'll kill me, too.*

"Okay, boys, let's go get ready for our guests."

Chapter Fifteen

"Are you sure this is a smart idea?" Mickale loped alongside Devlin, jumping over the low barrier separating the park's perimeter from the sidewalk along the street. "I mean, what're you thinking of gaining by meeting with this guy?"

Devlin slowed to a jog and started scanning the open grassy area for George. "Gain? Nothing except the joy in breaking his neck. Or, at least, scaring him so much he'll never bother her again. I'll take either outcome."

"But he's got to have something else going on. After the encounter you told me about, he's not going to meet you in a park to talk. At least, not by himself. He's not stupid, is he?"

Devlin skidded to a stop, pivoted on his heel, and attempted to head off in the opposite direction. "Crap. Let's get out of here."

"You! You, wretched, horrid man! Who let you out of jail?"

Mickale grabbed Devlin's arm before he could take off. "Bro, I think the lady means you."

Whose side was Mickale on, anyway? Caught, Devlin swiveled to face Cuddles and Mrs. Skylard. "Mrs. Skylard, I'm out on bail and have every right to come and go as I want."

Mrs. Skylard's voice radiated to the surrounding park visitors. "How can the courts allow an animal abuser like you to infest our park?" Clutching Cuddles against her huge bosom, Mrs. Skylard searched for help. "Police! Police! Oh, where is an officer when I need one? Poleece!"

Devlin cringed under the curious stares of the people milling around them. "Mrs. Skylard, you misunderstood the whole situation. I was helping Cuddles. Someone else put her in the bush."

"Looks to me like Mrs. Skylard's the one who should get stuck in a bush."

Devlin grumbled low, so only Mickale could hear him. "That's what I thought."

Her indignation at Mickale's remark heightened her calls for help. "How dare you?" Her upper lip twisted into a disgusted snarl as she scrutinized Mickale. "Do you know you're associating with a known animal abuser, young man?"

Mickale's mouth gaped as he faked a stunned reaction. "No! Really? I had no idea."

Mrs. Skylard smirked, satisfied with her characterization of Devlin. "You really should be more discriminating with whom you associate."

"Oh, you are so right." Mickale reached out to pet Cuddles on the head.

Unsure of his intentions, Mrs. Skylard tensed and clasped the poodle tighter. "Well..."

"I thought Devlin had stopped all the abuse nonsense." Mickale parted his lips, letting his fangs peek out. "I thought he'd moved on to eating them." Stretching his mouth a little wider to show more teeth, he added, "Like me."

Mrs. Skylard's eyes popped open as a small cry escaped her. She tried to shout, to let go with another one of her ear-piercing shrieks, her mouth working strangely, but she couldn't get more than a soft mumble to come out.

"Crap, Mickale. Are you trying to make things worse for me?" Devlin gripped Mickale's arm and dragged him along with him, down the path away from the lady, who stayed frozen to her spot. "I can't wait for the judge to hear this story."

"Please. As if you're even going to court. We'll have our attorneys take care of the matter and you'll never see the old coot again. Unless you've got a thing for Cuddles?"

Devlin rolled his eyes, dropped Mickale's arm, and glanced to where she'd stood. "Good, she's gone now. I'd hate to think of her having a stroke from the shock."

"So what? She's an uptight old bitty who'd have to pay someone to lay her." Mickale winked at a girl on rollerblades as she passed by them. "Poor Cuddles looked like she'd love a new mommy."

"It's about time you two showed up."

Devlin and Mickale swiveled together to find George leaning against a lamppost. Before he could say another word, Devlin's hands were around George's neck, his fingers pressing into his throat until the man couldn't squawk out a sound. With George's back against the pole, Devlin lifted him off his feet, propping him two feet off the ground.

"Look, you little asshole. I'm here. I did as you asked." Devlin let his fangs grow and the saliva flow in his mouth. He bared his teeth and pressed his nose against the squirming man's bulbous one. "But I'm warning you. If I ever even guess you bothered Tala, spoke to her, or came within twenty yards of her, I'll track you down and rip out your heart."

Mickale sidled up next to the two men and wiggled his fingers in greeting. "Hey, dude, how's it hanging?" He chuckled as he pointedly looked at the ground beneath him. "Or should I ask, how're *you* hanging?"

George gurgled at Mickale, an obvious plea for him to intercede. "Uh, Dev. He's turning blue, man. You may want to think about letting him live. Especially since there's so many people watching you."

Devlin, who'd locked onto George and forgotten the existence of anyone and anything else around him, took a moment to check out the spectators. A group of people stood gawking at them.

Mickale leaned in to whisper. "Too many witnesses, bro. Put the little man down."

Devlin growled, not wanting to ease the hold he had on George, but relented. The guy's face was a mottled purple and blue. "For now."

George rubbed his neck as soon as Devlin let him go, sucking in air as fast as he could. Once he'd coughed a couple of times, however, Devlin figured he was good to go. But the crowd lingered.

"Okay, folks. Show's over." Mickale flapped his hands, trying to shoo the people away. "Merely a little fuss between old drinking buddies. He's fine. No need to contact the authorities." Slapping George on the shoulder, he nodded and urged him to agree. "You're fine. Right, buddy?"

Devlin slitted his eyes at George, emphasizing his need to follow along with the story. "Sure, George. You're fine, right?"

He darted his gaze between Devlin, Mickale, and the onlookers. Although his voice sounded strained, he managed to croak out the words. "Yeah. Right. Fine."

Devlin nudged him, driving him to take it a step further. After the scene with Mrs. Skylard, he couldn't afford another one.

"No need for the police." George coughed again, but plastered a half-hearted smile on his face.

Playing the game to the finish, Devlin slid his arm around George's shoulder and pulled him onto the path. "What's more fun than a little rough-housing between friends, huh?"

Mickale took up step on the other side of George, wedging him between the two shifters. "Oh, for sure, bro. Good times."

As the three walked down the path together, the crowd they'd left behind dispersed. Devlin took a deep breath and patted his captive on the cheek. "Keep walking and start talking. What's this all about?"

"Tala's waiting for you."

Devlin missed a step, but Mickale's hold on George from the other side kept them moving forward. "What're you talking about? She's at her apartment." A cold dread, ice closing up his veins, hooked onto him and he had to fight to breathe.

"Your friends from the other day are with her."

Devlin stopped, swinging the shrieking, little man in front of him. Yanking him closer, Devlin snarled his words, his anger fighting a not-so-distant second to his fear. "Stop playing games with me and tell me what's going on. Where's Tala?"

"Keep walking, Devlin. There's a cop not far behind us."

Mickale's warning catapulted Devlin into motion again, taking George along with him. George, however, tried to drag his feet until Devlin let his eyes change color. Terror filled the atmosphere around them as George let out a small gasp.

"Keep your tone light and easy if you want to keep your tongue attached." Devlin sniffed and picked up a smell off of George. Shivers sprinted down his spine. *Hunters. He's been around hunters.* "Talk."

George's words were weak, but unmistakable, confirming Devlin's worst nightmare. "The hunters have Tala. They're keeping her in a house at the edge of town. If you, both of you, show up and turn yourselves over to them, they'll let her go."

*****

"Devlin, where are you?" Tala strained against the ropes securing her to the chair, but the cords held tight. Afternoon light poked through the sides of the blind and caught dust particles floating in the air. She puffed and saw her breath in a swirl of dust.

Maybe she could signal to Devlin somehow? Closing her eyes, she pictured him, tall and strong, wondering where she was. Concentrating, she sent a mental message to him and prayed he'd receive her plea. *Devlin, hear me. I'm in trouble. Danger. Get help.*

"Oh crap. I sound like I'm telling Lassie to fetch Timmy's dad."

Tala worked her wrists back and forth, hoping to find her ropes loosening a bit. But no luck. Could she get a message to Devlin some other way? Hadn't Devlin said she'd called him to her? Remembering how he'd told her about "hearing her call," Tala decided a howl was worth a try.

She took a few deep breaths so she could put as much force as she could behind her call. Just as she was about to take the final and biggest breath of all, a ludicrous thought struck her. *Who do I think I am? The big, bad wolf in* Little Red Riding Hood? *Although, blowing down the house like the wolf in* The Three Little Pigs *would really help right now.* The silly idea, along with her fractured nerves, gave her the giggles. Tears streamed down her cheeks as the giggles kept coming.

With the tears finally subsiding, she shook her head and resolved to do her best. "You can do this, Tala. You have to."

She squirmed in her chair a minute, trying to get comfortable. Taking some more deep breaths and keeping her mind off the idea of huffing and puffing...*No. Don't think about the big, bad wolf...* Tala sucked in a big intake of air, laid back her head, and howled.

Her throat ached as she pushed out the sound with all the strength she could gather. One howl ended as she slid into another. And another. All the while thinking, *Devlin, hear me. Come to me. Damn, it's hard to howl with ropes across my chest.*

The door banging open startled her, cutting off her last howl before she could finish.

"What the hell are you doing?" Carl scowled at her, confusion making his natural stupid expression seem imbecilic. "Are you howling?"

Tala put on her dumb blonde face. "Howling? Little ole me?" *Such a big mouth you have, Grandma.*

When he didn't seem to buy her routine quickly enough, she slid into *Plan B*, going into full flirtation mode. "Okay, you got me." Batting her eyes at the idiot striding over to her, she adopted the sincerest, yet sexiest, expression she could and gazed up into his malicious eyes. "I wanted some attention. You can't blame a girl for wanting a little attention, can you?" She stuck out her lips, hoping for a sexy pout. "From you."

Eck! Am I really flirting with this goon? Shit, how far will I go to save my butt? Not that far. But for Devlin? As far as it takes.

A glimmer of excitement sparked in Carl's eyes. Bending over, he licked his lips and got on his knees in front of her.

Oh, please, do not let this guy touch me. If he touches me, I'm going to upchuck. But at least she'd make sure she'd upchuck on him.

"From me?"

The creep nearly drooled on her. She swallowed the bile rising in her throat and fortified her game face. "Who else, handsome?"

He chuckled, a dirty chuckle filled with innuendo. "Yeah, I thought we had a vibe going on before. And I do like girls, too."

She smiled a coy, little smile. "Too? Me, too. Uh, men, I mean." Leave it to her to pick a bisexual. "I couldn't wait for the others to leave us alone. But then you left me and didn't return. So I had to do something to bring you back to me."

His hand skimmed over her breasts and a wave of nausea hit her. *Keep yourself together, Tala. Don't lose it. For Devlin's sake.* Doing the exact opposite of what she'd like to do, she thrust out her chest and let him cop a feel. "You know, if you'd untie me," she made sure he saw her glance at the cot, "...we could have some real fun."

His eyebrows slid between his noses. "Uh, I don't know. Skanland wouldn't want me messing with you."

Shooting him a disappointed look, she stabbed at his ego. "Are you telling me you're afraid of him? A big, strong man like you?" *God, please kill me now before my dignity sinks even lower.* Instead, she turned down the corners of her mouth and acted as if he'd told her she couldn't have a kitten for Christmas.

"'Course not. I'm not afraid of him. But Skanland runs things, you know."

"He wouldn't have to know. I promise I won't say a word. And afterwards, you could tie me up again." When he started to protest, she continued, making one last ditch try. "I'd love to run my tongue, and my hands, all over your body."

Score! After his jaw plunged to the floor, Carl couldn't get to the ropes fast enough.

"You promise you won't say anything?"

"Oh, I promise, my big, strong man." *Urgh! Blech! Vomit!!*

"Carl, you're dumber than I thought you were."

Tala's heart plummeted to her feet at the sound of Skanland's voice. *Damn him to hell and back.*

Carl, snatching his hands away from the ropes like they were laced with acid, jumped to his feet and headed toward the door. "I wasn't doing anything. I was just checking to make sure the ropes were real tight."

Skanland knocked Carl in the head and pushed him from the room. "You stay outta here." Turning to face Tala, he jabbed his finger at her. "And you shut the hell up or I'll shut your fat trap for you."

Fat? She tipped her head to study her body. *Sure, she'd shared a lot of pizza with Devlin, but she wasn't fat. Was she?*

The door slammed closed behind Skanland, leaving Tala wondering what to do next. She shook her head and discarded the idea of howling again. Skanland might do something drastic like stuff a rag in her mouth if she made any more noise.

"So what do I do now?" She slumped in the chair and let her mind wander. *If only Devlin was here. He could shift and take care of things.* The power he exuded when he shifted was twice a normal man's. If only she could shift.

Devlin had said she'd shift when the time was right. And Skanland had called her a shifter. Could the power be hidden inside her? Could she shift now? Deciding it was worth a try, even though she'd failed so many times before, Tala focused on one thought. *Shift.*

For several minutes, she chanted the word over and over in her mind. And waited. And waited some more. Tried again and waited. Yet after several attempts, nothing had happened.

Fighting the frustration boiling inside her, she stomped the floor, even as the ropes held fast. "Why can't I do this?" Why didn't shifters have a manual or a beginner's class?

As her mind thought about devising a workshop...*Shifting for Dummies*...she remembered another class she'd taken called *Anything is Possible with Visualization*. According to the teacher, if one could visualize something happening, like getting a promotion or mastering a physical challenge, then they could make any dream, any ambition come true.

"Shit, I can't do any worse than offering to sleep with Carl." Tala contemplated what she wanted to happen. She wanted to shift. To do so, according to the visualization class, she'd have to see herself as a werewolf.

Tala closed her eyes and imagined she was at home. Standing naked in her bathroom, she visualized her body in the bathroom mirror. *Whoa, maybe I am getting fat. No more pizza.* Shaking off the thought, she concentrated harder, forcing her mind to make the changes to her body, in her vision. Sweat popped out along her brow as she pushed harder, wanting the change more than anything else in the world.

Without warning, the form in her mind's vision altered. Her torso expanded, doubling the size of her ribcage. Her facial features morphed, elongating, stretching beyond human limits. Hair, golden and shiny, spread across her body as claws replaced her French-tipped nails. And fangs. Glorious, long, sharp fangs broke through her gums as she opened her mouth to snarl.

Tala snapped her eyes open, eager to experience the real transformation. Grinning, she widened her mouth, and yearned to feel the fangs she'd formed. Eager to see her claws, she glanced down.

"Skanland!"

Tala whipped her head around to see Carl standing in the doorway. Could she break free in time?

Skanland appeared next to Carl, paused, and hurried into the room. One look at his face told Tala what she'd hoped. She'd done it! She'd changed.

Carl joined Skanland standing in front of her, both of her captors gaping at the sight before them. Gaining his voice, Skanland cocked his head at her in wonder. "Holy crap. What happened to her?"

Chapter Sixteen

"This is the address George gave us."

Devlin surveyed the decrepit house. What little color was left on the exterior after years of neglect hung in strips of peeling paint. A broken down picket fence, sporting the same dismal gray coloring as the house, surrounded the yard. The yard, overgrown with weeds, left images of vermin and bugs crawling through its jungle. A mailbox, beaten and attached to a rotting piece of wood with yards of duct tape, bent at an angle from the dry, hard ground.

"Figures." Mickale spat on the sidewalk to show his disgust at the sight. "A hunters' hole in the wall."

"Yep. A rat hole, all right." Devlin reached for the swinging gate hanging halfway on the fence. "Let's get Tala." But Mickale's hand on his arm held him in check.

"Uh, bro. We've got company."

Vicious growls caught Devlin's attention and he rotated toward the sounds. Two large Dobermans stood a few feet away, their fangs dripping with saliva, ready to chomp on delicious flesh. "Aw, crap. Doggies."

"Big, mean doggies, bro. The type who'd chew up Cuddles and spit her out in one gulp."

"And then eat men as their main course." Devlin set his sights on the dog in front of him. "Good doggy. Nice doggy."

"Yeah, right. Can't you just feel the love, Dev?"

Devlin flung out his hand, whacking Mickale in the arm. Snarls erupted as the dogs lunged forward, stopping a foot away from the fence.

"Bro, don't make any more quick moves, okay? Which means, don't hit me."

Devlin nodded, keeping his arms close to his body. "Agreed. But we have to get past these guards." He bent down, getting eye level with the dogs.

"Dev? What're you doing?"

"Getting to know the leader." Devlin locked gazes with the bigger Doberman, diving into the mind behind the dark, angry eyes. Yet when fear ripped through his chest, halting his breath, Devlin wasn't surprised. Fear often hid behind anger.

He searched the other dog's mind and came to a similar conclusion. "Someone's hurt both of them. A lot."

A snarl came from Mickale, echoing the sentiments squeezing his chest. "Three guesses."

Devlin shook his head, dismayed at the pain he'd picked up from the lead dog. "The hunters keep them locked up most of the time with very little food or water. Keeps them mean." He twisted his head around to exchange a glance with Mickale. "Even if we didn't have to get past them to save Tala, I'd have to help them."

"I'm with you, bro." Mickale squatted beside him. "But after this is all over, we have to talk about pack leadership."

"Father made his choice."

"His chose wrong." Another snarl escaped Mickale.

"You think so?"

"I know so."

"So you thought by feeding Tala frightening stories, you'd keep her from mating me, putting you in line to rule?"

Mickale laughed a short bark. "Yeah, well, when you didn't go for the other women—"

Devlin gaped at his brother. "You mean the bar trio?"

"Hey, they were nice and they saved our butts, too. You should've stuck around for the rest of the night. Anyway, when you didn't go for one of them, I had to play the nutcase card. Besides, all this hunter business distracted me before I could come up with a better plan."

"Too bad she didn't believe you, huh?"

"I didn't know you'd already marked her. And shifted for her." Mickale fell to his knees. "But I'm not giving up. As first born, I deserve to be leader."

Devlin studied his brother for a moment. "Yeah, you do."

Without responding to the stunned expression on Mickale's face, Devlin renewed his focus on the dog. "Okay, boy. Let's understand each other." Going to his knees, Devlin poured his thoughts into the Doberman.

The dog cocked his head to the side, listening to Devlin. After a few minutes of this exchange, the dog whimpered, laid down, and rested his head on his paws. The other dog, having moved to one side of the leader, squatted down and placed her head on her paws, too.

Devlin smiled and reached through the fence to pet the bigger dog's head. "Thanks. I'll return the favor." Standing up, he opened the gate and stepped inside the yard. "Coming?"

"After you, bro."

Devlin took the lead as they passed through the gate and stalked to the house. The dogs rose, following on their heels.

"You know they've got to be watching, right?"

Devlin nodded without glancing around. "Shh. Probably, but then again, you know how arrogant hunters are."

"Yeah, but this is a setup. They know it and we know it." He pushed ahead of Devlin to stomp up the broken steps to the front door. "Let's quit playing games and get this party going."

Leave it to his brother to take the most direct approach. Although this time, Devlin couldn't argue with his brother's logic. Together, they stripped off their clothes, piling them in a spot by the door. "Hurry up. I have a feeling some old lady's spying on us from across the street."

"Then it's her lucky day, huh, bro?"

Devlin smirked as he joined Mickale in front of the door, ready to knock. After knocking for several minutes, the door flung open with two hunters standing in the frame, their guns poised and ready. Both hunters glanced down at the brothers' private parts, and then turned to check each other's reaction as their mouths fell open.

Devlin grinned. "Hi ya, boys. I hope we're not overdressed for the party."

*****

"What?" Tala scowled at Carl and Skanland as they gaped at her. "What're you rejects staring at?" Did they have to gawk at her like she was a three-headed frog?

"Damn." Carl stammered another couple of expletives before repeating Skanland's earlier question. "What happened to her?"

Skanland reluctantly inched forward, acting as though he expected her to be contagious. "I think she's starting to turn."

"You mean, like she's a little bit werewolf?"

"No, you moron. Being a little bit werewolf is like being a little bit stupid. Not possible. Either you're stupid or you're not." He rolled his eyes at his cohort. "And trust me, you are."

Who were these guys? The *Two* Stooges? Tala squirmed under Skanland's persistent scrutiny as other hunters joined them at the door. *Scratch that. The Four Stooges.* Why don't they stop staring at me? "How about telling me what you find so fascinating?"

He squinted at her and leaned closer. Reaching out with his index finger, he slid his finger along her jaw. "Weird. Really weird."

Tala whipped her head to the side and snapped at his finger, missing his digit by centimeters as he snatched his hand away. "Don't touch me, you pervert."

To her surprise, Skanland nodded as if agreeing with her. Until he spoke. "Oh, sure. I'm the preevert."

His short bark afterwards made her wince in disgust. "The word's 'pervert,' not pree-vert."

Fumbling in the pocket of his pants, he brought out a cosmetic compact. "I ain't the *per*-vert here. You're some kind of mutation." He opened the compact and held it in front of her.

What was this guy up to? Her stomach flopped, unsure if she wanted to gaze into the small mirror or not. *But knowing is better than not knowing, right?* Skanland snickered and she made her decision. She'd have to look.

With all the dread of a mother checking out her truant child's report card, Tala dipped her head and stared into the mirror. Shock shook her body as she turned her head to better examine the sight reflected in the glass.

Soft, golden fur covered the left side of her face, running from the curve of her jaw down to the middle of her chin. Fascinated, as well as stunned, she moved her head from side to side, comparing the two parts of her face. While the right side was clean and hairless as usual, the left side sported a virtual rug of animal hair. "Oh, God."

"God has nothing to do with monsters like you." Skanland thrust the mirror closer to the end of her nose. "Take a gander at yourself. You tried going wolf, didn't you?"

A spark of excitement sent her heart soaring. But why hadn't she shifted all the way?

Skanland saw her smile and whipped the compact into his pocket. "Just so you know. You go all the way, you die." He straightened up and headed for the door.

She coughed a sarcastic laugh. "Trust me, going all the way with you isn't happening." His lurch in her direction only deepened her resolve to piss him off. "Oh, Skanland?"

"What?"

She feigned an expression of interest before asking the question she knew he couldn't, wouldn't, want to answer. "Why do you carry a ladies' cosmetic mirror?"

An immediate stream of red burst up Skanland's neck and into his face. "Shut up, bitch!"

Carl was the only hunter bright enough...*now there's a frightening thought!*...not to snicker at her question. Instead, he covered his laughter by clamping a huge hand over his mouth. But the other two yokels laughed like they'd never heard anything so funny in their whole lives. And couldn't keep their mouths zipped.

"Yeah, Skanland. What's with the makeup mirror? My momma used to carry one like it."

"Gotta put on some lipstick? You gotta hot date tonight? Is he gonna get lucky?

The chunkier hunter nudged his friend in the arm. "'Course not, Rims. Skanland won't even kiss goodnight. He wouldn't want to mess up his makeup."

"But Skanland, sweetie, you can always bend over and take it in the a—"

Skanland's hands wrapped around the man's neck, cutting off his last word. "Shut the fuck up or I'm going to mess up your face. Do you hear me? Shut the fucking shit up!"

Carl gripped Skanland's shoulders and pulled him from the choking hunter. "They're just teasin', Skanland. They don't mean nothing by it."

Skanland, whose complexion was slowly returning to normal, broke free of Carl's hold. "I carry that thing because..." He paused, unable to finish his sentence.

The three men were as entranced as Tala by his possible reason. In fact, they were so anxious to hear what he had to say that none of them said a single word.

Skanland glanced around at their rapt attention and stumbled for an explanation. "I, uh, I have it because..." He squirmed a minute longer before tensing up and glaring at them. "None of your damn business. Get back to your posts. Those mutants could arrive any minute now."

A strong, loud knock reverberated through the small house, shaking the walls around them. Stunned, the men stared at each other a few moments before they raced from the room, leaving Tala alone to gape at the open door.

*****

"Devlin?" Tala strained against her ropes, trying to see into the hallway. Soon howls changed to growls, snarls, and barks. Shouts from human men mixed with the sounds of fighting as loud bangs and crashes came from another part of the house. "Hey, I'm in here!"

The Doberman, however, who skidded to a stop at the door, was not the rescuer she'd hoped for. "Right species. Wrong breed." Long, white teeth bared at her as she held her breath and prayed he'd turn around and go away. But the dog stood his ground, snarling and dripping saliva on the floor.

"Oh, damn it all to hell and back." Tala spoke as softly as she could, not wanting to incite the dog any more than he already was. "Good doggy. You're a nice doggy, right?" When he didn't leap and tear off her face, she took a shallow breath and dared to hope she could escape certain death. "Go find your master and leave the nice lady alone, okay?"

"Okay. But I don't call Devlin my master. He's always been more like a pest. You know, the typical younger brother."

Daring to take her eyes off the dog, Tala looked up to see a nude Mickale standing a few feet behind the brute. *Keep your eyes on his face, Tala.* "Mickale? Whew! Can you get rid of him?"

Mickale acted confused and pointed at the dog. "Get rid of him? What for?"

Was this guy ever serious? "So he won't chew me up and eat me alive?"

Mickale chuckled, flinched when a terrible crash came from the other room, and snapped his fingers. "Go along, Brutus. I think Devlin could use your help."

Twisting his massive head around to snarl at Mickale, Brutus took one last hungry look at Tala before heading down the hallway toward the noise.

Tala's heart skipped a beat. "Devlin's here? Well, don't just stand there. Untie me. Let's go help him."

Mickale shrugged and walked over to work on her bindings. "If you say so. But he seems to be enjoying his time alone with the boys."

As she stood up to pull the rest of the ropes off her arms, Mickale clasped her chin and examined the fur alongside her jaw. "Hmm. Looks like someone's tried going wolf. And didn't quite make it past the puppy stage." Bending forward, he sniffed at her, paused, and swiped his coarse tongue over her fur.

Tala lurched away from him. "Yuck. What the hell do you think you're doing?"

"Just welcoming you to the family, babe."

"I thought I already got the rump rub welcome. And don't call me, 'babe.'"

A loud boom echoed from the fight going on in another room. Tala jerked, startled by the intensity of the sound, and ran toward the sounds of battle.

After racing down a long corridor with Mickale on her heels, she tore into a larger room containing living room furniture. Or, at least, it contained furniture a few minutes ago. Now the debris of chairs, a sofa, end tables, and a television littered the room. Devlin in full werewolf splendor, stood in the middle of the fray as three men attacked him. The dog stood next to him, an unflinching comrade-in-arms.

Damn. Talk about magnificent. She stared at Devlin as he slashed one hunter while bending the arm of another. She heard the snap of the man's arm as it broke. Just as she concentrated on his face, Devlin raised his head and saw her. His howl, ferocious yet joyful, erupted from his lips.

A growl wafted over her from behind and she turned to find Mickale transforming and roaring his rage. He flew by her, picked up a hunter poised to smash a chair over Devlin's head, and hurled him across the room.

Where's Skanland? Tala whirled in a circle, searching for the lead hunter. A yelp from the other room sent her spinning to the right.

Tala raced into the kitchen and skidded to a stop, horrified at the sight before her. *No!* Skanland stood over another, slightly smaller Doberman, a butcher knife in his white-knuckled hand, as blood dripped down his wrist. The dog, whimpering and wild-eyed, locked eyes with Tala.

Help me.

Had she just heard the dog speak? Tala's mouth dropped opened as she gaped at the canine. She hadn't spoken, but she'd heard her cry for help, nonetheless.

A ferocious anger grabbed her as she stared at the dog, too furious to even think. But no thought was necessary. Instead, she let the power within her build, surging through her veins at an impossible speed. Her breath shortened as fangs grew in her mouth and claws sprang to replace nails.

Tala turned her head to the right and glimpsed her reflection in the mirrored door of the microwave. She widened her mouth to expose long, sharp fangs.

I'm shifting.

"It's about time." Glorious elation filled her as she lifted her head and howled.

At Tala's howl, Skanland turned, brandishing the knife at her. "Damn bitch is trying to shift again."

What's he mean trying *to shift?* Tala pivoted enough to catch her image in the glass of a large picture hanging on the wall. Hair grew in tuffs all over her human-shaped face, but didn't cover the entire area. Her mouth, however, was contorted to make room for the long fangs protruding over her lips, but not much else had changed. *Oh, come on, already! What's a girl gotta do to get a little hair on her chest?*

Holding up her hands, she studied the claws pointing out from the ends of her fingers, but the rest of her body remained human and unchanged. *Why can't I get the hang of this?*

"I should have killed you when I had the chance."

Torn from her disappointment, Tala looked up in time to deflect the knife from puncturing her breast.

She roared, both from fear and anger, and instinctively struck out. Skanland flew across the room, banging against the wall with enough force to rattle the pictures. He scrambled to his feet with the butcher knife still clutched in his hand.

At least I'm getting stronger. Tala leapt over the injured dog and grabbed Skanland's wrist, driving his knife-wielding arm over his head. His hot breath hit her face, making her stomach revolt, but she held on and squeezed.

His eyes widened at her strength and a small cry escaped him. Although he tried to throttle her with his other hand, she thwarted the move, twisting his arm behind his back. She howled, delighting in her power.

"Talk about Call of the Wilde. Want some help?"

Tala glanced over her shoulder at Devlin, Mickale, and Brutus standing in the doorway. She considered the offer and hurled Skanland's body at them. "Yeah. You take care of him." The hunter flailed, trying to regain equilibrium as his body landed against the two waiting wolves.

Devlin caught one side of him while Mickale twisted one of the hunter's arms. "You want to do the honors, Mick?"

Mickale's eyes glittered with delight. "Thanks, bro. Don't mind if I do." Snarling, Mickale dragged the struggling man into the other room.

Tala watched as Mickale left with his victim and turned to the dog lying on the floor. She hurried to her side and knelt down on her knees to examine her wounds. "Damn, this looks very bad."

Coldness skimmed the side of her arm as Brutus lay down next to his mate. His pitiful whimpers cut a slice through her heart. "Don't worry, boy. We'll do everything we can for her."

Devlin fell to the floor beside her, now in human form. Very naked human form. Very naked, sexually erect human form. "Devlin, this isn't the time or the place."

He followed her gaze and cupped his hands over as much of his shaft as his hands could cover. Jutting his chin toward the female, he broke the hold his manhood had on her rapt attention. "Will she live?" Yet before she could answer, he pulled her to him. "Are you all right? Really all right?"

The concern, the worry she heard in his voice made her search his face. His arm around her sent warm tingles racing down her spine while an overwhelming impression of safety filled her soul. *He loves me.*

"Uh, I can tell you're glad to see me." She giggled, the high-pitched titter of a girl in love.

Snuggling her closer, he whispered in her ear. "Kind of hard to hide my happiness in my present condition."

Tala's pulse raced as the adrenalin of a hormonal kind flowed through her. The familiar hot flash burned around her abdomen as visions of Devlin sucking her tits, as he stroked her, pulling her on top of him rushed through her brain. But the following images of Devlin holding her close, cuddling against her through the night, made her head reel and her soul soar.

Another stronger whimper came from Brutus, coaxing her to return to her patient. Smiling, she pulled away from Devlin to examine the female's injuries.

Keep your mind on the dog, Tala. This is no time to think about jumping Devlin's bones. But later...

She licked her lips and noted she was still in wolf form. Or, at least, partial wolf form.

"Is she a friend of yours?" If she'd asked this question about a dog at any other time before meeting Devlin, she'd have thought it a joke. But not now.

"Yeah, you could say so." Devlin reached out to put his hand on the dog's head. "She's hurting a lot."

"I know. I can sense it." She placed her hand on Devlin's arm. "We need to get her medical attention right away or she won't survive. Go find something to wrap around these wounds to stop the bleeding."

Devlin nodded and moved away. She knew he wouldn't fail her or the dog. Murmuring soft words of comfort, she held her palms over the worst wounds and waited for Devlin's return. She didn't have to wait long.

"Here." Devlin dumped a few rolls of bandages and tape on the floor beside her. "The hunters had a first aid case in the bathroom. Seems only right we're using it on the dog and not wasting it on them." He started tearing off a strip for her. "Besides, I don't think there's enough bandages in the world to put them back together. Not that anyone would want to."

She gritted her teeth at the sudden fury whipping around inside her, nodded at the dog, and started bandaging the most severe wound. "I sure wouldn't."

"How're you two doing?" Mickale stood over them, in clothed human form, a frown covering his face. He dropped a wet cloth and a pile of clothes onto Devlin's lap. "I thought you might need these."

Devlin rose, wiped the signs of the fight off his body, and started pulling on his jeans. "Good thing we stripped before we came to the rescue."

Tala couldn't help but groan as Devlin covered his magnificent body. "Hey, don't cover up on my account."

Devlin grinned his any-time-any-place grin and finished getting dressed. Growing somber, he glanced from Tala to Mickale, and to the male dog. "You take care of the hunters?"

"Yeah. They're all gone."

What does he mean? Tala checked each of the brothers, but decided she didn't want to know everything. Not yet. She wrapped the last of the bandages around the dog and wiped her bloodied hands on a cloth. "If you two have finished, uh, cleaning up, let's get this poor girl to a vet. In fact, let's take her to my office at the zoo. She'll get the best possible care from them."

Moving with the utmost tenderness, Devlin slipped his arms under the wounded dog. As he lifted her, his eyes locked onto Tala and shot her a pointed look. "You might want to go to full human form before we get to the zoo. I'm not sure how you'd explain those teeth and your pitiful patches of hair to your coworkers."

"Yeah, you look like you mated with a poodle."

Mickale's chuckle heightened her frustration level. Why was this so funny? She snarled at him and followed Devlin from the room. "Tell me why, Devlin."

Mickale ran ahead of them, opening the front door, and the gate. "I found a set of keys to the hunters' car." He tossed them at Tala who caught them with one hand. "I think you'd better drive, don't you?"

Cradling the dog, Devlin slid into the back seat with Mickale piling in after him. Tala jumped into the front and looked into the rearview mirror in time to see her fangs recede into her mouth. Her hands turned back to human as she gripped the steering wheel.

"Why what, Tala?" Devlin held the dog to him, but looked out the window at Brutus standing alone in the yard. As if signaling to Devlin, Brutus raised his head and yelped a few short, sad barks. "We need to come back for him as soon as we're done."

Tala caught his eyes as he turned his head away from the bereft dog and stared straight ahead. A silent message zipped between the two of them as their gazes met and held fast. *Why can't I change all the way?*

The look in his eyes softened, changing from a hot desire to a comforting warmth. "Don't worry. You will. But for right now, concentrate on getting all the hair off your face."

*****

"So? What'd your coworkers say?"

Mickale leaned forward in the rear seat as Tala and Devlin slid into the front of the car. "I didn't give them time to ask. Besides, Devlin's presence intimidated them so much they couldn't get a word out, what with their chins sitting on their chests. But they'll take good care of our friend."

"Yeah, I thought old Jim was about to keel over from a heart attack when I snarled at him. The lightweight." Devlin laughed and buckled his seat belt. "You're gonna have some 'splainin' to do later, Lucy."

"Lucy?" Mickale's forehead creased as he glanced at Devlin and then Tala. "I thought your name's Tala."

Tala threw Mickale an oh-puleeze expression. "You know it is. I think Devlin's watched too many old television shows." She pulled the car onto the road and headed toward town. "We've got some unfinished business to deal with."   "Like taking care of a certain disgruntled ex-employee?" Devlin followed his words with a low, mean rumble in his throat.

"Exactly. Now if only I knew where to find him. I can't remember George mentioning any friends or favorite hangouts." She paused, and snapped her fingers. "Wait a sec. I think I know where we can find the slug."

Devlin crooked his neck to shoot Mickale a look before leaning toward her. "So? Spit it out. Where is he?"

"When the hunters had me tied up, one of them came in and said something about meeting George at some place called *The Lucky Lady*."

"I know the place. It's a hole-in-the-wall strip joint downtown."

Tala's bemused glance caught Mickale in the mirror. "You a regular there?"

"Not so much. Only when I'm trolling for lowlife humans."

Devlin twisted to face forward again. "Well, since the hunters won't be able to keep their appointment with old Georgie, I think we should go in their place."

"Hell, yes." Tala laughed and high-fived Devlin.

"That's my girl."

Tala headed the car downtown, following directions from Mickale. Before long, they'd managed to park and make their way inside the hovel of a bar. "Wow." Devlin crooked his head to the side to follow the stripper's act as she held her body upside down on the pole. "How does she do that?"

An uneasiness clenched Tala's stomach. Recognition of the sensation dawned on her, stunning her in its passion. She was jealous. Plain and simple. Green-eyed, hot-tempered, stay-away-from-my-man jealous. "Uh, yeah. She's limber and strong. I think we've established as much."

Mickale grinned as he scooped up a drink off the tray of a passing topless waitress. He flipped her a twenty-dollar bill as she started to protest, and her glower morphed into a practiced smile. "Limber and lusty. Just the way I like 'em."

Tala swallowed, hoping to keep breathing. A dense layer of smoke, stale air, and cheap perfume threatened to enclose her in a shell of bad smells. She wrinkled her nose and peered through the blanket of smoke at the dimly lit stage where one stripper worked the pole and another gyrated at the end of the platform. Neon signs promoting various alcoholic drinks hung on walls of an indeterminate mud color while topless waitresses cruised around the room with trays expertly balanced on one hand. A long bar, filled with male customers, ran the length of the wall on the opposite side of the room.

Devlin and Mickale stood side by side, both of them transfixed, mesmerized by the two women on the stage. Neither one's attention left the dancers, except when a third stripper swayed out from behind the stage curtain.

"Okay, boys. Let's keep our eyes on the prize." She tugged on Devlin's sleeve twice before he noticed her. "Our ball's in play." She winced at his chuckle. "You know what I mean."

"Um, sure. Whatever you say. I only have eyes for you anyway."

A snort from Mickale didn't help her declining disposition. "Shit, bro. You're already pussy-whipped."

Tala slid her tongue over her mouth in a mocking sexual come-hither gesture. "You wish you were so lucky."

The unexpected sparkle...*from a tear?*... in Mickale's eyes threw her off balance. "Yeah. I do."

She paused, unsure of what had just happened, unsure of what he'd just said. Smoke swirled around their heads and, for a moment, she blamed his uncharacteristic confession on the polluted atmosphere. Was he dizzy from the smoke? "Don't get sappy on us, Mickale. We're here on a mission, remember?"

Cocky Mickale returned in an instant. "Sappy? Me? No way." He coughed, pivoted away from her, and pointed toward the bar. "Check him out at two o'clock. If I'm not mistaken, that's our little squealer making a meathead sandwich between two big blobs of silicone."

Tala scanned the bar, but with the crowd as thick as it was, she couldn't see where Mickale meant. "You mean next to the blonde waitress?"

"Blonde?" Mickale narrowed his eyes as if seeing the woman for the first time. "Oh, hey, yeah. I guess she is blonde. Didn't notice before."

Of course, all he'd noticed were her gigantic breasts. "Urgh. Men are such animals."

Devlin slid his arm around her shoulders and squeezed her to him. "Some more than others. But in a good way, huh?"

Mickale and Tala rolled their eyes and spoke the same thing at the same time. "Oh, puleeze."

Glancing between the two of them, Devlin shook his head. "You two are getting too chummy for my comfort."

She and Mickale exchanged a telling look and all three of them, in sync, turned toward George. He raised his head from in between the breasts and took a swig from his drink resting on the bar. Tipping the glass, he poured a little of the clear liquid onto the blonde's boobs, grabbed the woman's large breasts with both hands, and plunged his head down to hold the breasts on either side of his head. Men on either side of him cheered and slapped him on the shoulder, urging him on.

Tala shuddered. She snarled, a wave of nausea almost knocking her off her feet. *And to think I used to think he was an okay guy.*

"Tala? You okay?"

Devlin's velvet tones broke through the bad thoughts and she waved away his concern. "Yeah, I'm okay. Just thankful I don't have to deal with the asshole any longer. At least, not after tonight."

"Well, okay then. Let's get the creep before he hires the bitch for a backroom session."

"A backroom session?" Tala cringed, fearful of the answer, yet guessing it already.

"You don't want to know." Devlin started toward George with Mickale and Tala following on his heels.

As they neared the bar, the wall-mounted television flickered, replacing the scene of a football game with one of Tala's public service messages. Her face, smiling at her from the set, unnerved her a bit, even before George voiced his reaction.

Pointing at the screen, he shouted in a very loud and drunken voice. "Hey, there she is. Bitch of the Beasts."

A few men guffawed at his remark as the blonde waitress took the roll of bills George clutched in his hands. She peeled off almost half of the roll and stuffed the rest into his shirt pocket.

"I'm telling you guys, stay away from her. She may look hot, but she's cold as ice inside. Even if she is great in bed. The broad can suck the skin right off your dick and you'll love every minute of it."

Tala stopped, frozen with shock. Damn him to hell and back, telling lies about her. Especially lies about having sex with him. Numb, she stared at him, unable to think beyond hearing his words repeated in her head.

George's voice rose as his audience responded with titters and jeers. "And to top it off, she loves animals. Especially the big wolves. In fact, it wouldn't surprise me if she got some doggy action once in awhile. If you know what I mean."

A roar of laughter exploded around him as he gyrated, pretending to hump an invisible Tala. Grinning, he downed the rest of his drink and called for another.

"Too bad she'll never get the chance. 'Cause right about now she's giving it up for some friends of mine. And it's going be the last time she ever spreads her legs. For anyone."

A fat, balding man next to George swiveled away from the counter and saw Tala gaping. He studied her, scanning her from top to bottom. Soon, a slow leer slid across his blubberous features. Nudging George, he stuck out a chubby finger and asked in a voice loud enough to rise above the raunchy music filling the bar. "Think again, man. Looks like the animal lover's tracked you down."

As George twisted around, his bleary eyes socked into Tala. "Tala? How the hell did you get away—?"

His last words never made it past his lips as Devlin's fist connected with his mouth.

Chapter Seventeen

George's head jerked backward and forwards in a weird mimicry of a Jack-in-the-Box. Blood ran out of his nose, staining the front of his paisley shirt. "Argh!"

Devlin, Mickale, and Tala formed a semi-circle in front of him, trapping him in front of the bar. The men around George scattered, unwilling to get involved in the dispute.

Snatching several napkins from the counter, George clutched them to his nose and held up his other hand, begging them to stop. His eyes bugged wide and he stammered, trying to keep Devlin from attacking again. "Wait! Hold on."

Devlin snarled and stepped toward him, drawing back his arm for another blow. Tala, however, hooked a hand under his arm, keeping him near her. "No, Devlin, you can't beat him up."

The force emanating from Devlin struck Tala, hyping the power growing within her. She chanced a glimpse at him, but saw no visible signs of him shifting. At least, not yet.

George called to the people surrounding them. "Someone call the police! Get help! This guy's trying to kill me!" When no one budged to come to his aid, he whimpered, calling to the bartender. "You! They're going to wreck the place if you don't get some cops in here. Now!"

But the bartender shook his head, picked up a baseball bat lying on top of the counter behind him, and moved around the bar to stand beside Tala and her men. Waving the bat in the air, he demanded the spectators keep their distance. "Everyone keep a safe distance. I wouldn't want my customers or my girls to get hurt." He skimmed his eyes over George before adding, "But I'll make an exception with you."

"You really want someone to call the police, George? So you can answer all the animal abuse charges I'm going to file against you?" At George's cringe, Tala smiled an wicked grin. "I didn't think so." Maybe now wasn't the time for the cops with Devlin around, but later she'd file those charges. She wasn't letting George get away with hurting animals.

"Looks like you're on your own, Georgie. Defenseless. With no one to help." Devlin rubbed his hands together. "And all mine." Without turning his head, he asked her, "Why can't I beat him up?"

Tala caught the shared look Devlin and the bartender exchanged. Did they know each other? Or was their connection just a guy thing? *Do you know him?* She mouthed her question to Devlin who acted as though he hadn't seen her.

George's bloodied mouth curved into a pitiful half-smile as he reached one hand to her. "You won't let him, will you, babe? Don't let him hurt me."

Tala arched a brow, and slapped his hand down. "One last time. Do. Not. Call. Me. Babe." She delighted in his wince at the tone of her voice. "Dev, I didn't mean you couldn't beat him up. I meant you shouldn't do it right here. You know. In front of witnesses."

"Oh, right." Devlin jutted out his lower lip, adopting an understanding pose. "Gotcha."

The bartender chuckled and elbowed her. "Don't worry none about witnesses, sweetheart. These folks know better than to talk about anything that happens at Jake's. Isn't that right, folks?" He nudged her again and winked. "I'm Jake."

A low murmur from the crowd confirmed his claim and Tala, once more, thought she noticed a bond, a kinship pass between Devlin and the man. She asked out loud this time, "Do you two know each other?"

Mickale, however, jumped in, not giving Devlin a chance to answer. "George, you're going to do exactly what I say."

Tala sensed the change in Devlin and Mickale at the same time. Raw power undulated in the stale air around them as the brothers' transformations reached the critical point. Peeking out of the corner of her eye, she saw each of them allow a partial shift to happen. Two sets of fangs, each as dangerous as the other's, replaced teeth and full lips curled back into similar snarls. Captivated, she watched as two sets of deep brown eyes morphed, replacing the raging darkness with brilliant, furious amber.

Concerned about the crowd seeing them, she checked Jake's reaction and was shocked to find him smiling at the brothers. And pushing the people farther away from their group. Again, he winked at her, sending her the unmistakable message to not worry.

"You're not good enough to lick my brother's boots." Mickale's already stretched lips widened into an evil smirk. "But do it anyway."

Surprised at the command, Tala watched in awe as the terrified George didn't hesitate to fall to his knees. Crawling over to Devlin, he bent over and licked the dirt from his boots. Between licks, he sobbed, sniveling as tears dropped to the dusty floor.

The crowd behind them burst into jeers, taunting the groveling man. Laughter joined the jeers, making George cry even harder.

"I don't believe what I'm seeing." Tala's mouth dropped open as he continued to lap up the grime on Devlin's boots. The sight should have thrilled her. Yet, she couldn't help the uneasiness clenching at her stomach. The plea, the order, burst from her lips before she'd even thought the word. "Stop."

George halted, but didn't move. His body shook with unbridled fear as he waited for the next command.

Tala placed her hand on her chest, knowing she couldn't allow this to continue. Grasping Devlin's arm, she hoped he'd understand. "I don't want him tormented. I don't want you sinking to his level. He's the real animal. Not you." She looked down at the pitiful man at their feet.

She watched the amber anger in Devlin's eyes fade for a moment as she gazed into the soft brown eyes she loved. "Let him go. He won't bother us any more."

"Now hold up. Don't I have a say in this?" Mickale growled at George, sending him into another volley of shakes. "How about we have a little more fun first?"

Devlin pulled Tala to him. Warm comfort, mixed with the ever-present attraction, flowed through her, followed by an intense rush of uncontrollable lust. She inhaled his masculine, dangerous aroma, drinking in everything he was, everything he had to offer. "Let him go. We can go home and make up for lost time in bed." Rising on the tips of her toes, she slipped her tongue inside his mouth.

He groaned a half-human, half-animal sound and held her chest against his. "Whatever you want." Bending over, he yanked George to his feet. "If you ever come within a thousand yards of Tala, I promise you I'll pluck out your eyes and have them for appetizers."

"Blech, bro. Talk about nasty food." Mickale scrunched up his face and swiveled away from his brother to ogle one of the strippers. "I can think of a dozen other things better to eat."

"Get." Devlin flung the trembling man away from him, leaving George to stumble toward the back area of the club.

*****

Devlin good-naturedly jostled Mickale, recalling the day's events. "You and me, big brother. We take care of our own."

"And what about this guy?" Mickale hooked Jake in a headlock, playing with the brawny bartender. "I knew he was one of our kind the minute he picked up the bat."

Jake broke free, sauntered back behind the bar to pour three drinks, and set them on the counter. "Here's to the pack. Whoever's pack it is." Raising one of the drinks in a salute, he waited for Mickale and Devlin to join him and all three downed the booze in simultaneous gulps. "I haven't had this much fun since I went hunter-hunting."

Devlin offered his hand in greeting. "Devlin Morgan of the Morgan Pack. And this ugly mutt is my older brother, Mickale."

Jake accepted the handshake and offered one to Mickale. "Jake Branson. Swift Pack. Glad to be of service." Jake poured another round. "Should I pour one for the lady? Providing she wants one when she returns."

"Sure." Devlin turned to check for Tala. "Where'd she go?"

"She headed off toward the ladies room a minute ago." Jake jerked his head toward the neon sign over the adjacent hallway. "Is she a new convert?" He poured them all another drink. "I can smell shifter in her, but she hasn't completed a total transformation yet, has she?"

Devlin scanned the hall for Tala. *Guess she needed some time to herself. After all, like Jake said, she's new.* "Not all the way, but the full transformation won't be much longer." *Yet I wish she hadn't gone in the same direction George had.*

"Is she yours?" Jake scooped up a towel to mop up a wet spot, while other customers inched toward the counter.

Devlin studied Jake's face, a mask of uninterested control, yet his seemingly nonchalant question was more loaded than a sawed-off shotgun. And Devlin didn't like it one bit. "Yeah, she's mine. I've marked her and she's agreed." *So don't even think about it, man.*

Jake's eyebrows hopped up and down as if taking Devlin's words to heart. "Good for you, buddy. She's a hot one."

"And mine." The low rumble in his throat slipped between his teeth.

Jake held up his hands. "Message received and understood." When Devlin eased up a bit, he added, "But does she have any sisters?"

Mickale wasn't one to be left out of any conversation about women. "If she did, I'd have taken them. One or all at once."

The three shared a laugh together and let a comfortable silence envelop them. Each of the brothers lifted a glass, nodded at the other, and gulped down their drinks. Jake left the bottle on the bar, winked, and moved off to serve another customer.

Devlin swallowed a mouthful and cleared his throat, hoping to dislodge the growing knot of unease resting there. "I want to thank you for all your help. You really came through for me, big brother, and I appreciate it."

"More than once, if I do say so myself. I saved your butt a couple of times, at least." Mickale laughed at Devlin's scowl. "Hey, just like when we were kids. I'm going to pick on you as much as I can. But that doesn't mean I'll let anyone else run over you. Or your mate."

"Yep, you said it. She's my mate. So don't try and break us apart any more. No more crazy stories about me, right?"

"Hell, the girl knows the truth. And the truth in our family is a whole lot crazier than any story I can dream up."

Devlin scrutinized his brother and wondered if he dared do what he thought was best. Now that he and Tala were together, the time had come to tell his father, his brother, and the pack about his business. "Mick, let's make a deal."

Ever suspicious, Mickale squinted at him, careful with his words. "A deal?"

"A deal. Like how about I take pack leadership?"

Mickale scoffed, interrupting him before he could go on. "Some deal. And, uh, no deal."

Devlin shouldered him, prodding his brother to shut him up. "If you'll keep your pie hole closed for a second, I'll explain." *Where's Tala?*

Mickale waved his hand for him to continue and refilled their glasses. "Okay, so spill your guts. I'm listening."

As much as his brother wanted the pack's leadership position, Devlin wasn't sure his plan would work. Yet if there was one thing he'd learned in recent days, it was that he could trust his brother with his life. Now it was time to trust his brother with the future.

Maybe, just maybe his plan would make both his father and his brother happy. Of course, the pack might not go along with the idea. He'd have to make them see the wisdom in his proposal. Though some obstacles stood in his way, he thought he could pull it off.

"You want to lead the pack. And I don't."

"Yeah, that's what I always thought. But then why—"

"Because our father wouldn't see it any other way. But I have a different idea. I propose we both lead the pack."

Mickale dropped his drink on the counter, splattering alcohol everywhere. He flicked the wetness from his hands. "You want to rule together? Are you fucked up?"

He'd expected a better response from Mickale. *Some gratitude. Hell, at least some civility.* "Why the hell not?"

"Because packs have a one leader, not two. Okay, two if you count your mate. But one male leader."

"Who says?"

Mickale stared at him as if he'd grown another head. "Because that's the way it's always been."

"Doesn't mean that's the way it has to stay." If he couldn't persuade Mickale on the idea, how would he convince the others? "Tala and I will rule on our own until you find your mate. Your true mate and not just some female picked at random. Once you do, we'll rule together."

"All four of us? I don't think so, bro. Too many heads for one job."

Devlin glanced in the direction of the restrooms. *Where is she?* The uneasy emptiness in his stomach morphed into full-fledge concern. "Not if one team is on the other side of the mountains."

Now he had Mickale's full attention. "A second camp?" He pivoted, his eyes squarely on Devlin's now. "We've always talked about setting up another location. A second pack within the pack."

A nervous tingle ran down Devlin's spine. *She's taking too long.* Still, he needed to finish his conversation with Mickale and put their rivalry to rest.

"You and I make a damn good team. Dealing with these hunters proved we do. And with Tala and then your mate, we'll make an even better team. Two teams, two home packs within the larger, greater pack. We'll make decisions for our individual groups and rule for the whole pack. And I'll get to run my company the way I've been running it. Only out in the open."

"You've got a business going?" Mickale narrowed his eyes even while a knowing smile formed on his lips. "I thought you were up to something."

"Yeah, and I'm not giving it up."

"So what happens if we disagree on a decision affecting both groups?"

"We'll let the council of elders make the final decision." He could see Mickale's mind working, letting the idea take root. Holding up his drink, he went on to close the deal. "What do you say? Partners? Co-leaders?"

Mickale paused, grinned, and lifted his glass. "Deal."

They clinked their glasses together to seal the bargain. "Good." With the agreement made, he leveled his focus on the hallway again. "I don't like this. Tala's taking way too long in the restroom."

"Why don't you—"

Before Mickale could finish his sentence, Devlin strode over to the hallway and headed down the long, dark hall. A flickering neon sign boasting the word, "Bitches," hung lopsided over the girls' restroom door. Devlin hurried over to tap the shoulder of a young woman leaning on the wall next to the door. "Do me a favor, will you? Go inside and check on my girlfriend."

"In there?" The passion pink-haired woman blinked at Devlin before shooting him a take-me-home-and-fuck-me smile.

Just how dumb was this female? Hiding the annoyance churning inside him, he returned her smile and hoped he kept his tone light. "Uh, yeah. In there.

She went inside awhile ago and I'm worried about her. Maybe she fell in the toilet?" He chuckled through gritted teeth. *Come on. Gather what few brains cell you have and think.*

As he'd half expected, his joke went straight over her head. "Really? You know what? My roommate, Missy, fell in the sink once. Hi, I'm Stacy."

Attention, World. Dumb and Dumber are roomies.

"How does a person fall into a sink?" Devlin punched an elbow into Mickale's arm as he sidled up next to them.

The girl flipped her hair over her shoulder and reached out to skim her fingers over Mickale's chest. "Missy and me went out partying one night and got like really drunk. So by the time we made it home, we had to like pee like really, really bad. And since I got dibs on the potty first, she decided to use the kitchen sink."

"We don't have time—"

"Hush, Dev. The lady's telling a story."

Stacy flashed Mickale a flirtatious smile and continued. "Anyway, she got up on this like really, really tall stool and turned around. But when she tried to squat over the sink...you know, how girls squat over potties...she lost her balance and fell into the sink." She ran both hands over Mickale's shirt when he joined in with her giggles.

"Then what happened? Did she get out?" Mickale pressed closer to Stacy and leered down her low-cut blouse.

"No. But she bruised her butt up like really, really purple."

Their joint laughter raked over Devlin's last nerve. "Very interesting. Now can you check on my girlfriend?"

"Trust me.   A woman was in there, but not now. And some freaky guy was in there with her." She batted her long, fake eyelashes at him. "I'll take her place, if you want."

Panic leapt through Devlin as he shoved past the girl and Mickale into the dirty bathroom. Open doors showed three empty stalls. "Tala? Where are you?"

Checking under the other two closed doors, Devlin's nerves prickled along the top of his skin. He rotated in a circle as if he could have missed seeing anything in the tiny restroom. His hands clenched and unclenched as the same line kept chanting through his brain. *Tala's in trouble.*

"Bro, take a look."

Devlin followed Mickale's gaze to an open window against the far wall. It was large enough for a person to crawl through. Or be dragged through. Devlin stared at the window, saw the dark patch, and moved to the windowsill to get a better view. Holding his breath, he ran his finger along a line of red on the bottom of the frame.

His stomach lurched as he brought his fingers to his nose and sniffed the all-too familiar smell. "Blood."

"Shit, bro. Is it Tala's?"

The pounding of his heightened pulse throbbed in his head as Devlin answered his brother's question. "Yeah."

"You think he took her out the window?"

Devlin raised his eyes from the smear on his finger to stare at the parking lot outside. "Yeah, I do. But I can see her car from here. So either he had a car or he's dragged her off." Anger, stronger than he'd ever known, ripped through him, churning his stomach as the power within him started rising. His eyesight clouded momentarily as the fury took over. "Shit, the air in this place is so foul I can't catch her scent." Growling, he wiped his hand across his pant leg. "Except in her blood."

Shedding his clothes, he shifted, turning to Mickale once again for help. "You go back into the club and make sure she's not still inside. Check the dancers' rooms. When you're finished, wait out by her car. Let's hope we get lucky and have this pegged all wrong. In the meantime, I'm going to search the surrounding area in case the bastard hurt her and left her…"

"Don't go there, bro. We don't know that anything has happened to her."

Devlin coughed, refusing to let his throat clog up with emotion. "I know. But I need to find her. If I don't find anything outside the club, I'll head back to her apartment. If you find her, go home with her." At Mickale's curt nod, Devlin leapt, throwing his body through the window.

*****

"Ow!"

"Oh, shut up, George." Tala touched her head where blood oozed from a gash across her forehead. After entering the restroom, the world had gone upside down as George had thrown her against the window, knocking her head on the sill. But she hadn't gone down. Much to his surprise she'd returned his greeting.

George's wide eyes told her the change she felt coursing through her body was a total transformation. *Finally.*

The power roared alive in her, but this time she was ready. Instinctively, she directed the force, letting it ebb and flow through her veins. Forcing herself not to think, only to react, she waited for what would come.

Bones grew, crunched, and bent as her body changed with the conversion. Hair sprouted, not in small tufts, but all over her as George whirled and headed for the restroom door.

Reaching to her forehead, she no longer felt the gash. Instead, her fingers...*claws*...skimmed over ridges forming her new brow, her alternate face. Fangs, glorious, long, razor-sharp fangs jutted out from her elongated jaw and she grinned a different grin, a wolfish grin.

Her hair shortened, leaving fur in its place. George pulled on the doorknob, but couldn't get it open in his fear. "No! Stay away from me!"

Heat inside her, glorious and untamed, burst into a full flame as she snagged his ankle and yanked him to her. His scream sent chills over her, not from the horror of the sound, but from the delight she experienced hearing his cry.

As she clamped a paw around his ankle, tugging him to her so she could flip on top of him, she glimpsed her image in the full-length mirror at the end of the room. Sitting astride the wiggling George, she cocked her head to the side, and stared at the sight.

Wow. That's me. Cool. Very cool. Although I've made a real mess of my clothes. Crap, my favorite t-shirt is shredded.

"But it was worth it." The golden wolf in the mirror lifted the corners of its mouth in a welcoming smile. She'd definitely shifted. And definitely all the way.

Damn, if only Devlin were here to see this. To see me. Because I look good. Damn good.

She stretched the grin wider as her paws gripped George, holding him down and limiting his movement. She shook her head, liking the way her soft fur bounced around her new face. "Talk about the windblown look. Eat your heart out, Farrah."

With difficulty, she broke her gaze from her reflection and dropped her head close to his cheek. A snarl, deeper and more vicious than she'd ever managed before, snaked out of her as she blew hot breath against his neck. Piercing her fangs into his skin, she growled again. Ecstasy raced through her at his scream. Until, that is, a warm wetness slid along her leg.

"Oh, damn it all to hell and back." She sneered and hopped off of him. "Get yourself some Depends."

As a terrified George tried to scramble away, she wiggled her fingers at her image and giggled. Without glancing at him, she hooked one long claw under his belt and lifted him to her.

Blowing a low whistle, she brought her gaze to him. "So? What'd ya think, George? I make one gorgeous wolfie, don't I?"

When he didn't answer...unless the incoherent babble was an answer...she shook him a little. "As much as I'd love to stay like this..." She glanced longingly at herself as she stood, taking him along with her. "I've got a better idea. Come on."

She shifted, in one quick, continuous move, before flinging the door open and stalking out, almost knocking a pink-haired woman down in her haste. Ignoring the expletives the girl hurled at her, Tala headed toward the rear of the building, found the strippers' changing room, and pushed George inside.

Several pairs of eyes fell on them, although no one acted surprised to see them. Curious looks bored into her as she held George two inches off the floor.

"I guess nothing much surprises you ladies any longer, huh?"

A heavily rouged, bleached blonde rose from her stool in front of the large vanity mirror to stride over to Tala. Dark, seen-it-all eyes scanned them while she hoisted a tight-fitting bustier over ample breasts. "Got that right. I'm Maggie." Maggie slipped her rhinestoned fingers under one of the slits in Tala's shirt. "But I've never seen an outfit like this one."

"Uh, it's the new shredded look." George squirmed in Tala's hand, but still couldn't form words that made any sense. "I was wondering if you'd like to have a new act tonight." She tilted her head at him and added, "A comedy act."

A penciled-in eyebrow arched in response. "You talking about him?"

"Hey, I know this guy." A chubby, little brunette who looked like she'd be more at home in a high school pep squad than in a strip joint, pointed at

George. "He's a real creep. Always treats us like dirt and doesn't tip."

Tala clucked her tongue in sympathy. "Figures." Would the young stripper help her? "Do you think you might have some clothes to fit him?" Other strippers gathered around as Tala waited.

"You mean like stage clothes?"

"Exactly. Like maybe a hot pink thong or something? Granted, he'll stretch it out, but I'll buy you new clothes. I promise. You see, George here wants to go on stage." Shaking him a little elicited a small squeak from him. "Don't you, George?"

The ladies checked each other's reactions before turning to dig into their personal stashes of costumes. Within minutes, Maggie handed Tala a large brassiere and thong panties. A pink robe and feather boa completed the ensemble.

Holding them up against George's skin, Tala leaned back and nodded. "Oh, my. Pink is your color, Georgie. You'll be pink perfection in this outfit."

Tossing her captive to the floor behind her, she turned away from the strippers, allowed her fangs to peek through her stretched lips, and snarled her command. "Put them on. Now. You've got a show to do."

"And if I don't?"

"Hey, he can talk, after all." Maggie chuckled as the girls around her threw barbs at George. "We're waiting, man."

Tala widened her lips more, adding a low growl for emphasis. George, horror paling his complexion, unbuttoned his shirt, swapping it out for the big bra.

"Keep going, George." Tala crooked her finger at his slacks.

"Yeah. Get the panties on. I paid good money for the lacy thong, but it'll be worth it to see you in them." The little brunette wiggled her butt as if shimmying into the thong.

George, seeing Tala's warning look, dropped his pants in a hurry, stripping his jockey shorts along with them. But Tala stopped him as he started to take off his socks.

"No. Leave those on. I think we'll add a pair of high heels, too."

A pair of silver, four-inch heels appeared on cue, tossed at George's feet.

Once dressed, the strippers clapped their approval, giggling at the chubby, short man shivering before them. The tight bra pinched into his man-breasts while the thong showed what little package he had to offer.

"Hmm. Maybe we should pad his crotch some. He sure doesn't fill out my thong much."

Tala helped him slip on the silky robe and wrap the feathery boa around his neck. "Maybe some makeup would do the trick?"

Three girls jumped for their cosmetics. While one girl added rouge to his cheeks, another added eye shadow, and the third applied an apple-red lipstick to his lips.

After letting the women have their way, Tala crossed her arms and admired their work. "Okay, Georgie. Show time."

The whole group of women followed Tala as she pushed George out of the dressing room, down the dimly lit hall, and onto the stage area behind the red curtains.

Loud, raunchy music ended as a stripper broke through the curtains, and stared at the man standing before her. "What the shit?"

"Don't ask, Stella. Just go out there and announce a very special act." Maggie studied George for a moment before adding, "This is Gorgeous Georgina, the Pal Gal of the West."

Stella paused for a moment, shrugged and spun around. Flinging the curtains aside, she swayed onto the stage.

"Please, Tala. Don't make me do this. I won't do this."

"Lookie, lookie. He speaks again."

Tala ignored the ladies as they picked up Maggie's taunting. "Do this. Or I'll finish what I started in the restroom."

George blanched at her threat, turning toward the stage as Stella's voice rang out.

"Gentlemen! We have a very special treat for you tonight. Straight, or maybe not so straight, from his life in the closet, *The Lucky Lady* proudly presents for your amusement, Gorgeous Georgina, the Pal Gal of the West."

A generous applause filled the air as Maggie drew the curtains out of the way. Stepping behind George, Tala placed both hands on his shoulders and pushed him on stage.

Pandemonium broke out as catcalls, insults, and boos erupted from the male audience. The disc jockey, catching on to the joke, broke off the fast-beat music he was playing, substituting it with the typical bump-and-grind stripper music.

Tala poked her head through the split in the curtain and hissed at George. "You better start dancing or they're liable to get really mad. Not to mention how mad I'll get."

A forlorn George glanced at Tala before scanning his gaze over the audience. Slowly, in gawky, awkward movements, he moved his hips to the rhythm of the song. Soon the men surrounding the stage got involved in the prank and took up a chant. "Take it off, babe. Take it off."

Tala laughed as George baby-stepped to the middle of the runway, stopped, and clutched the boa close to his chest. Yet even as he cowered in front of the boisterous crowd, his hips continued to bump to the left and right, hitting with the beat of the music.

As a few of the strippers gathered around her to sneak glimpses of the show, George loosened up, growing bolder with each second. Tossing the feather scarf in a flamboyant gesture, he twirled around, executing a perfect pirouette.

Although the move was unexpected, his expression was what surprised Tala the most. "Oh, my God. He's enjoying this."

"Looks like Georgina may have started a whole new career tonight." Maggie guffawed, slapping Tala on the arm.

"Damn, Tala, Dev and I were going crazy with worry and all the while you're busy making a diva out of a dickhead."

Tala turned toward Mickale, not surprised to see him circled by four strippers and enjoying every bit of the attention. "Worried? I figured you two were having a great time out at the bar congratulating yourselves on how well you handled George. Or as he's now known, Georgina. I

didn't think either one of you would notice my absence."
She glanced over the women hanging onto Mickale,
searching for the brother she really wanted to scc. "So if
he's so worried, why isn't Devlin with you? Yo, Mickale.
Can you keep your mind on our conversation for a minute
longer?"

 Mickale forced his gaze away from the brunette
thrusting her breasts against him even as his arm slipped
around the stripper's waist. "What'd you say? Oh, Devlin?
Yeah, well, he sent me to check out the back rooms while he
scours the neighborhood for you. Then he's headed back to
your apartment. The guy's so freaked out with worry that
he's not thinking clearly."

 "I'll say since he sent you to search the strippers'
dressing room. That's like sending a bank robber into Fort
Knox and asking him to ignore the money and find a
paperclip."

 "Hey, I found you, didn't I?"

 She grinned, unable to resist his mischievous charm.
"True. So Devlin's gone back to my apartment? Then I
need to get back there before he does. I guess we'll see
which is faster; four wheels or four paws." With Mickale's
attention back on the girls surrounding him, she didn't wait
for the answer she knew wouldn't be coming. Instead, she
hugged Maggie, thanked all the girls for their help, and
headed for her car.

Chapter Eighteen

He needed to learn how to drive. Before anything else happened, he'd learn how to drive. Jogging down the streets, even in wolf form, was slower than traveling in a car. But at least as a wolf, he could cut through yards. The full moon above beckoned him, calling him to hunt, but he couldn't let anything keep him from finding Tala.

He'd been positive that George had dragged Tala through the bathroom window, yet a fruitless search outside the strip club hadn't found anything. Still, he'd hoped he'd catch her scent outside. Yet, again, he'd found nothing. Sensed nothing except an urgent need to return to her home. How could she have vanished into thin air?

Sending Mickale back into the club hadn't given him any hope that Tala was there. After all, if she were, wouldn't she have returned to the bar and him? No. Something had happened. He'd head home and pray she'd get in touch with him or return safely. If she didn't, then he'd find one ex-employee and tear him apart, inch by slow, agonizing inch.

He bounded toward Tala's building, her scent hitting him, almost knocking him off his feet with the relief rushing over him. *She's alive.* Rounding the corner, he glanced at the one lamppost shedding a hazy, yellow glow over the area behind her apartment. Another light shone from the second story window of her apartment, highlighting a shapely shadow on the blinds. He inhaled, caught the spicy, tantalizing aroma of her, and smiled.

Her form played across the blinds, gliding back and forth, arms outstretched, as if in flight. The enticing shape, alluring in silhouette, dipped and weaved, dancing in time with the familiar, sensual music. Her movements entreated him, flaring the desire within his soul to a fever pitch. Grinning, he flew up the stairs, and burst into the apartment.

The music, seductive and sultry, played over him as his mouth fell open at the sight of her naked body floating around the room. His shaft rose as she slid her hands along her body, skimming over her firm, round breasts. She flicked her tongue over her top lip and moved her hands up and through her hair.

She was more beautiful than ever. His shaft throbbed for her, but it was his heart that swelled with love.

Spinning again, she performed a perfect twirl, and landed with her arms outstretched, welcoming him home. "What took you so long, Devlin?"

*****

His hand slid over her breast, tweaking her nipple. Tala laughed and slid on top of Devlin. "When do we leave for the mountains?"

He busied himself, playing with the already tight and taut bud. "Next week. Mickale's gone home to relay our plan to our father and the elders."

She studied him, wanting to make sure he was all right with the idea. "And you don't mind giving up part of your power to Mickale?"

He shook his head and toyed with a strand of her hair trailing across her chest. "I never cared about the power like Mickale does. Besides, my business is thriving and I'm ready to show my father what I've accomplished on my own. This is a good solution for both of us. And for the future of the clan. You and I will rule alone until he mates. Then we can come back into the city if you want."

She nibbled at his ear wanting to hear him groan in pleasure. "I'll go wherever makes you happy. But continuing my work is important, too."

"This way you can do both. Think of the first-hand experience and knowledge you'll gain about wolves."

She rubbed her breasts against his skin enjoying the way her nipples felt against his hard chest. "I shifted, you know. All the way."

Devlin fondled her breasts as she wiggled her bottom over his crotch. No harm in teasing him a little more. He groaned and tried pushing into her, but she resisted.

"I'm trying to talk to you. To tell you what happened with George."

"I can't concentrate with your pussy on my dick. I am, after all, only human." He grinned and attempted to force his way in again. "Well, sort of."

Giggling, she leaned over so he could suck on her tits. Now she found it hard to talk. "You should have seen me. I was amazing. And one hot bitch."

"My bitch." He mumbled around her tit, unwilling to let go. "You're always amazing. And beautiful."

"But as a werewolf? Who knew?" She gasped as his hands clamped onto her rump.

"I knew." He let go of her breast and pulled her mouth to his. His tongue scorched its way into her mouth, while he lifted her rear high enough to slide his dick into her wetness.

All thoughts vacated her mind as his shaft plunged deep within her. Breaking free of his kiss, she placed her hands on his chest and leaned back, tossing her hair over her shoulders. Hot lust shot through her as she matched his pounding with her own.

"Take me, Devlin. Mark me again."

He grunted, working his hips against her. "Again?" The gleam of love in his eyes brought tears to hers.

"Yeah. I don't want your pack to have any doubt I'm yours."

He shoved her off him, landing her on her back. Without hesitation, she opened her legs again, ready as he slid into her again.

Growling in pleasure, he panted and drove into her harder. "Admit it. You like me to bite you."

She echoed his growl. "Okay, yeah, that's part of the reason."

"Good."

His teeth dug into her shoulder as his arms wrapped around her, pulling her to him. Tala squealed, lust and love joining as one. Again, she shouted, this time from the searing pain and answering delight. Blood trickled down her neck, but she didn't care. All that mattered was the mark.

They came together, each of them crying out at the same moment. His body's shudders matched hers and she clung to him, desperate to keep his shaft inside her. "Stay, Devlin."

Grasping the side of her head, he rained light kisses over her face. "I can't stay on top of you forever."

Tala took his head with her hands, copying his gesture. "No one has forever. So we'll just have to make the most of our time."

Devlin chuckled and licked a drop of sweat from her chin. "Maybe I should have mentioned this earlier, but shifters live a really long time. In fact, some might say we're immortal. Think you can handle being immortal?"

"With you, I can handle anything."

Collapsing to her side, sweat running along both of their bodies, he took her hand in his and brought her palm to his lips. "Tala Wilde, you are mine. All mine." He twisted onto his side and kissed her palm again. "And I'm all yours."

She turned his hand around and copied his gesture, feathering kisses along the long lifeline of his palm. "Then you'll do something for me?"

"Anything."

Laughing, she flung her body out of the bed. "Come with me, Devlin Morgan." Swiveling with a little wiggle of her butt at him, she snatched up her robe and skipped through the living room. Pushing open the sliding glass doors, she went to the railing of her patio, and waited for him to join her.

His arms slid around her waist, while the towel he'd used to cover his body tickled her calves. A happy shiver slid up her neck as he licked her already-healing wound.

"The scar will get bigger this time." He continued to lick her, holding her next to him.

"Dance with me, Devlin. Dance with me in the moonlight."

Together, they swayed to silent strains of music, drifting along with the breeze of the summer evening. Pausing, Tala angled her body so she could gaze into his eyes, smiled, and lifted her eyebrows at him in a question. When his quiet response came, she altered her gaze, raising her eyes to the creamy moon above them.

As one, they lifted their heads and howled at the moon.

Epilogue

"Yeah, I know. I miss you, too. But my meetings won't take much longer, I promise. Then I'll head straight home faster than greased lightning."

Tala scrunched down into the cushions of her sofa as she listened to Devlin's strong voice on the other end of the phone. Two weeks was too long. She agreed with Devlin's complaint and nodded her head before speaking. "I've almost finished relaying my research to the group and a lot of the information I've uncovered is blowing their minds. Of course, they don't know that I'm closer than any human has ever been to a pack."

She giggled at Devlin's retort. "Yeah, you're right. I'm not entirely human any longer. But what they don't know won't hurt them."

Devlin's masculine tone caressed her ears as she savored the warmth of his voice. "Mickale's in the city, right? Too bad I don't have time to get with him. Maybe do a little barhopping? Not that I'd introduce that hound dog to any of my girlfriends. Even if he is a gorgeous immortal."

She basked in Devlin's laughter, filling her with delight and longing, until the doorbell interrupted her reverie. "I've got to go, Dev. I'm expecting an important package from our affiliate zoo in Chicago." She blew a kiss into the phone. *Wow. Have I gotten sappy or what? Watch out, World. Woman in Love.* "Talk to you soon. *Babe.*"

She giggled at her joke as she closed the cell phone, rose and strode across the apartment. Images of Devlin's first appearance in her apartment so many weeks before kept the grin on her face as she swung open the door.

As expected, the postman stood before her holding a large package. Tala signed for the parcel, took it and checked the return address. Yet unexpectedly, the package wasn't from the zoo.

"From my cousin? I wonder what she sent me?" Tala's cousin lived across the country and rarely communicated with her. Except during their brief visit when her cousin had told her about how she and her friends had "summoned an immortal." Following her cousin's example had brought Devlin to Tala. "I've got to remember to send her a thank you card for her idea."

Settling onto the couch again, excitement rippled through Tala as she tore open the package. A large, brown book, wrinkled and weathered through age and use, rested in a cardboard box. Although she couldn't see any dust on the book, a musky aroma drifted up to her nose.

"A book?" Tala lifted the heavy volume from the box. "She sent me an old book?" Tala read the words out loud as her fingers slid over the intricate lettering. *"The Still Sexy Ladies Guide to Dating Immortals."*

Tala studied the title several times before placing the book on her coffee table. "A guide? Like a manual?" Again, she stared at the title, taking the book back onto her lap. "Oh. My. God. This is a manual for dating immortals." Eagerly, she flipped open the book, her hand landing on the Table of Contents. "Let's see. *Chapter One. Summoning An Immortal.* Hmm, been there and done that one. What else is there?"

Her grin grew wider as she scanned the chapter headings. *Dating the Demanding Demon. Teaching a Greedy Leprechaun the Value of Love."* Tala chuckled and read on. *"Don't Let Your Vamp Suck You Dry. Bringing Your Greek God Down to Earth."*

As she continued, her heart beat faster, knowing what she would find. The tip of her index finger flew down the list, skipping over the other headings. "Come on. There has to be one for werewolves." Finally, her finger and eyes found what she hunted for. "Ah, ha! I knew it." She wet her lips, enjoying the moment. *"Howl If You're Horny."*

Quickly, she flipped to the chapter on werewolves, her eyes devouring the first page in minutes. She read on, gasping and nodding, mumbling to herself to help her remember the advice.

At long last, she finished the chapter, took a deep breath, and closed the book. She stared at the wolf posters covering the walls, her mind sorting everything she'd learned.

"Cuz, I sure wish you'd sent this book to me earlier." She could have avoided so many of the mistakes she'd made in the first few weeks of her relationship with Devlin. How could she have known shifters don't like cream in their coffee because it reminds them of cats? How could she have known certain smells affect male wolves differently than females? And, oh, if she'd only known not to touch a wolf's ears while making love! Damn it all to hell and back, if she'd had the guide as a reference she *would* have known!

"Well, at least I have it now. Thanks again, dear cousin." Tala hugged the book to her, vowing to read the chapter on werewolves again. "I wish I had time right now, but I'd better get my butt back to the zoo and find out what happened to the other package."

Carefully placing the book in her briefcase, she hurried to the door, and rushed to the parking lot. Her mind raced with the suggestions in the book, making her unaware of the dark figure jumping out at her from a nearby bush. Unaware until it was too late.

Snarling, she started to shift, but the blow to her body knocking her off her feet, aborted the transformation. She crashed to the ground with her breath rushing from her, forcing her to let go of the briefcase. The case flew into air, straight at her attacker who snatched it, whirled in the opposite direction, and fled into the woods.

"No!" Tala's cry ripped from her lips as two of her neighbors hurried over to help her to her feet. She started to dash after the thief, but Caroline held onto her, holding her back.

"Tala, you can't go after that guy. He's dangerous."

She growled her anger, shoving down the power aching to burst free. "I'll show him who's dangerous."

"Caroline's right. We should call security and the police. I learned my lesson about messing with intruders after that experience with the animal-man. So I'm sure not letting you chase a thief now." Bobby Lee took her other arm, securing her between her two well-meaning friends.

"But he took my briefcase. And, oh no! He took the book!" Tala gave up struggling against the two, realizing her attacker was long gone.

"What book?" Caroline gawked at Tala. "Who cares about a book, anyway?"

Tala heaved a sigh and puffed out her frustration. "A very special book from my cousin. And I doubt I can get another copy at any bookstore."

"Well, no book's worth getting hurt. Come inside with us and you can call the police."

Tala shook her head slowly. "No, that's okay. They'll never find him. Besides, I only had a few unimportant papers in the case. And, of course, the book." She fought to keep the tears in check. "But no credit cards or money. So, I guess I'll just have to live and learn on this one." *Thank God I read the chapter before this happened.*

"If you say so." Caroline rubbed Tala's back, giving what comfort she could.

"Something tells me this jerk doesn't read much. He'll probably just throw it in the trash." Pain at the thought of losing the guide tore into her chest, but she forced a smile at her friends. "Maybe someone else will find the book and get some use out of it. Thanks for your help, guys, but I'm all right. And I need to get to work."

Caroline and Bobby Lee nodded, uncertainty in their faces. Ever the mother-type, Caroline had to check one last time. "You're sure?"

"I'm sure."

"Well, okay." They paused yet again before they turned and crossed the lot toward their apartment.

Straightening to her full height, she made it to her car on wobbly legs. Tala slid into the driver's seat, locked her doors, and groaned. "Damn it all to hell and back."

THE END